GUARDING HER LOVE

THE SONOMA SERIES

SHELBY GUNTER

For Jonathan, for your unfailing support. I love you with everything.

TABLE OF CONTENTS

PROLOGUE

I am unseen.

I am the shadow that slithers across your window in the dark of night. I am never noticed and stay hidden within your world to remain unknown. The anonymity gives me powers beyond anything ever felt before. Building and guiding me to places undiscovered.

Patience has allowed me to quietly watch, until now. Your choices have consequences and you will learn them.

I watch you walk to your car, oblivious to what awaits you. Your taillights shine onto the darkened street as you drive, allowing me to see your progress. I follow through the shadows, waiting for the moment when my message is received.

A boom. A ball of orange and red fire. And your lesson has been learned.

The glow against the night sky is beautiful, and a thrill runs through my system as the darkness grows inside me.

You don't know who I am, but I walk among you, and one day, you will know my name.

QUINN

PRESENT DAY

This is it, ten years of my life packed in boxes and on its way to North Carolina. I feel like I should be stressed out right now, but I've honestly never been happier. Growing up, moving was second nature to my family because my parents were traveling doctors who discovered a rare genetic disorder.

I got to live in some exceptional places and saw a lot of extraordinary things, but as I got older, I always felt like something was missing. Looking back, I think it's because those places didn't have that sentimental feeling you get from living in the same house your whole life.

The only place to ever come close was my grandparents' house in Sonoma, North Carolina. I'd spend three months with them every summer, and I looked forward to it the entire year.

They lived in that quintessential small town where everyone knows everyone and seems like it should only exist in a movie. It always felt more like home than any city my parents ever moved me to, and it was my one chance to feel like I belonged somewhere.

Now, as I stand in my empty studio apartment, I look at

the big windows I've always loved and the dark hardwood floors running throughout. The kitchen with its dark cabinets, the exposed brick on the walls, and the industrial-style pipes should make me feel sentimental but standing here, I feel oddly detached.

Shouldn't I feel sad about leaving the place I've called home longer than anywhere else I've lived? Surely there should be some nostalgia or reminiscence of times spent here, but as I think back, there's nothing. I was in my office more than I was in my apartment, so the memories that should've been made never were.

I guess if anything, that's what I'm most sad about. I didn't take the time to create a home here, but I'm determined to fix those mistakes when I get to Sonoma.

I pick up the box closest to the door and start down the five flights of stairs to load my car. After three trips up and down, the boxes containing things I didn't want to be ruined in the moving truck are loaded into the car I'd only recently bought.

I sit down in the driver's seat, and with all of the excitement flowing through me, I barely notice the ache in my muscles when I reach for the gear shift, put my car in drive, and pull away from the insanely lucky parking spot in front of my building.

Looking in my rearview mirror, watching as my apartment building grows smaller, I smile with the knowledge that I'm finally on the right path. Up until this point, I had been passively going through the motions of life, and now, sitting in New York traffic heading south, I feel the buzz of adventure in my body. I know this is going to be the start of something big.

I stop a few hours outside the city to fill my gas tank and buy food because a road trip is not a road trip without snacks. I have another six hours before I arrive, and plenty of the time is spent listening to the songs of my youth, but for the majority of the drive, I think about my time in New York.

I came to the city for my undergraduate degree as well as law school at NYU. I kept my head down, studied hard, and graduated at the top of my class.

While my parents were disappointed I didn't follow in their footsteps and become a world-renowned doctor, they were still proud of me. Hell, I was proud of myself. I never imagined I'd be capable of succeeding in law school, but I was determined to make a name for myself that wasn't associated with my parents.

After graduation, I was offered a position at one of the top law firms in the city. It was the job every law student would have killed for, and I landed it with ease. All of my carefully laid plans were lining up perfectly and going way better than expected.

After only six years at the firm, I was on track to make partner because I was damn good at my job. I spent long nights and weekends in my office pouring over cases and doing everything in my power to win—even if my client was slightly less deserving of the alimony payout.

Then, a few months ago, I was sitting in my office several hours after everyone had already left for the day, and I thought, what am I doing here? What is the point of this career I've busted my ass for? I have more money than I know what to do with because I never do anything other than work. I'm slaving toward a promotion that would most certainly result in even more hours than what I'm currently putting in, and I'm no longer in love with my job.

Had I ever been in love with my job?

I didn't have a good answer to that question.

Despite being one of the best family lawyers in the company, I no longer had any desire to go to battle for a client. It didn't feel like I was making a difference anymore because one minute, I would be gushing over a brand-new baby about to be adopted by the most deserving family, and the next minute I watched as broken-hearted parents were forced to give the baby back to people who weren't capable of caring for him.

My entire career had always been this endless loop of soaring highs and horrible lows. Recently, I had been in the lowest of lows. Between incredibly selfish clients, coworkers who suddenly had it out for me because of the promotion, and the minimal desire to do my job, I was just done.

But how could that be? I had the dream job. I was moving up faster than anyone in my graduating class, and I was working in the specialization I cared the most about. When did my goals and achievements suddenly stop being what I wanted for myself?

I sat there contemplating my life and realized the last time I was genuinely happy was the last summer I spent with my grandparents before they died. I was eighteen, about to go to college, and I knew, deep down, it was the last time I was going to be there with them. At the time, I thought it was because I was going to school, but they died three months after I started my first semester at NYU, and I couldn't bring myself to go back after the funeral.

My grandmother went first and very suddenly. My grandfather followed her a month afterward from what they call "broken heart syndrome". I like to think he couldn't continue living without my grandmother, so instead of mourning her for the rest of his life, he joined her.

They left the house to me because they knew how much it meant to me, and it also came with a decent inheritance since I was their only grandchild. My parents and I hired a company to help take care of the house while I was in school, making sure it didn't fall into disrepair, and because of that, I've got a place to live when I get to North Carolina.

So, after having had the epiphany of a lifetime, in the middle of my office alone, I realized I no longer wanted the illustrious career of a high-profile city attorney. It wasn't my dream anymore, and while I had no idea what would be waiting for me, I knew I needed to go back to the only place I could always count on in order to figure out my next step.

The dinner when I told my assistant and best friend, Hailey, I was quitting the firm and moving to North Carolina will be a night I remember for a long time. I'd made reservations at Frank's Steak House, which was our favorite restaurant to go to after a win in court. I had arrived before Hailey and ordered our usual—two glasses of pinot grigio and an appetizer of bruschetta.

I LOOK up after chastising myself for the third time to wait and not eat the food in front of me when I see her breeze in with the elegance and grace of a model walking on a catwalk.

Hailey's blonde hair is swept back in a low bun, and she has killer blue eyes that are the envy of many because they look like sea glass. Her sharp features make her seem intimidating, but in reality, she's the furthest thing from it.

She sits down, immediately taking a drink from her wine glass, and says, "Hey girl, I'm sorry I'm late. I got stuck talking to Peter who doesn't seem to understand that I would rather stick an ice pick in my eye than go out with him."

"He can't take a hint, can he?"

"Of course not. What woman in their right mind would say no to Peter the douche?" she says with the most disdainful look I've ever seen from her.

"He gives me the skeeves."

"Tell me about it. So, what's up? What's with the dinner? You weren't in court today, so I know we aren't celebrating."

Yikes, she's jumping right in here before we even have our main course.

I'm suddenly nervous, and my heart starts beating so hard I'm pretty sure the neighboring table can tell I'm going to have a heart attack in a minute.

Am I having a heart attack?

No. Focus. Stop being ridiculous. I should've known she'd see through the dinner ploy and know something was up. Why did I think I'd have more time to prepare before I laid everything out for her?

"Hello?" she says, waving her hand in my face. "What's happening here? Why are you sweating? I've not seen you like this since your first day in court."

That was a rough day, let me tell you. I spent thirty minutes in the courthouse bathroom throwing up my breakfast and stuttered through presenting my case. Thank god it was a straightforward win because I think I would've quit the firm that day if I'd lost.

"Right," I clear my throat. "I'm just going to throw it out there and hope to God you don't keel over."

She looks at me like I've got two heads and nods for me to keep going.

"I am quitting the firm and have decided to move to my grandparents' house in North Carolina," I say quickly.

Hailey tilts her head and her eyebrows furrow. "You want to run that by me one more time?" she asks.

I straighten my shoulders and, after taking another drink of my wine, I say, "I am not happy anymore, Hailey. I haven't been for some time, and I've decided I need to make a change. I realized that I'm not living the life I want, so I'm going to move to my grandparents' house in North Carolina and slow my life down for a little while."

"Holy. Shit. Seriously? Are we on Punk'd right now and someone is going to come out and say 'Ha, you fool' and then proceed to laugh in my face?" she asks, looking around behind me and over her shoulder, apparently hoping for a camera crew to come out.

"No, Hailey," I say, shaking my head and laughing. "You're not

8

on Punk'd. I know it seems sudden and drastic and insane, but I've never felt more sure of a decision in my life. This is what I need."

"Honey, if you need an emotional boost, that's totally understandable. We've been working non-stop for a while now, so I get it, but why don't we just take off and go to the Hamptons for the weekend or something?"

"Because come Monday, I'd have to go back into the office and pretend like I enjoy my work. Pretend like little pieces of me aren't dying every time I open a case file."

"But what are you going to do instead? From what I remember you telling me, it's a small town. I doubt many people there need legal services. And don't get me started on the living environment. It's all moo-cows and howdy-dos and god knows what else."

"Have you ever actually been to a small town, or are those just examples from movies?"

"They might be from the movies, but my description is not the point. The point is, what are you going to do there?"

"I don't know yet, maybe paint or get a retail job. All I know is, it's time to take a step back."

"What about the partnership the firm has been hinting at? You're just going to walk away from that?"

"I don't want it. I don't want to have to work more than I already am. I'm just...not happy," I say, shrugging my shoulders.

"Quinn, are you absolutely sure about this? This is huge and more than likely career suicide. You wouldn't be able to come back whenever you wanted."

"Yes, I've been thinking about this for a while now. I know what the consequences are, and I also know I won't ever want to be a lawyer again."

"I guess you're the only one who knows that," she says with sympathy in her eyes.

"My lease is up in three months, and I've already started the process of transferring my case files to Lisa and Nicole. I'm hoping to have everything packed up by early June before my lease officially ends."

"Well, all I can say is I better not see you in a pair of cowboy boots. Those are not flattering on anyone no matter where you live," she says, and I just laugh at her.

IT TOOK about a month for Hailey to get on board with my plan and, being my best friend, I wouldn't have expected anything less from her. We've been each other's support system and fiercest allies since I started at the firm. Having spent the last six years together, at work and in life, this is going to be tough for both of us.

She knows my disdain for mushrooms, that I'm a serial first-dater, and I'm incredibly socially awkward. I know when she's coming in from a one-night stand or when she's biting her tongue from saying something mean just by looking at her. Usually, the scathing remark is not directed at me, although when you work closely enough with someone, it tends to happen occasionally, and it only has made our relationship stronger.

I know I will miss her terribly, but I also know she supports me one hundred percent, and because of that, I'm ready to begin my new journey.

2

QUINN

I pull off onto the exit ramp towards Sonoma and start taking inventory of my surroundings. The town is a few miles off of the highway, and as I turn onto Main Street, I'm reminded of how much I love this place. Planter boxes housing beautiful flowers are stationed between timeless black lampposts. Awnings cover the sidewalks on both sides of the street, and I know they'll be decorated for the fourth of July soon.

There are shops on both sides of the street, and as I slowly drive by them, I see how much things have changed over the years. There is a clothing boutique next to the barber shop that still has the striped pole outside its door. Matthew's Furniture Store has a beautiful chair and end table display in its front window, and where there used to be a laundromat, there's an adorable pet store called Waggin' Tails. I drive a little further down the street and see my favorite building located in the town center.

Town Hall is a two-story building with red brick walls, white trim windows, and beautiful white stone columns lining the front entrance. I've always loved the building's architecture and have wondered on many occasions what it would be like to work in a place that beautiful.

I keep driving towards my grandparents' house, and as I make the turn onto their street, I see the big moving truck out front. It all feels surreal right now. It hasn't quite sunk in yet that this town is my home, and I am going to start building a life here.

I pull into the driveway, and my heart gives a little lurch. The two-story cottage looks exactly the same as I remember. There are three steps leading up to the white front porch, and an empty planter box hangs on the railing. The wooden porch swing sits to the right of the black front door and is missing its cushion. The windows are trimmed in white, and the siding on the house offsets the windows in a steel grey. I feel a sudden pinprick of tears behind my eyes knowing my grandparents won't be waiting for me inside. Even after all this time, it will still be immensely difficult to be in the house without them.

I park my car in the driveway and get out to grab one of the boxes from the back of my car. The movers are quickly unloading the truck and will be finished soon. I watch them move like a well-oiled machine, proving they do this on a regular basis.

I pick the lightest box packed in my back seat and head inside. As I walk up the front steps and over the threshold, I am hit by an onslaught of memories. My grandpa chasing me up and down the hallway, the smell of my grandmother's spaghetti sauce simmering in the kitchen. I always felt so comfortable with them, and the sadness of knowing they're no longer here swamps me.

I close my eyes, letting the tears pass, and when I take a deep breath, I can almost hear my grandparents say you're going to be just fine. I open my eyes again and know they are right. They're here with me even if I can't see them, and I make a vow to myself to make new memories.

I walk out of the entryway and see the french doors to the office on my left. It was always one of my favorite rooms because one wall has floor-to-ceiling shelves that used to hold every book I could dream of reading, and the rest of the office would be turned into a painting studio for me to use while I was visiting.

I look to my right and see the living room which is open to the dining room and kitchen. The stairs face the front door, and a bedroom and a half bathroom are on the left side down the hallway. I walk upstairs, passing another bathroom and bedroom, and head toward the master.

It's a huge room with large windows on the left, facing the backyard. The en suite bathroom is to the right as well as the walk-in closet of my dreams, but I would have never been able to afford it in New York. The cream carpet and white walls will allow me to put my stamp on the space without making me feel like I'm erasing my grandparents.

I set the box down in the middle of the room and walk back downstairs to start organizing the boxes the movers have already brought inside. I delegate where I want the furniture to be placed, and after a few hours, all of my things are in the house and the movers have left.

I look around and realize how empty the house still feels. My entire apartment in New York was about the same size as the kitchen, dining room, and living room. The furniture I brought seems dwarfed in this massive space, and I start giggling at the ridiculousness of the whole thing.

I didn't even consider that I was moving into a three-bedroom house from a tiny studio apartment. Still giggling, I spin in a circle taking in my sparse furniture and boxes when I hear a knock on the door.

Wondering who in the world would be visiting me already, I walk out of the living room and down the hallway. I open the door and see the only person I could've wanted to see there.

Hailey stands on my porch with a suitcase the size of Texas on one side of her and three bottles of wine on the other side. She's staring at her phone, brows furrowed, looking every bit as lost as I'm sure she feels.

"Hailey? What are you doing here?"

"Oh, thank god! I was worried I drove nine hours and ended up in the middle of nowhere outside some stranger's house." I rush towards her and envelop her in a huge hug. My five-nine height to her five-two makes it so I feel Amazonian next to her, but at this moment, all I'm thinking about is that my best friend is standing on my porch.

"I can't believe you're standing here. What's going on? Why are you here?"

"You know I couldn't let you move to Nowhere, USA all by yourself, so I took a couple of weeks off from the many weeks I've accumulated and decided to come and help you get settled."

"This is amazing. I'm so glad you're here."

"Well, with you gone, I didn't have much to do at work, and it took all of two minutes for me to realize I missed you way too much to not come and spend time with you. Now, show me this adorable house that's stolen you away from me." I lean down and pick up the wine bottles and nod my head towards the house.

"Do you think you brought enough wine?"

"I was still worried you'd gotten yourself into a mess, and I figured if it was awful we could drink until we forgot how bad it was. Right now, I think we can use them to celebrate because this house is beautiful." I walk her into the living room and she leaves her suitcase by the entryway.

"Did you get robbed or something? Where's all of your stuff?"

"No, I didn't get robbed." I chuckle. "You know what my apartment looked like, it was tiny, and now all of my stuff feels small because none of it fits here." Hailey looks at me and gasps, eyes wide and a smile growing across her face. "Do you know what this means?"

"No, what does this mean?" I ask, slightly worried about her response.

"It means we get to go shopping." She squeals, making me laugh.

"Of course it does. Actually, there is a furniture store in town that looked promising. Do you want to go check it out? We can also look into getting furniture for the guest room since you're going to be staying for a while."

"A brilliant idea since I'm not about to sleep on a couch. That's a little too rough for me."

"Then let's go find you a bed," I say as I grab my purse and lead her back out to my car.

3

COOPER

"Hey, Coop, I'm headed out. I'll see you later?" Todd, my best friend and deputy chief asks, peeking his head around my door.

"Yeah, I'll be heading out here soon. I'll see you at Donna's," I respond, referencing our favorite bar. It's been around since before I can remember, and it's pretty much the only place to go on a Friday night to get a drink.

This will be the first weekend I've had off in a while and I'm taking full advantage of the time. Being the police chief of Sonoma, my days usually only consist of paperwork and patrolling the streets for reckless teenagers thinking they're invincible, but these past few weeks have been rough.

One of the neighboring towns has had a string of breaking and enterings, or B and Es, and the most recent ones have resulted in huge amounts of damage. To help out, my deputies and I have been lending them a hand with their crime scenes on top of running extra patrols in Sonoma to ensure everyone is kept safe.

We haven't had any issues so far, but it would be fool-hardy to think our town is safe. The worst part is, we're nowhere near being able to solve these crimes. I'm doing what I can to help, but since it's not my town, there isn't much I can do except lend a hand when needed and hope the perp doesn't try anything in Sonoma.

I pack up my stuff, lock my office, and walk down the hallway to the lobby. It's a small station with a few offices, a bullpen, and a main waiting area. We have a few cells in the back but we don't normally need to use them.

There's only been a few times I've had to put someone back there. Once because a fight broke out at Donna's over a bad bet during a football game. I put the guys in the cells to cool off and sent them home the next morning.

Another time, a college kid decided to streak across the football field during homecoming. We caught him before he made it all the way onto the field, and we just put him in there to scare him. The dude freaked out, so we didn't keep him in there for too long.

We still have a good laugh about it every now and then.

I wave to the deputies in the break room who are getting ready for the night shift and walk out the front door to my truck. Driving towards my house, I stay alert of my surroundings. Sometimes it feels like I'm always on guard, and it can be exhausting.

Growing up, I was the rule follower. I liked the control it gave me, and it drove me nuts when my little brother, Levi, would rope me into one of his schemes. I was always the one who got in trouble when we got caught, but eventually, I learned to stop going along with his antics.

When I got into high school, I realized my rule following was a pretty good indication I should go into law enforcement. Plus, my dad was the police chief, and I've never wanted to be anything other than exactly like him.

I pull into my garage, jump out of my truck, and walk into the laundry room that leads into the kitchen. Piper, my fifty-pound mutt, comes bounding into the room to say hello. She's a mix of German Shepherd, lab, and pitbull, and she's my best friend.

I like to think she picked me to be her buddy because one day, I was sitting on my back porch and all of a sudden, this little tan puppy came barreling out of nowhere and started biting my shoe laces.

I took her to the vet to make sure she was healthy and to check if her owner was looking for her. Come to find out, she was a stray the shelter had been trying to catch for months, so I took her in, and she's been my best friend ever since.

That was four years ago, but it seems like it was just last week she bounded into my life.

I sit down on the bench in my laundry room to take off my boots and hang up my tactical belt. Walking into my kitchen, I grab a water bottle from the fridge and let Piper out into the backyard to run around. Most of the time my Friday nights are spent hanging with Piper, but with all the stress over these last few weeks, I'm needing more of a distraction to keep from constantly thinking about the job. I let Piper back in and head upstairs to shower. Throwing on a pair of jeans, a shirt, and my boots, I'm ready to go out.

Driving towards Donna's, I do my best to clear my mind off work so I can have a good night. It's tough with all of the unknowns right now but I do my best.

I pull into the gravel parking lot and see a ton of cars already parked. It shouldn't be surprising since there's nowhere else to hang out on the weekend.

I walk in and immediately look for Todd and Megan. It's not the easiest task because it's loud and feels like everyone is stacked on top of each other since it's so crowded, but I finally find them standing at the bar with their heads bent together. They've been together since high school, and even after all this time, they're still just as in love as they were when they were seventeen.

Of course, they also still look exactly the same as they did at seventeen too. Todd's black hair is wavy and he keeps it long on the top and short on the sides. He's tall, standing well over six feet, and is all muscle. His dark brown eyes and sharp features give off a menacing look when in reality, he's the nicest guy. Megan is Todd's opposite in almost every way. She's petite with a soft face, blonde hair, and blue eyes. She's every bit as nice as she looks, and they're the perfect pair.

I've been the third wheel of our group since they first got together and, even though most of the time I don't mind, I do have moments where I wish I had someone to bring along with me when we go out. Unfortunately, living in the same town your whole life gives you limited options on partners. Don't get me wrong, I've dated and had my share of fun, it just gets harder when you only have so many women in your age range to date.

Todd looks up and sees me walking towards them and gives me a wave. "Hey guys," I say as Megan leans in to give me a hug.

"Hi, Cooper. How are you doing with everything? You guys have had a long couple of weeks," she says with a measuring look like she's trying to read my mind and make sure I'm okay.

"It's definitely been one for the books," I say.

"Let's get him a drink before we pepper him with questions," Todd says, motioning for the bartender to come over while Megan sticks her tongue out at Todd, making me chuckle.

"What can I get ya, Chief?" Cheryl, who's been the bartender at Donna's since we were in high school, asks me. Despite not being in uniform, the town still typically addresses me as my title no matter what I wear or how many times I've asked them not to when I'm not on duty.

"Whatever you have on tap tonight would be great, Cheryl. Thanks." She grabs a glass and pours my drink. As soon as she slides it across the bar, Megan asks, "Anything new on the B and Es?"

Megan's been part of our team since Todd and I graduated from the academy. At this point, she should be deputized which we joke about doing every now and then. She says she'd rather step on nails than do the fitness routine Todd and I go through to stay in shape.

"No, unfortunately, and Westlake's chief is already wound up about needing the extra hands, so they aren't interested in our help solving the cases," I say.

"Well, then it's their problem if they don't want our help," Todd says, shrugging his shoulders.

"Yeah, I guess. It's frustrating because the perp has started escalating. Half the house was smashed with this most recent one. I'm worried they'll come here when they run out of houses in Westlake."

"If he does, then we'll do the jobs we were born to do and hope to God he doesn't escalate past breaking into empty houses," Todd says with the strength and conviction I've relied upon for a long time. He's always been the steady rock I can count on no matter what situation we're in.

"Okay, let's talk about something else so we can start enjoying our Friday night," Megan says with a pointed look at both me and Todd.

"Good idea, babe." Todd looks at her with a dopey smile on his face.

"Did you hear someone moved into Dan and Carla Johnson's old house?"

"Oh really? Do you know who it is?" Todd has to lean in so Megan can hear his question over the noise of the bar.

"Their granddaughter, I think, but I don't know what her name is. I was going to stop by this week and see if she needed anything."

"When did she move in?" I ask.

"Sometime on Monday. I saw the moving truck in the

driveway, and Mrs. Holliday said she was buying furniture at Matthew's with another woman." Mrs. Holliday is the town's busy body. If it's worth knowing, she will have already heard about it and shared it with every person she knows.

"Well, when you go see her, make sure she knows we're around if she needs anything," I say, knowing Megan would've done that whether I told her to or not.

"You know I will."

The conversation shifts to the high school football team's chances of getting into the championships and ebbs and flows as it always does with the three of us. I want to spend some time with Piper, so I head home early even though I don't have to work tomorrow.

I walk outside and the warm air is jarring compared to the A/C inside. As I'm about to get in my truck, I get this weird feeling in my gut telling me something is off. I look around the parking lot, and it's full of cars just like it was when I got here.

Since everyone's inside, the lot is empty of people, but it still feels as though someone is out here with me. I do one more scan and don't see anything, so I chalk it up to the stress I've had this week and get in my truck to head home.

Piper is waiting for me in her bed in the living room when I walk in the door. Since I haven't been home much, I spend a little extra time playing tug of war and working on her find and retrieve skills. I hide treats in different areas, and she'll usually sniff out where I've hidden them.

We're going to take advantage of my rare day off and go fishing tomorrow. It's been a while since I've gotten out to the lake, and it would do us both some good to get some fresh air. As I get ready for bed, I give one fleeting thought to the uneasiness I felt when I left Donna's and then quickly drift off to sleep.

4

QUINN

Hailey and I found some amazing furniture at Matthew's and had it delivered to the house the same day. I told Hailey she could have free reign over decorating her guest room since she will be the only one staying there, and she did not disappoint. She decided on reds and blues for her theme with a white bed and nightstands. The girl has some serious style and has made decorating the rest of the house a breeze.

After the furniture arrived, we spent our time unpacking boxes and organizing the things I brought from the city. Hailey has been vital to keeping my sanity together throughout this whole process. Her organizational skills are legendary, and without her, I would've just thrown things in cabinets and moved on. The only room I confidently put together by myself is my painting studio.

Every summer, my grandparents would convert my grandfather's office into a studio, and I would spend hours there painting anything and everything. I didn't get to paint throughout the year because it was too hard to move all of my materials each time my parents relocated, so I had to make up for the lost time during the summers.

Hailey and I have gotten a lot unpacked and put away, and I've only got one more week with her. The time is going by so fast already. "Are you sure you can't stay forever?" I ask her while I flip through the movie channels on TV.

"Darling, I know you can't live without me, but I am not cut out for this small-town life. I need my city to survive. I've gone a full week without smelling the sweaty summer scent of New York. I think I might be having withdrawals." Hailey walks into the living room and drops down onto the couch next to me.

"Oh, that's so gross!"

"You know you miss it," she teases.

"I absolutely do not miss the smell. It was always the worst part of summer. But I am going to miss you when you have to leave next week."

"And I will miss you too, but that is what Facetime and airplanes were designed for."

"Okay, okay. I see this is a losing battle with you. What should we do today?" Since the house is basically unpacked—with the exception of my bedroom which is still a disaster area—our whole afternoon is wide open.

"How about we check out the bar tonight? You're going to have to make friends at some point, so you might as well start there."

"I guess that's not a bad idea. Plus, I'll have you to run interference when I say something stupid."

"Shut up, you will not say anything stupid," she says, giving me the stink eye.

"Come on, Hailey, you know how I am. I suck at social interactions. I'm always awkward and uncomfortable; nothing ever comes out of my mouth the way I want it to." This has been a lifelong struggle for me. I've never been one to make friends easily, and I tend to avoid social interactions in general. Hailey was forced to be my friend since she was my assistant first.

"I know you get uncomfortable but you're not awkward, and you always do great after the first few minutes. You just need to pluck up the courage. Plus, I'll be there with you the whole time." As she continues to encourage me to be more social, the doorbell rings, and I stand up to answer. I can see through the glass framing the door it's a woman holding a basket.

"Hello, how can I help you?" I ask the petite blonde woman.

"Hi there! My name is Megan Montgomery. My husband, Todd, and I live a few streets over, and I thought I would stop by and introduce myself. You're Dan and Carla Johnson's granddaughter, right?" she asks.

I'm immediately overwhelmed by this woman and, at the same time, oddly at ease. She's beautiful in a wholesome and endearing sort of way, and she exudes kindness. I'm the exact opposite of her in personality and looks but feel as though she could already be my friend.

"Yes, I am," I confirm, holding my hand out to her. "Quinn Lawson."

"It's so nice to meet you!" she says, still holding the ginormous basket of goodies and grabbing my hand at the same time.

I wave her into the foyer. "Please, come in."

"Wow, all of the updates you've made look amazing. I knew your grandparents pretty well and we were all so sad when they passed," Megan says with genuine sympathy.

"Thank you. They left me their house after they died, and I hired a company to help me take care of it while I was in school. When I decided to move here, I thought it would be good to update the place," I respond.

The house hadn't been updated since before my grandparents were alive, so after I put my plans into motion, I had a contractor help me renovate it while I got everything squared away in New York.

We walk into the living room where Hailey is sitting on the couch. "This is my best friend, Hailey. Hailey, this is Megan. She and her husband live a few streets over, and she stopped by to say hello." Hailey jumps up from the couch and walks around to shake Megan's hand.

"This is amazing! I was just telling Quinn she needed to find friends in this town and here you come along. It's so nice to meet you," Hailey says, much to my mortification.

"It's nice to meet you too!" Megan grins and shakes Hailey's hand.

"What's in the basket?" Hailey asks.

We walk into the kitchen, and Megan puts the basket on the counter.

"Oh, just the essentials for unpacking. Wine, chocolates, crackers, and cheese."

"This is so nice of you, Megan, thank you," I say, checking out the contents.

I still can't get over how nice people have been to me, and I've only been here a little over a week. It would've been so easy for the town to ignore me since I'm the new person, but they've been so welcoming and kind. Everyone has made sure I had everything I needed while moving into the house.

Apparently, my grandparents were well-loved in this town, and that has extended to me by default.

"Of course. Todd and I wanted to say welcome to Sonoma, and if you need anything, please let us know. Todd is the deputy chief of police, and our best friend, Cooper, is the chief. Either one can be here in a heartbeat if you need them," Megan offers.

"That's really sweet. I will definitely reach out if I need anything," I tell her.

"We were just talking about what we wanted to do tonight. Donna's seems like the place to be on the weekends, is that true?" Hailey asks.

"We love Donna's! We've been going there since we were legally able to walk in," Megan says.

"We will have to check it out then." Hailey grins at me.

"Actually, Todd and I are having a barbecue tonight at our house with some friends. We would love to have you both come over and meet some of our group if you want," Megan offers.

"Yes, yes, yes! That sounds amazing," Hailey says, jumping up and down and clapping her hands.

"Are you sure, Megan? We wouldn't want to impose on your time with friends." It's kind of hard to believe they would invite random strangers to come over, but Megan seems like the outgoing person I've always wanted to be, so maybe this is a normal occurrence for her.

"Oh my gosh, of course, I'm sure. This will be so much fun. You can meet everybody and kill their curiosity at the same time." Megan laughs.

"We will be there. What's the dress code?" Hailey asks.

"We are completely casual around here, so wear whatever's comfortable."

"Perfect."

"Let me write down our address and my phone number," Megan says, grabbing a pen off the counter and jotting down her info. "We'll eat around seven, but come anytime."

"We'll see you tonight then." I'm still not entirely sure what just happened, but with Hailey around, it's not a surprise.

We lead Megan toward the foyer and wave as she walks out. I close the door and turn to Hailey.

"Hailey, I can't go to this barbecue. Everyone is going to bombard me with questions, and you know how I get. I'll be babbling like an idiot the whole night, and no one will want to be my friend, and then what am I going to do? I can't live here and be the social outcast. I won't survive!" I yell at her as I hysterically pace between the living room and the kitchen.

"Whoa, whoa, whoa, hold on there. Back up twenty paces and take a breath, girlfriend," she says pushing me down on the stool next to the island in the kitchen.

"First of all, you are wonderful, exceedingly smart, and can handle anything. Second of all, I'll be with you the whole time and can deflect anything you don't want to talk about. Third, it's time to pull up your big girl panties and get to know people because if you want this to be your home then you're going to need friends." I look at Hailey and take a huge deep breath to calm my racing heart.

"You're right. I need to do this. I can do this." I say with determination I don't really feel.

"You're damn right you can do this."

"But what am I going to wear?" All of my courage flies right out of the window.

"Oh, darling, that's why you have me," Hailey says, taking my hand and leading me upstairs to my bedroom.

5

QUINN

Hailey helped me pick out the perfect outfit for tonight. I'm wearing my favorite cutoff shorts and a sleeveless, red gingham shirt that ties at the bottom. It's casual but super cute, and it makes me feel comfortable which is a bonus in these situations. "Hailey, are you ready to go?" I yell as I walk downstairs and into the kitchen.

She comes breezing into the room looking very New York chic with skin-tight black shorts and a sleeveless, white flowing top with a bow at the neck. I wouldn't have expected anything less from her.

"Yes, primping is done, and I am ready. How are you? Are you ready?"

"Yes, I think I am," I say with a determined nod. For the first time in my life, I have a chance to build friendships, and I am both terrified and thrilled.

"Then let's do this," Hailey cheers.

We walk out to my car and drive the few minutes it takes to get to Todd and Megan's. Pulling onto their street, you can tell they're having a party as several cars are parked around their house already. We find a parking spot and walk up the sidewalk to their gorgeous two-story craftsman-style house. It's got grey siding that almost looks blue, and grey stone wrapping around the bottom. The front porch is lined with columns that are also covered in stone.

We knock on their front door and can hear people talking and music playing inside. Megan opens the door with a wave and a great big smile. "I'm so glad you guys are here. Come in and meet everyone."

"Hi, thanks again for inviting us," I say as we walk into their house. It's completely open, and you can see all the way through to the windows in the back of the house. Two white columns stand in the middle separating the left side from the right. The living room is on the left and opens up to the dining room while the kitchen takes up most of the right side of the house.

Everyone is either standing or sitting around a huge island in the kitchen. The room is warm and inviting in creams and whites with little splotches of black perfectly scattered.

"We brought wine, but it's probably only enough for me to be happy," Hailey says, handing the bottle to Megan.

"That's perfect. We'll add it to the mix." Megan grins.

She leads us toward the kitchen and people start noticing we've arrived. "Everyone, Quinn and Hailey are here!" They all look up at us as Megan starts pointing to people. "That's Lucy, Max, Todd, Sara, Natalie, and Levi. Cooper, Levi's brother, was here a minute ago, but I don't know where he went."

They smile at me and Hailey, and I smile back, giving a little half-wave. Todd walks up to me and reaches out to shake my hand. He's tall with dark hair and dark eyes and is incredibly handsome. "It's nice to finally meet you. Cooper went out back to check the grill," he says with a welcoming grin. I shake his hand, and he turns to Hailey and he shakes hers too.

"It's nice to meet you too," Hailey says. "Your house is gorgeous! Are you guys from here originally?"

"Thank you. We bought this house about seven years ago and have done a ton of work on it, but we've lived in Sonoma our whole lives," Todd says.

"Wow, I can't imagine living in one place my whole life. That seems so odd to me," I say.

"Almost all of us have lived here all our lives. I grew up here and met Max at UNC, but we both knew we wanted to move here after we graduated," Lucy says as she shares a smile with Max. She has straight blonde hair that hits her shoulders, and her brown eyes seem kind and genuine. Max looks back at her with dark chocolate eyes full of love for her. "Where are you both from?" she asks.

"I moved here from New York which is where I've lived the longest. My parents are traveling doctors, so I grew up moving all over the place."

"I've never lived anywhere else but New York, and I wouldn't trade it for anything. You just have to walk a few blocks and it'll feel like another country. Trust me," Hailey says, making everyone laugh. God, I wish I had her ease and charm.

"Where are some of the places you've lived?" Levi—I think —asks me.

"Oh, um, I've lived in most states across the country. My favorites being Washington and Virginia, but I've also lived in other places across the world like Dubai, London, Sydney... It would probably take most of the evening to tell you all of them," I respond.

"Who's ready to eat?" A booming voice calls as he walks in from the back patio. I turn towards the voice and am suddenly staring at the most gorgeous man I've ever seen. His eyes are almost amber in color, growing darker towards the middle, and they suck you into their depths. I'm not even standing very close and I feel like I'm drowning in them.

"Oh, there you are, Cooper. Come and meet Quinn and Hailey. Quinn is Dan and Carla Johnson's granddaughter and just moved here from New York. Hailey's here helping Quinn get moved in," Megan says.

Suddenly, I'm panicking. I'm going to have to talk to the most beautiful man I've ever met.

He's got light brown hair that's just long enough on top to run your fingers through it and is shorter on the sides. He has a hint of a five o'clock shadow on his strong jaw and looks like every fantasy man I've ever dreamed of.

Okay, get it together, Quinn. You are smart and strong and are fully capable of talking to a gorgeous, sexy man. Thank god I learned how to mask my facial expressions in law school.

"Hey, it's nice to meet you," Cooper says, stretching out his hand to shake mine.

As soon as I touch him, I feel this electricity shooting up my arm. Cooper's eyebrows furrow as though I'm not the only one who feels the odd charge. He holds on to my hand as I stammer, "Hi, yeah it's, uh, nice to meet you too."

Shit. I sound like an idiot. I turn to look at Hailey, desperate for a reprieve from my whirring thoughts and complete stupidity. She seems as cool as a cucumber as she says hello and shakes his hand.

"Is everyone ready to eat? The burgers are done," Cooper says and looks at the group around the kitchen. He looks back at me, and a shudder moves through my body. I've never had such a physical reaction to someone before.

Sure, I've met plenty of attractive men throughout my life, but none of them have ever thrown my entire body and mind into such chaos like Cooper did with one touch.

He shakes his head as if to get rid of whatever thoughts he was having and steps back as everyone starts filing outside with shouts of hunger and excitement to eat. Once we're outside, we fill our plates in the outdoor kitchen, and everyone finds a place to sit between the dining table and living space.

I'm having serious backyard envy right now. Megan and Todd have obviously put a lot of time into their space with perfectly placed greenery and flowers around their fenced-in yard, and the entertaining space looks like it came from a magazine.

"Holy hotness, Batman. Can you believe that Cooper guy?" Hailey whisper yells to me as we sit down on a loveseat. "He is like sex on a stick. Almost makes me want to stay here."

"Shhh... he'll hear you," I admonish.

"I don't care if he hears. A guy doesn't walk around looking like that and not know he's sexy." I look over at Cooper who is talking with Levi, Megan, and Todd. She has a point.

He is definitely sex on a stick, but there's something about the way he carries himself that exudes a confidence I would never be able to emulate.

I've always envied people who are able to stand in a room and know exactly how they fit into it. It usually takes me a significant amount of time to figure out the dynamics of the group before I feel comfortable. I will say, it's made me a great listener because I end up wanting to hear people's life stories instead of talking about myself.

"So, where's the coolest place you've lived outside of the U.S.?" Natalie asks, interrupting my thoughts. She sits down in a chair across from the couch Hailey and I are sitting on while we eat. She has beautiful auburn hair that hangs in soft waves around her face. Freckles dance across her nose, and her gorgeous green eyes sparkle with life and humor as she smiles at me.

"That's a tough question for me to answer. I've lived in some really neat places. The farthest away I've lived was Sydney, Australia for a year while my parents did a lecture series at the university, but I think Florence and London are a couple of my favorites."

"What kind of doctors are your parents?" Sara, who has soft brown hair and hazel eyes, asks.

"My dad is a cardiologist and my mom is a family practitioner. They discovered a genetic disorder about thirty years ago, and since then, they've traveled across the world researching and presenting their results. They also do some clinical work to help medical centers set up diagnostic and treatment practices," I respond, mostly by rote memory at this point. I've shared this story so many times throughout my life.

People are always so fascinated by my childhood, but they usually don't understand the toll it took on me. As a young kid, it was incredibly difficult trying to fit into a new place all the time.

"Wow, that's pretty intense. I can't imagine living in all of those different places. How long did you live in New York?" Sara asks.

"I lived there for a little over twelve years. Initially, I moved there to go to NYU, and then, being the black sheep of the family, I stayed for law school. After I graduated, I practiced family law where Hailey and I worked at a firm together," I respond.

"Yeah, this one's a real ball-buster, but I love her anyway," Hailey teases.

"Hey! I wasn't that bad."

"No, of course not. You just make it so easy to tease you." She winks.

"Don't I know it," I tell her with a roll of my eyes.

"How are you settling into small-town life?" Natalie asks.

"It's been a lot smoother than I anticipated. Hailey has helped a ton with unpacking, and the people I've met have been incredibly nice, albeit a little nosy. It's super refreshing compared to New York though."

"That's so good to hear. I'm sure everyone is just excited there's a new person in town, but don't worry, something else will happen, and they'll move their attention away from you," Natalie says.

"I honestly don't mind too much, but that's good to know." It's been a huge adjustment having people come up to me and want to talk; New Yorkers do not do idle chit-chat. One day, I spent an extra hour at the grocery store because a couple of ladies started asking about my life. Hailey thought I got lost when I didn't come home.

"I'm going to get another drink, does anyone else need anything?" I ask, getting up off the couch. They all shake their heads, so I walk back inside to the kitchen. It's amazing how quickly I've felt comfortable in this space and with these people. It's only been a couple of hours and I'm more relaxed here than I have ever been in a social setting. Even talking about myself hasn't bothered me like it normally does.

I start perusing the wine selection, picking up the pinot Hailey and I brought because it's one of my favorites. As I'm pouring my glass, I hear the door open and turn to see Cooper striding inside. Everything inside me tenses up.

It's like a live wire has touched me, and the air seems to sizzle. Am I the only one feeling this? I guess I could be going crazy. That would make the most sense since I've never once in my thirty-two years ever had a reaction to a man like this.

"Hi there," Cooper says as he walks towards me. "I was coming in to grab another beer. What are you drinking?"

"Yeah, me too. Uh, wine. Not beer. I'm not drinking beer. I like this white wine I brought for Hailey because she doesn't like red wine anymore after getting incredibly sick one night in college... and that's more information than you asked for... sorry." I cringe, my eyes closing and I shake my head. Why can't I have a normal conversation with this man? He's just a guy that also happens to be sexier than any man

I've ever seen. Ugh. *Okay, Quinn, pull yourself together and focus.*

"No red wine for Hailey, got it," he says with a smirk as he grabs a beer from the fridge. "Are you getting settled in okay?" Whew, a topic I can handle. Maybe I won't make a fool of myself twice in one conversation.

"Thanks to Hailey, I am finally settled, I think. We got some new furniture and everything is moved in. Now, all that's left is organizing, which is the bane of my existence. I'm the worst at knowing where things should go. The only thing I'm confident in is my studio."

"Studio?" Cooper asks.

"I turned my grandfather's office into a painting studio. I didn't get to paint much when I was in New York because I never had time, and now that I'm here, I'm hoping to start again." I don't normally tell people about my paintings. I've never shared them because they were my escape. Art was always my way of expressing myself, and once a painting was finished, I would just put it away somewhere.

"What do you paint?"

"Mostly landscapes, but when I'm in the zone, I paint whatever comes to me at that moment. I'm usually really bad at interacting with people, so I use it as a form of expression. My embarrassing story about wine is an example of my social ineptitude." My nose scrunches up in embarrassment but Cooper throws his head back and laughs. Jesus, Mary, and Joseph is that a sight to behold.

His smile lights up his face, and his eyes turn golden with humor. It makes me feel incredibly lucky to be on the receiving end of it. "Now that I'm settled, I'm hoping to do some exploring around town and at the lake. There are so many things here I'd love to paint. It's such a beautiful town, and it has changed a lot since the last time I was here."

"That's right. Megan said you used to come and visit your

grandparents in the summers. I'm sorry you lost them, they were great people."

"Yes, they were. I miss them a lot, but being back in their house has made me feel closer to them than I thought it would," I say with a small smile.

When I first contemplated moving here, I was worried about how difficult it would be to live in their house without them, but with all of the happy memories made, I can't help but feel like they're here with me, encouraging me to finally live a life that makes me happy.

"Well, I'd be happy to show you some of my favorite spots in town if you're interested. I know a place on the lake I could show you. You can get a great view of the sunset there, and not many people know about it."

"That's nice of you to offer, thank you. I'll probably take you up on it since I haven't been out there in about fifteen years."

Cooper reaches into his back pocket and pulls out his wallet. He hands me a card and says, "That's my cell number, let me know when you want to get together, and I'd be happy to show you around."

Holy jumping cactuses, the hottest man on the planet gave me his phone number. I've never had something like this happen before. I know he's just being nice since I'm new here, but still, he actually gave me his card and expects me to call him.

"I will definitely reach out once everything in my studio is ready. I don't think I could handle seeing something I want to paint and not being able to paint it right away," I say, trying to sound nonchalant even though I'm screaming on the inside.

"Sounds good," Cooper says, grinning at me, and then turns to walk back outside.

I think this town just got a whole lot more appealing if I have Mr. Hot Pants showing me around.

6

COOPER

I t's been four days, and I think I've officially lost my mind. I've checked my phone no less than ten times in the last ten minutes and have gotten zero work done in the last two days. All because of a woman with the most striking blue eyes I've ever seen. I can't get them out of my head.

She's consumed me, and I'm dying for her to call. I thought maybe she'd call me yesterday since she needed time to set up her studio, but she never did, and now I'm trying my hardest not to go straight to her house and beg her to go out with me. She captivated me from the first moment I saw her. There was something behind her eyes, a calmness I wanted to fall into and get lost.

After giving her my number, I tried so hard not to follow her around like a puppy. I wanted to be close to her the whole night but I knew it would scream creeper, so I took the moments I got with her and tried to be happy about it.

The way she interacted with everyone there was amazing to watch. She was so focused on the person she was talking to, like she was invested in what they were saying and genuinely listened with everything she had.

She made everyone gravitate towards her and not

because she was someone new. By spending a few moments with her, she could make you feel like the most special person in the world.

"Cooper, are you listening?" Rachel, my secretary asks.

"What? Oh, sorry, Rach. I was zoned out there for a minute. I didn't see you come in. What did you need?"

"Chief Roberts called and requested you call him when you can."

"Got it, I'll call him now. Thanks, Rachel."

"Are you okay, Cooper? I've never seen you quite so spaced out before." A valid question from those who know me best, and Rachel is one of those people.

She's been my secretary for the last four years and followed me from deputy chief to chief. The transition went much smoother with her help. She's been essential to keeping me afloat as I've gotten into my role as chief these last couple of years.

"Yes, I'm fine. Just had an interesting weekend that's still distracting me. Did Steve tell you why he needed to talk to me?"

"No, but he sounded strained on the phone," Rachel says with a wince.

"Okay, hopefully, it's not a new case."

"Yeah, I wouldn't hold my breath. Let me know if you need me for anything. I'm going to head to lunch in a minute." Rachel waves as she leaves my office.

I call the chief back right away in case he needs some of my men, and as the phone rings, my mind drifts back to Quinn's ocean blue eyes and if I'll get a chance to see them again soon.

"Chief Roberts," he answers in a gruff voice. Steven Roberts has been the chief of Westlake's police department since before I even decided to join the force. He's a surly man who always seems to be in a bad mood no matter the situation.

"Hey, Chief, it's Cooper Jackson. What's going on?"

"Cooper, we've had another B and E. The damage on this one is even worse than the others."

"When did it happen?" I ask, standing up from my desk to get ready to leave. If it's worse than the last one, he'll need extra hands going through the evidence.

"We think it happened on Saturday night. The home-owner was out of town for the weekend and got back on Sunday. Can you round up some guys to come help us sift through this mess? We've already started cataloging, but we're nowhere near done and could use the extra hands."

"Already heading out the door. I've got a couple of my deputies with me. We'll be there in thirty minutes." I round up Derek and Liam, leaving Todd and a few other deputies to handle anything that comes in while we're gone. We'll probably be there all day and most of the evening.

When we arrive at the scene, there is a flurry of activity happening. A few cruisers are parked in the driveway and on the street. There's crime scene tape across the porch and an officer standing outside with a man who, I'm assuming, is the homeowner.

We nod at the officer as we walk up the front porch and into the house. From the outside, you wouldn't believe anything is wrong, but as soon as we step into the entryway, the destruction becomes apparent. There are shattered mirror pieces everywhere, a broken vase litters the floor of the living room, the couch cushions are shredded, and the kitchen is in complete disarray.

We walk further into the house where Steven is standing, talking with one of his officers. "Chief, what do you have so far?" I ask as we approach the two men.

"Not a damn thing," Steven says on a growl. His full mustache flutters as he breathes out of his nose. "They've escalated from a few broken picture frames to complete mayhem. I don't understand how there isn't a shred of evidence in this mess."

"He may be escalating, but he sure as hell isn't getting dumber. He's getting angrier, and with each break-in, he needs to do more damage in order to fulfill the need that's driving him. Have you found a connection between the victims?"

There is so much destruction here it's hard to tell what the end goal was. The escalation is what's scaring me the most. He won't be able to continue this level of destruction in the same town. He likely has one more shot before he'll need to move on or get caught, and he doesn't seem stupid enough to make that mistake.

"No, they all went to different high schools, hung out with different people, have different backgrounds. The only thing they've had in common is they're all in their mid-thir-ties and male."

"Other than a target type, not exactly helpful," I say. "Look, Chief, I know you don't want our hands in this, but you know as well as I do he's not going to stay in your town for too much longer. Based on the pattern, he's either going to head to Denton or Sonoma, and I'd like to help you catch him before that happens."

"I know, you're right. Why don't you come back to the station with us, and we can start laying out what we've got," Steven says, and I nod my head.

I walk over to Derek and Liam to check in before heading out. I know they'll be at the scene for another few hours at a minimum collecting evidence.

"You guys good? I'm going to hitch a ride to the Westlake station with Chief Roberts."

"Yeah, we're good. I'm glad they're letting us in on this. Now we'll have a lot more to go on if the perp decides to come to Sonoma," Derek says.

"Tell me about it. Will you take my truck and pick me up

when you're finished here?" I ask, handing Derek my keys when he nods at me. "Call if you find anything." I walk back over to Steven and let him know I'm ready to go.

We walk out to his truck and head to the Westlake police station which is almost identical to our own station, just laid out a little differently. It's quiet inside since a good portion of the deputies are at the crime scene. Steven and I head into their conference room and start laying out what they have so far on the whiteboard and the table.

Steven starts talking through what evidence they've collected since the B and Es began. "At first, there were broken window latches, and items inside would be out of place. There was no major destruction or permanent damage inside the house. Over the last five instances, three have been committed within Westlake city limits, the others just outside of town. The damage has escalated with each break-in, culminating in this last one with complete destruction. From what we can tell, they're not stealing any items, just destroying them."

As Steven talks, he places pins on a map and hands me pictures of crime scenes. There's a clear escalation pattern but there isn't anything else pointing to a potential person of interest.

"Any DNA evidence collected from the scenes? It would be hard to not leave anything behind during these last break-ins," I ask, examining each photo, hoping something jumps out at me.

"No, we haven't been able to get anything from the scenes. They have to be wearing gloves, masks, shoe covers, the whole works to not leave anything behind," Steven confirms.

"And the only connection between the victims is their age and gender. These last two, they were both out of town when the perp broke in?"

"Yes, they had both gone away for weekend trips when the break-ins occurred."

"Hmm, that means either the perp knew their schedule or got incredibly lucky. Since there isn't a connection between victims, I'd venture to guess they got lucky, and that's why the destruction was so bad," I conclude.

Sorting through these photos there's still one thing I don't fully understand, "What is this guy getting out of breaking in and destroying things? He's not stealing, so there's no financial gain. There's no connection between vics, so revenge is more than likely out. There has to be more to it, right?"

"Absolutely, but I can't seem to put enough of the pieces together to figure it out," Steven agrees.

"Any thoughts about next targets?"

"Other than the demographic? None. And the kicker is I never realized how many males in their mid-thirties we had living in this town. Trying to warn over one hundred men to stay vigilant is like trying to persuade a rebel teenager to follow the rules—almost impossible," he says with a shake of his head. "We've stepped up patrols, but there's not much more we can do without sending my deputies into an early grave with all of the extra hours."

Steven goes back to the whiteboard and looks over the maps and photographs pinned up. We've drawn a timeline indicating when the B and Es occurred, and I've been staring at it, trying to see a pattern. I don't see anything in the evidence, and that's really concerning. My phone chimes with a message from Derek, letting me know they're on their way to pick me up.

We've been here for about six hours now, and I'm ready to head home. We aren't getting anywhere at this point, and all we can do is hope they get something from the evidence collected today.

"Derek and Liam are on their way here. I guess they've wrapped up what they can at the scene," I say as I stand from my chair, my body aching from sitting for so long. Steven looks at me and nods his head.

"Can I count on you to help me with this?" he asks.

"Of course. You'll call me when you get the results back from the evidence we collected today?"

"Yeah, I'll call you, but I doubt there will be anything we can use. I'll keep you updated and let you know if we need anything more from you in the meantime."

"We're at your disposal, Chief, so use us if and when you need us." I reach out to shake his hand. I know it's not easy having to rely on other people for help. He's the police chief, it's his job to protect his town from any threat, and I can only imagine the weight he has on his shoulders right now. I'm going to be in the same boat if this perp decides to move on to Sonoma.

I walk out of the station as Derek and Liam pull up in the truck. I jump in the back and settle in for the drive home. We're all beat from the long day, so the ride back is mostly silent. Each of us are in our own heads and decompressing after the shitstorm we walked into at the crime scene.

Derek pulls into the parking lot of the Sonoma station, and I jump out of the truck and walk around to the front. "I'll see you both tomorrow morning, and thanks for your hard work on this. I know it makes for long days, but it'll be worth it when we get this guy."

They both nod and head towards their own cars as I get into the driver's seat. I'd normally debrief with them before heading home, but we're all exhausted, and it won't do any good to go over everything we've already gone over a hundred times.

The drive home is quick, and I am greeted by an excited Piper when I walk inside. After getting my stuff put away, I sit down on the couch and turn on the sports highlights I missed from last night's games. My phone chimes and I grab it thinking it's going to be Todd responding to my text letting him know we made it back.

43

Unknown: Hi, Cooper, this is Quinn Lawson. I got my studio set up and am wondering if the offer to show me your secret spot on the lake is still good?

A grin stretches across my face and my heartbeat picks up speed when I realize she finally texted me. I'd like to say *can I come over right now* but I know that would be met with crickets or more likely a restraining order, so I type out the next best option.

Me: Hey, Quinn. I'd be happy to show you around the lake. How does tomorrow evening work for you?

Quinn: That works great. Where should I meet you?

Me: How about I pick you up? Say around 6:30?

Quinn: Okay, sounds good. Do you need my address?

Me: No, I still remember where the house is.

Quinn: Right. I forget how small this town is sometimes. I'm so used to the anonymity of the city where very few people knew my name or where I lived.

Me: It can be annoying just how much people know about you, but at the same time, it's nice to live in a place where they care enough to want to know you.

Quinn: I never thought about it like that. Makes me love this town even more.

Me: It's an awesome place to live, that's for sure.

Quinn never texts me back, and despite the late hour, I

44

am more wired than when I drink too much caffeine. To burn off some of my excess energy, I do a quick workout in the home gym I set up in one of my guest bedrooms.

Otherwise, I'd never be able to fall asleep. After my workout and a shower, I fall into bed, and I'm immediately immersed in dreams of ocean blue eyes and chocolate brown hair I can't wait to have my hands in.

7

UNKNOWN

The darkness surrounds me as I get closer to my target. The silence of the night guides me, and the stillness of the air blankets me in comfort. I do not hurry because there is no need to rush. I already know what to do and how to do it. My small purges go unnoticed but because they take more skill, my need for release is diminished.

I slip inside and make my way through the house. My anger burns bright and strong as I create chaos. It would be so easy to allow my urges to take over but I have to be smart. Do the most damage without being noticed. That's the goal and one I have succeeded in many times over.

Through my destruction, people have recognized what I'm capable of, and while they may not know my name, I've never felt more seen.

I stand in the blackness of the last room. Power coursing through me as steady and strong as my beating heart. All I do is watch, but it's enough. For now.

8

QUINN

"**B**ut what do I say?" I whine for the umpteenth time. Hailey has been pushing me to text Cooper for the last two days, but I haven't been able to get myself to actually send him a message.

"Quinn, I might strangle you right now despite how much I love you. You can do this. It's not like you're asking him to have sex with you. Think about it like you're doing this for your art and not for yourself." She shoves another handful of popcorn into her mouth.

We're sitting on the couch watching a reality show Hailey loves. I'm not paying attention because I've been staring at the new message window for the last twenty minutes, trying to find the right words to say. I know I'm being ridiculous about this whole thing, but the man just frazzles me.

"God, I'm so pathetic," I groan. *Okay, focus. It's not like he's asking me on a date. He's just helping me out. I can do this.*

As I type out a message, I have so many self-doubts running through me. I'm normally a pretty confident person, albeit shy in social situations, but in this moment, texting the most beautiful man I've ever seen... oh god. He really is the most beautiful man. Why would he want to hang out with me?

No, that's ridiculous. I am smart and brave—most of the time—and I can do anything.

Pep talk for the win, I type out what I want to say. "Okay, I typed it out. I'll read it one more time to make sure things are perfect." I look back down at my phone to read the text again but it's not in the text box anymore. "Oh no. Shit. Hailey, I sent it. I didn't even proofread it!"

"What did you say? Let me see!" she yells, sitting up and grabbing my phone out of my hands.

Me: Hi, Cooper, this is Quinn Lawson. I got my studio set up and am wondering if the offer to show me your secret spot on the lake is still good.

"Aw, you're even grammatically correct with your commas. Well done. Very light and casual."

"What if he texts back and says, *sorry you took too long, idiot, I don't want to hang out with you anymore...*? I don't know if I can handle the rejection."

"Oh stop. He wouldn't say that, and what's the big deal if he does say no? You and I will go to the lake together, and it'll be fine. But I don't think he would have offered if he didn't want to hang out with you, so he's going to say yes." I feel my phone vibrate in my hand and look down, suddenly nauseated at what I'll find.

"Ah, he texted me back! That was so fast."

Cooper: Hey, Quinn. I'd be happy to show you around the lake. How does tomorrow evening work for you?

"Tomorrow? He so wants to date you," Hailey says with a smug grin.

"He does not. I'm sure he just wants to get it off of his to-do list." I can't let myself go there. Thinking about dating Cooper is unfathomable.

"He wouldn't have texted you back so fast and would have suggested a day much later if he didn't want to date you."

"Oh, whatever. I highly doubt my awkward conversation with him would make him want to date me. He probably thinks I'm a weirdo and is just being kind."

"Well, if that's the case, then we have to plan the perfect outfit to show him you aren't a weirdo," Hailey says with a glint in her eye that screams scheming. "Should we have a movie night tonight since you'll be out tomorrow?"

Ignoring the look, I only respond to our evening plans. "Yes, movie night sounds perfect. I'll make more popcorn and you pick the movie." I know Hailey has to leave me in a couple of days, and I am dreading that very much. It has been so nice having her here, making me feel less alone.

If anything, this outing—that I'm refusing to call a date—with Cooper will be helpful in my mission to make friends. I should also ask Megan about going out one evening. I really enjoyed spending time with her and the other girls at the barbecue. I could absolutely see us becoming friends which is new for me as I don't usually make friends easily.

I WAKE up the next morning, and as soon as my eyes open, I remember I'm seeing Cooper today. I hope I'm not a complete dunce when I see him. I enjoyed hanging out with him and the rest of his friends, so if I make things weird tonight, it will ruin any chance I have of fitting in with a group of genuinely great people.

I roll my eyes at myself. This man has turned me into a melodramatic child, and Hailey was right the other day. I need to pull up my big girl panties and make some friends. At the very least, I can go into this with that goal in mind.

I get out of bed since there is no hope of me falling back asleep. I put on some painting clothes and go downstairs to make some coffee. Getting lost in a painting will keep me from ruminating on my outing this evening which is just what I need to get through the day.

With my coffee in hand, I walk into my favorite place in the whole world. Set up along the right wall of my studio is a reclaimed door I found at a flea market. I had it customized to lay horizontally like a table. I put a storage unit under-neath to hold my tubes of paint and a piece of plexiglass on top so I can mix and blend my colors. I hung bins on the wall above the door to keep all of my brushes organized and clean, and my easel sits to the left of my paint station.

The left side of the room is set up as a comfy reading area. The floor-to-ceiling bookshelves run along the entire back wall and are packed with books. I have two wingback chairs set up in front of the windows and a soft grey and yellow rug underneath. The room is the perfect combination of the two things I love to do the most.

I dig through my paint baskets trying to decide what I want to paint today. After I lay a few tubes on my worktop, I squirt a few colors on the glass and start combining them.

Mixing paint is one of those mindless tasks that also takes every ounce of concentration you have. If you use too much of one color then you end up with something totally wrong but add just the right amount and you've created something brand new.

Once my brush hits the canvas, I'm gone. The feel of the paint as it glides across the woven fabric lulls me into a place where my imagination takes over. A place that comforts and guides me, never seeming to let me down. It's beautiful and raw and something I have missed terribly these past few years.

I'm brought out of my musings when I hear the french doors open and turn to see Hailey come into the room. She's wearing running shorts and a tank and is still breathing heavily.

"How was your run?" I ask, setting my paintbrush down on my worktop.

"Pretty great, actually. The scenery is much better here than in New York, but I do miss running in Central Park. How long have you been up?"

"A while now. I woke up early and couldn't fall back to sleep, so I decided to paint." Hailey walks over to my canvas, and I step back to look as well. I don't think I even realized what I was painting until this moment.

"Quinn, this is amazing, and the colors are beautiful. You started it this morning?" Hailey asks, and I nod.

"Thanks, it just sort of came out of me." I take in the browns, yellows, and golds across the canvas. The realization of what I painted makes me feel a little uneasy, but I've also been seeing them in my dreams.

"You've recreated his eyes beautifully, Quinn. You captured the light and sparkle of them while keeping the soulful wisdom he exudes. It's brilliant."

Cooper's eyes shine off of the canvas. They are so different from any others I've ever seen, and he's taken up a lot more of my brain space than even Hailey knows about.

He's captured me.

"I didn't set out to paint them, but it seems my brain needed an outlet. Now that I step back, it feels a little creepy," I tell Hailey.

"It's not creepy, you're capturing something beautiful. Are you about done, or are you going to keep going?"

"I think I'm done for today. I'll let this dry for a while, but I don't want to add anything else." I look at the painting I've created. I've only painted his eyes and it's unfinished around the edges. I've never been one to paint portraits, so finishing this one won't be likely for me.

"How about I go make us some pancakes while you finish up here?" Hailey starts towards the door.

"Sounds great. I'll be out in a minute." I set to work cleaning my brushes in the little sink my grandpa had installed long ago. My grandmother wouldn't allow me to bring my paints out of this room, so we installed the sink to not drag paint through her house.

Once everything is cleaned, I walk out of my studio and into the kitchen. Hailey is standing at the stove with an apron covering her clothes and a spatula in hand. There's a stack of pancakes sitting on the counter and more coffee in the pot.

"Get 'em while they're hot!" Hailey says with a flip of a pancake. I refill my coffee cup and grab a plate with some pancakes. I load them with butter and syrup and sit at the counter to eat.

"What should we do today?" I ask Hailey as I shovel the delicious morsels of cake into my mouth.

"I was thinking we should check out the shops in town. There were a couple of cute boutiques I saw when we went furniture shopping. Maybe we'll find a cute outfit for you to wear tonight."

"I love that idea. It's a nice day, too, so we can eat lunch on the patio of the café," I add.

"Yes, perfect."

We finish breakfast and get ready for our day. Shopping was always something I enjoyed doing in New York. Hailey and I would often try to find the hole-in-the-wall stores in unexplored areas of the city. It was one of our favorite things to do when we'd get a day off.

We get into town and find a parking space near the café. We walk down the awning-covered sidewalks and peek into different stores selling antiques and other tchotchkes.

"Oh, here it is!" Hailey exclaims as we near a shop with eclectic window dressings. There are vintage cameras and mannequin bodices with adorable outfits put together. Shoes with hand-painted designs and matching knick-knacks. I'm already in love, and I haven't even been inside.

We walk into the store, and a bell chimes signaling our entrance. There are clothing racks lining the middle of the store and shelves hanging on the walls holding artwork and other handcrafted pieces.

"Hi there! Welcome to Blossoms and Bows. I'm the owner, Trish. All of the artwork and crafts are made by local artists, and if you need a different size we might have it in the back, so just ask," Trish says to us with a kind smile. She's in her late forties and has black kinky-curled hair.

"Thanks, Trish!" My eyes wander across the room. It's not a large space, but it has two levels with a spiral staircase in the middle of the room leading up to the second floor.

Hailey and I go in separate directions and start browsing the clothing racks, periodically showing each other items we like and hanging on to things we want to try on.

Once we gather a collection of clothes, we head back to the dressing rooms with our items. We try on outfit after outfit, giggling and strutting around while Trish tries to keep up with us. She's constantly bringing us more clothes to try on as she figures out our styles.

"Oh my gosh. Quinn, that's it!" Hailey squeals as she comes out of the dressing room wearing a red fitted dress perfect for going out. I have on a burgundy top that criss-crosses in the front and shows off my cleavage without being too revealing.

"Are you sure it's not too simple?"

"That's what makes it perfect. It's not a fancy shirt you'd wear on a date, but it's just sexy enough to make him take notice. Pair it with your ripped, cut-off shorts and some

53

sandals, and he won't be able to take his eyes off you. Plus, you'll be comfortable enough to get the photos you need."

"Who's the guy?" Trish asks.

"Quinn has a date with the hot police chief," Hailey says, wiggling her eyebrows.

"It's not a date. He's taking me to the lake to get some shots of the sunset. I like to paint, and he offered to show it to me. It's nothing more than him being friendly."

"You're going out with Chief Jackson? Damn, girl, way to land the big fish your first few weeks in town." Trish grins. "He's the guy every single girl in this town wants to date." I roll my eyes and shake my head at Trish, but I don't doubt her statement in the slightest. He's so good-looking, I'm sure women just melt at his feet.

Myself included, if I'm being honest, and it makes me even more nervous. He probably has a whole harem of women he could take out, and I'm not entirely sure I want to be a part of that.

"I did not land anything. You both are being silly, but I do think I'm getting this top and the white dress with the flowers on it."

"You are absolutely getting the top. The dress will be perfect for when Cooper asks you out on a second date." I roll my eyes again, knowing full well that's not going to happen. "I think I'm getting this dress and a few of the tops I tried on too. I can't pass up these prices, and they'll be perfect for going out when I get back to the city." She twists, checking out her dress in the trifold mirror.

"You both chose perfectly. Leave the items you don't want in the dressing rooms, and I'll take the ones you want to keep," Trish says.

Hailey and I both get dressed and head back up to the front counter. Trish wraps our clothes in tissue paper and puts them into bags for us. We pay for our items, and as we collect our things, Trish stops us, "I just want to say that

Cooper is a great guy. Being the police chief in a place like this comes with a lot of responsibility, and he's such a great leader. He genuinely cares about this town and we all love him for it. All teasing aside, I hope you have fun tonight."

"Thank you, Trish. I appreciate you telling me that." She could've let us walk out and said nothing about him but she took the time to stick up for him, which tells me he is a genuinely nice guy.

Hailey and I walk to the café and find a table on the patio. We both order summer salads and settle in to eat lunch.

"I can't believe you're going home tomorrow," I pout at her.

"I know. I'm both ready to go and not ready to go."

"As much as I want you to stay forever, I know the city is your playground. It's where you belong."

"True, and you know I'll never live anywhere else, but after seeing this town, I understand why this place feels like home to you."

"It's had my heart since the first summer I stayed here when I was nine. It's not going to be the same without you though. The house is going to feel so quiet," I tease.

"I feel like that was a dig at my constant sound level, and honestly, it's completely accurate," Hailey says with a laugh. I smile back at her despite the sadness I feel radiating in my chest.

"What are you going to do when you get back to the city?"

"Well, I actually have news. The firm is promoting me to executive manager since I know everything about your cases and everyone else's cases for that matter."

"What? Hailey, that's amazing! When did this happen, and why didn't you tell me?" If I wasn't so happy about the promotion, I'd be mad at her for not telling me sooner. Hailey is incredibly bright and should've been a lawyer herself, but she says she didn't want the responsibility or the loans.

"They asked me before I came here, and I was going to tell you when I arrived, but we got so busy getting you settled, I couldn't find a good time to bring it up."

"Now I feel like a selfish cow. You deserve to be celebrated. This is a huge deal, and I'm so glad the firm finally realized how pivotal you are to them."

"You are not a selfish cow. You had a lot going on. It's going to be an adjustment for sure but I'll have a little more control over my schedule and what I'm doing. It'll be nice not to be at some bitch's beck and call." She winks at me.

"I'm going to pretend like you aren't talking about me and are referring to an old lawyer you assisted way before me," I huff, but a smile tugs at the corners of my lips.

"You know damn well I'm not talking about you. The promotion couldn't come at a better time either. I'll be super busy and won't have time to miss you now."

"You'll still miss me just as much as I'll be missing you."

"Yeah, but now you'll have Mr. Hot Pants to distract you while I have sleazy Peter to keep me company. Life is not fair sometimes," Hailey says wistfully. I throw a wadded-up napkin at her as she busts out laughing.

"You're ridiculous and could have your pick of men if you wanted." And I'm not exaggerating.

Anywhere we went in New York, men would notice her. It didn't matter if we were shopping or out for drinks in the evening, Hailey drew the attention of every male who walked by.

Despite drawing their attention, she never goes out on dates. If a guy came up to her she would be polite but ultimately would turn him down. The only thing she is interested in is one-night stands. I always wondered if it had something to do with the boyfriend she lost when she was in college, but she doesn't talk about it, and I've learned not to bring it up with her.

"It's almost four-thirty now, should we head home and get you ready for your date?" Hailey asks, looking at her phone.

"Two hours early? Do you really think it will take me two hours to get ready?" I'd normally only need about an hour. Two seems a little excessive.

"Yes, it will. Trust me on this because I know you, and I know what's about to happen," she replies, seeming to understand something completely lost on me.

"Well, I guess we can go then." I stand and grab our shopping bags. I still think it's too early to get ready, but what do I know?

9

QUINN

Hailey was most definitely right. As soon as we got home, I took my bags upstairs and got in the shower. Suddenly, I only had an hour until Cooper would arrive. Then, I was blow-drying my hair and putting makeup on when I realized I was down to thirty minutes. Now, I'm freaking out because I have no clothes on, and he's going to be here any minute, and holy shit, I might pass out.

I sit down on my bed before I fall over and hurt myself.

Why am I freaking out right now? I can't remember a time I've ever been this nervous before a date, and yes, I realize I've started calling it a date.

I mean, first dates are my thing. I've been on plenty to know what's expected, so why is this date making me lose my mind?

I usually pride myself on being calm and collected. I don't let my emotions take over in stressful situations, even if they are raging on the inside. Outwardly, I can appear unemotional and detached from the situation. It's how I succeeded as a lawyer. I knew when to play on emotions and when to hold them back. But right now, I might be losing my marbles. I can't seem to find any calmness or get my shit together.

It's at this moment, I finally acknowledge that Cooper has affected me more than I thought, or maybe more than I allowed myself to think. Something is telling me he is going to mean something big, and all of my nerves and worries about this evening are adding to my knowledge that this guy is unlike any other I've encountered before.

I take a couple of deep breaths to calm down and start getting dressed. As I'm pulling up my shorts I hear Hailey say, "Hello, Hot Pants." I quickly throw on my sandals and fly down the stairs only to find Hailey with her nose pressed up against the window like a kid at an aquarium. Thank goodness she didn't call him Hot Pants to his face. I was a little worried there for a minute.

"What are you doing?" I ask as I walk further into the living room.

"Chief Sexy Pants is outside and looking yummy in his uniform. He's talking on the phone right now, pacing back and forth, giving quite the show of his front and back side."

"Could you get any closer to the window?" I tease, walking over to see the view. I look out and there he is in all of his muscular glory, just like Hailey said.

The navy-blue button-down shirt is stretched across his broad chest showcasing his cut upper body. It's tucked into pants that mold to his thighs and highlight his tight backside in the most flattering light. He does look pretty yummy out there.

"Come on, let's move away from the window so he doesn't see us ogling him." I grab Hailey's arm to pull her away from the window.

"Too late," she says with a wave and a smile. Mortified that he's caught us gawking at him, I walk over to the front door just as there's a knock. I open it and there he stands on my front porch, just as beautiful now as he was when I first saw him. It almost takes my breath away.

"Hi," I say when I finally locate my tongue and get it to produce words.

"Hi there." He gifts me with a heart-stopping smile, and I almost swoon right there.

"Do you want to come in for a minute, or do we need to get going?"

"We've got a few before the sunset will start, and I'd like to see what you've done with the place since you moved in," he says.

I wave him in, and as he crosses the threshold, the entryway suddenly feels much smaller. He's not even standing close to me, but I feel like we're on top of each other. I can smell his spicy cologne, and I think I could get drunk off the scent alone. It takes every ounce of strength I have not to lean in and take a deep whiff.

"Well, there's my studio. Down the hall is a bedroom and a half bathroom, and upstairs is another bedroom, bathroom, and the master. The place only needed some cosmetic updates since it sat empty for about ten years."

"It looks great. Can I see your studio?" he asks, looking through the windows of the french doors.

"Sure." We walk into the room, and I realize I never took down the painting of Cooper's eyes. I quickly grab it and set it down by the wall, hoping he didn't see it when he walked in. I turn to look at him, and he's looking around the room, so I don't think he saw it, thank god.

"You've got a great setup in here. What's the door for?"

"That's where I store and mix my paints. I use mostly oil paints, and the large surface on top gives me room to create different colors from the paint I have."

"I'd like to see that sometime. I never realized you had to mix your own paint," Cooper says.

I smile at him. "I would be glad to show you, but just as a heads up, if I start mixing, I'm going to want to paint, and then I'm not much company. I tend to zone out when I paint or do anything creative."

"I'll remember that when you're showing me the ropes."

I nod because I'm not sure what else to say. This guy wants to watch me paint, and I'm not sure what to do with that information. We walk back out of the studio and into the living room where Hailey is sitting on the couch watching tv.

"How are you, Hailey?" Cooper asks as we walk into the room.

"Oh, I'm great, Cooper. How are you?"

"Doing fine, thanks. Quinn, we should get going. Are you ready?" The sound of my name in his deep voice has my body lighting up. I can imagine him growling it in my ear as he hovers over me.

I shake my head to stop those thoughts from getting out of hand.

"Yes, I'm ready. Let me grab my camera bag and we can head out," I manage to squeak out.

"Camera bag?" Cooper asks while I walk over to the couch and grab my things.

"If I'm going to a location I can't paint in person, I always bring my camera with me. That way, I have something to refer back to if I need a reminder. The photos are never quite as good as painting in person, but they're better than going off memory."

"So, not only can you paint, but you're also a photographer?"

"It's more of a necessity, really. It comes in handy when I can't remember the little details of the landscape." I sling my bag over my shoulder and turn to look at Hailey, "I'll see you later?"

"Yeah, or tomorrow. Whatever. You two kids have fun, and don't do anything I wouldn't do." She winks.

I feel my cheeks heat, and I hear Cooper chuckle behind

me. I walk back over to where he's standing, and he motions for me to take the lead. We leave the house and head toward his white truck parked in the driveway.

Cooper walks to the passenger side and opens the door for me. I smile my thanks and climb into his truck. He closes the door once I'm settled, and the smell of his cologne envelops me as I watch him walk around and get in on the driver's side.

I feel the butterflies in my stomach dissipate and give way to excitement with the realization that I'm getting to spend the evening with the most drop-dead gorgeous man, and he just gave me his million-dollar smile. I smile back, feeling electricity in the air between us so thick I could cut it with a knife.

"I picked up some sandwiches and stuff to have for dinner when we get to the lake. I hope that's okay," he says as he starts the truck and backs out of the driveway.

"That sounds perfect. I'm excited to see the lake. I haven't been since the summer before Gram and Pap died."

"I'm sorry you lost them. How old were you when they died?"

"I had just turned nineteen and was a few months into my first semester at NYU when my parents called me. It was one of the worst days of my life."

"I can't imagine how hard that phone call was. The whole town was pretty upset when we heard they passed."

"Yeah, it was horrible. After they died, I didn't think I'd ever come back here, but they left me their house, and, for some reason, it made me feel like I could always come back if I needed to. It was a comfort while I was in school."

"What made you move here now?"

"Well, I was living the dream of being a big city lawyer, making stupid amounts of money and working nonstop—because I had no other choice—when I suddenly realized I was no longer happy. I have no idea what my dream is now, but it doesn't involve being a family lawyer anymore. Some of those people are horrible."

"I bet you've got some great stories."

"Oh, I have some doozies. I once had a client fight tooth and nail for this 5x7 photo frame that wasn't worth ten bucks, but I have to say, there were some great moments too. My favorites were adoptions. Helping couples begin the families they'd always wanted was the best part."

"I bet that was rewarding."

"It was incredibly rewarding, but those moments were few and far between. Which led me here."

"I'm glad it did," Cooper says, seemingly hesitant by his own words. I can feel the heat rising up into my cheeks as his eyes meet mine for a second before turning back to the road.

"I am too." Maybe this isn't just a friendly interaction like I thought. Maybe Cooper shares my feelings that this could lead to something bigger. I've never wanted something like this before, but right now, with him, it seems like a possibility.

In New York, I didn't have the desire to be in a relationship. I'd go out on dates if I was asked or had the time, but they didn't go anywhere past dinner. Usually, it was because I was never interested enough to pursue a relationship.

I already want to go on another date with Cooper, and we haven't even finished the first one. For the first time in my adult life, I actually like a guy, and I am scared shitless. I don't know how to be in a relationship. I don't know what it's like to have another person be a permanent fixture in my life on an intimate level.

I'm going to pause right there. I'm getting ahead of myself. We've barely even left for this first date. Who's to say he will even want a second date by the end of the night, but god, do I want that with him. We've spent a grand total of a few hours together, and I already know one evening will not be enough for me. I just hope he feels the same way.

10

QUINN

We pull into the parking lot of the lake and I jump out of the truck before Cooper can open my door. I need a minute of fresh air before my senses are invaded by his delicious smell again. I swear it makes my brain fry and the stupid come out of my mouth.

I look around and am hit by a wave of memories flooding my mind. The lake stretches out for miles, and leafy green trees surround the perimeter. The noise of beach goers splashing in the lake along with the smell of fresh air and a hint of gasoline brings a smile to my face.

On the far left is the tackle shop that sells everything from sunscreen and snacks to wakeboards and fishing supplies. The sandy beach extends out from the tackle shop and is lined with picnic tables and umbrellas. The dock sits farther off to the right so people can load and unload their boats safely, and behind the dock are rows upon rows of slips holding boats of every shape and size.

"It's just as pretty as I remember," I say as Cooper comes around the truck.

"I love this place. We'd come on Saturdays when my dad

64

wasn't working and stay the whole day skiing and fishing. I still come out here to fish when I can." He reaches in the bed of his truck and grabs a cooler and tote bag holding various items I can't quite make out.

"Can I help you carry those?" I ask as Cooper turns towards me with his hands full.

"Nah, I got everything," he says and takes off towards the marina.

"Are we getting on a boat?"

"Yeah, my favorite spot can only be accessed from the lake. Is that okay? I guess I should've asked first."

"It's fine. I haven't been on a boat since I was little. We usually stayed on the beach and spent the day swimming," I tell Cooper as he walks onto the platform that leads to the boats lined up in the marina. I follow along behind him, giving myself a little pep talk so I don't freak out when I have to get in the boat.

Cooper leads us to one of the boat slips and sets down the items he was carrying. He starts to take the cover off of one, and as he does a sparkling blue motorboat comes into view.

It's not huge by any means, but it's definitely not a tiny boat either. The front is V-shaped and has cushioned benches. The captain's chair is on the right side, a co-captain's is on the left, and the back has an L-shaped bench seat with storage underneath. It's the perfect size for four or five people to be comfortable with room for more if you don't mind sitting close.

"You want to jump in and I'll hand over the stuff?" Cooper asks.

"Sure," I say with way more confidence than I'm feeling. It's not that I'm afraid of the boat itself, it's more that I have this fear of either falling over or falling out of the boat. Either scenario would be mortifying.

He walks toward me, holding out his hand to help me

step inside. I grab on, and the moment he closes his big hand around mine, I feel this energy pass between us. I have to hold myself back from jerking my hand out of his from the intensity of it.

I get into the boat and gesture for him to hand over the tote bag and cooler. Once those are in the boat and settled, Cooper steps in and sits in the captain's chair, starting the boat at the same time. I sit in the co-captain's chair and take the opportunity to stare at Cooper as he does his thing.

He looks so confident and sexy as he maneuvers us out of the slip and away from the marina. His police uniform takes him from being sexy to panty-melting. I need to stop thinking about what's underneath the uniform before I embarrass myself.

Cooper looks over, catching me in my thoughts. A blush creeps up my face and he smirks, making me feel like he knows exactly what I was thinking.

I turn forward, not allowing him to read my wayward thoughts anymore, and watch as we break away from the marina and out onto the open lake. Cooper speeds up the boat, and we skim across the water, bouncing when we hit the wakes of other boats. The wind is whipping my hair back, making me wish I had a hair tie.

We take a curve into one of the offshoots and away from the main arm of the lake. The cove goes back quite a ways, and Cooper starts to slow down. We make it around another curve, and suddenly the trees open up, and all I can see is the horizon.

The view is breathtaking even without the sunset. It's like the lake sits up on a hill, and everything below it is forest and skyline.

Cooper comes to a stop in the middle of the cove. He lets down the anchor, turns off the boat, and all at once, it's silent. It feels like the world just stops and the sounds of nature echo around us. The wind blows softly through the trees as the crickets sing and the birds chirp. It's awe-inspiring.

"This is beautiful," I whisper because speaking any louder would disrupt the calm surrounding us.

"Yes, it is," Cooper says, and I look over at him, but he's not looking at the lake, he's looking at me. His amber eyes darken as they roam across my face. I can feel a blush move across my face as I run a hand through my hair, knowing full well it's a knotted mess after speeding down the lake.

"I'm going to take some pictures now, and then I'll take some more as the sun is going down," I say as I stand up and dig into my camera bag, pulling out everything I need.

I picked up photography when I was about fifteen. My parents knew how much I loved painting and felt bad that I couldn't because of their job, so they bought me a camera for Christmas. They thought if I could capture the views I saw while traveling, I could use the pictures as inspiration when I painted over the summer. It made a huge difference, and while I enjoy painting more, photography has become a passion as well.

I find it fascinating how changing little things, like the camera angle or lighting, can alter the entire mood of the picture. It's another way I get my thoughts to slow down and allow myself to notice the beauty around me.

The way the wind blows through the green leaves of the surrounding trees, the stillness of the dark lake that expands into the rocky shore, a heron swooping down to catch its dinner, it's all captured through the lens of my camera.

After taking a few shots, I put my camera down and seek out Cooper. He's relaxing on the back bench, looking delicious.

"All done?" Cooper asks with a smile.

"Yes, sorry for checking out for a minute. I told you, when

I zone out, I'm usually completely unaware of what's going on around me until I come back and it's been two hours," I say jokingly.

"It's only been about twenty minutes, so don't worry."

"Wow, I'm so sorry. I'm sure you've been incredibly bored."

"It was actually really cool watching you work." His eyes heat as he looks at me, and I'm pretty sure I can feel my entire body melting. How does he do that with one look? "Are you hungry?" He gestures to the cooler.

"Starving," I say, sitting down next to him on the bench seat.

"I have sandwiches, chips, and some fruit. Oh, and some snack cakes for dessert because they are the epitome of a lake snack." Cooper looks at me with the cutest grin on his face.

"That sounds perfect. I haven't had a snack cake in years." Cooper's head whips up to mine with wide eyes.

"Seriously? These things are my only vice. I don't let myself buy them unless I'm on the lake because I'd eat ten a day if I bought them regularly," he laughs. "Okay, I have turkey or ham and I have no preference, so it's your choice."

"I'll take the ham, please," I say, holding out my hand for the sandwich. "Can you pass me the chips as well?"

"Sure," Cooper says with a curious look on his face. I know what I'm about to do is odd, and anybody else would have just eaten the sandwich as is, however, I don't like regular sandwiches, and I'm starving, so here goes. I take the top off of my sandwich and start layering the chips across the middle, making sure the whole thing is covered, and then place the top back on.

"Really?"

I pause, my sandwich halfway to my mouth, and look over at Cooper whose eyes are wide with shock. "You're really going to eat a sandwich with chips on it?"

"Well, I don't like them without the chips so yeah, I guess I am. Why?"

"That is so gross. You're ruining the sandwich."

"No, it's actually quite delicious. You want to try it?" I ask, holding my sandwich out for him to take a bite. He looks dubiously at me and wrinkles his nose. "I promise it's not as gross as it seems." I grin.

"I am so going to regret this." Cooper sighs as he leans in to take a bite. I watch as he closes his mouth around the sandwich and then pulls back. His jaw starts working around the bite, and he swallows. I think it's the most erotic thing I've ever seen. Am I drooling? *Get ahold of yourself, he's just eating like a normal human being.*

"Well?" I ask him, realizing Cooper had his sexy mouth on my sandwich, and now I'm going to have my mouth on it too.

I think that may be the most juvenile thought I've ever had.

Willing myself to settle down, I take a bite. Yep, chips on a sandwich, just as good as I remember and completely worth the look of horror.

"That was fucking disgusting." I can tell he's trying to hide his smile because his lips twitch, and his eyes shine with humor.

"You're such a liar! You loved it and just don't want to say I'm right." I grin, pointing my sandwich at him to offer another bite. "Want some more?"

"No way, you'd have to force-feed me to take another bite of that abomination." Cooper teases, winking at me. I feel my smile widen as I watch him take a bite of his own sandwich.

Despite the fact that he's made fun of how I eat, I've never felt more comfortable around another person. I usually feel slightly off balance when I'm with new people, like I'm on the edge of the group, never fully belonging. I haven't even remotely felt like an outsider with Cooper. It's like he's always been in my life, like we've been friends for years instead of a few hours.

It's refreshing, and at a minimum, I know I've made a close friend in Cooper. I hope we can become more, but even if we don't, it's nice to know that I've officially found a good friend in Sonoma.

11

COOPER

She's beautiful. Fucking breathtaking, and I can't stop staring at her. When she opened her front door, it took every effort I had to keep my mouth closed and my eyes from bugging.

Okay, they might've bugged a little.

Her long legs shown off in those cutoff shorts just about brought me to my knees. I knew I needed to focus on something else besides her legs if I was going to make it through the evening without embarrassing myself.

I thought I might've ruined everything before it even began when I realized I didn't tell her about getting on the boat. I could tell she was nervous when I helped her in, but she was amazing and pushed past her fears without saying a word. I could see the determination in her eyes and the set of her shoulders as she sat down in the co-captain's chair. When we got out in the middle of the lake and I opened up the motor, her smile was radiant, and I knew she was going to be okay.

This whole evening has been incredible because Quinn is so easy to be around. She's quick to laugh and mesmerizing when she does; I've never met a girl like her. I feel like I should be freaking out over how comfortable we are with each other, but I'm not.

It's like she's always been in my life, and I can't wait to learn everything about her. I want to know what she dreams about, what her fears are, even things as small as how she takes her coffee, and what's more, I want her to know everything about me, which is a novel feeling.

We finished up our dinner right as the sun started to go down, so Quinn is taking pictures of the lake again. Watching her work is fascinating. She's so sure of herself. I have no clue what she's doing as she presses different buttons or flips switches on her camera, but the confidence she exudes is the sexiest thing I've ever seen. I can't wait to see what she does with the pictures.

"Hey, Quinn, I'm sorry to interrupt, but we should start to head back. It's going to be dark soon, which will make getting back to the marina a little more difficult." Quinn looks up at me from behind her camera, and I watch as she switches gears from creative mode to normal mode. She smiles and nods her head as she starts packing up her camera, carefully placing everything in her bag and tucking it underneath the co-captain's seat.

As Quinn packs her stuff, I pull the anchor up and go to sit down in the captain's chair to start the boat. The roar of the motor interrupts the peacefulness of the evening and seems to burst the little bubble we've been surrounded by since we got here.

I'm not ready for our night to be over, but I also know we shouldn't be on the water for too much longer. I don't want to risk our safety or the safety of others since my boat isn't large. Smaller boats are much more difficult to see when it's dark, which could easily lead to an accident.

I maneuver us back out into the main arm of the lake and open up the throttle. I don't go quite as fast going back as I did coming out since dusk is settling in and my visibility is lower. Luckily, we make it back to the marina before it's completely dark out.

The lights are on at the dock, and they help guide me into the slip. We both jump out of the boat once we are stopped, and Quinn helps me get the cover on, already comfortable with navigating the dock and being around the boat. It's a big difference from how she was when we got out here.

We don't say much as we get everything packed up, and instead of being awkward, it's more of a companionable silence making me feel connected with her. The motors of other boats echo across the dock, and the chatter of people from the beach packing up their belongings fills the silence.

Quinn looks up at me, and it's only then I realize I've been staring at her as she's been getting things organized.

"Everything okay over there?" Quinn asks, a little smirk pulling at her lips as she puts her hands in her back pockets. It's like she can see all the way through me, and I'm not sure if I feel vulnerable or reassured by that.

"Yeah, I was just thinking I've had a really great time tonight."

"Even though I barely talked to you and only focused on my camera?"

I laugh because that's exactly the reason I've had so much fun. Watching her do her thing was the highlight of the evening, even if I didn't get to learn much about her.

"Definitely. I enjoyed watching you take pictures tonight. I can't wait to see what you create from the photos," I say as I walk toward her and grab all of the things I brought for our dinner. We head back to the truck, side-by-side, and I wish my hands weren't full. I'd love to know how it feels to have her hand in mine.

"The sunset was beautiful. It was everything you said it would be; I'm excited to start painting."

"Will you show it to me when it's done?"

"I think that's the least I could do since you spent this

73

whole evening with me just for one painting," she says as we get back to the truck. I put all of the stuff in the bed of the truck and help Quinn up into the cab. I walk around the front and get in on the driver's side.

I don't want to take her home yet, but I'm not sure if she feels the same way. We never established if this was a date, and no matter how desperately I want to hold her and kiss her, I'm not confident my advances would be wanted.

"You ready?" I ask, hoping maybe she might not be ready to go home.

"At the risk of putting myself out there, I'm not quite ready to end the night yet." She bites her lip like she's nervous about being honest. I, on the other hand, feel relief wash over me and my smile grows now that I know I'm not the only one who wants this to continue.

"Thank god. I wasn't ready for the night to be over, but I was afraid you didn't feel the same way."

Quinn grins at me, and I watch the nerves dissipate from her eyes. She's stunning when she smiles, and her eyes get this sparkle to them that lights up her whole face. It's now officially my mission to keep that smile on her face and the sparkle in her eyes.

"What do you want to do then?" Quinn asks.

"How about ice cream? I only ate one snack cake, so I think we deserve ice cream."

"You only ate one? Where did those other two wrappers come from then?" Quinn asks with a lift of her eyebrow. I love that she's calling me out on my bullshit.

"I don't know what you're talking about. You must've eaten those because it was definitely not me. I think you might have a problem. Eating three snack cakes in one sitting is kind of a lot," I tease, knowing full well it was me.

"I'm the one with the problem?" she asks incredulously. "Who's the one that isn't allowed to keep them in their house?"

"Yeah, you mentioned that issue. Maybe you should see someone about it. I don't think it's too late to get you help. I'm sure we can work through it together." I have to bite my cheek to keep from smiling.

Quinn narrows her eyes at me. "You are something else, aren't you?"

I can't hold it in any longer and burst out laughing.

I look over at her and see she's laughing, too, while rolling her eyes at me. I can't keep myself from touching her anymore, and I lean over and squeeze her thigh. "I'm sorry for teasing you. I couldn't help myself."

I keep my hand there longer than necessary because her skin is so soft, but move it eventually. I'd like to keep it there indefinitely, but I don't want to mess up this amazing night because I couldn't keep my hands to myself.

I turn the truck on and pull out of the parking lot. It's fully dark out, so my headlights are on and the dashboard lights fill the cab with a digital glow. We're quiet as I drive us back into town, and it's nice that neither of us feels like we need to fill the silence.

I've never been on a date where I don't feel like I have to go out of my way to impress the other person. You know how first dates usually go, you get dressed up and you're so formal with each other. Trying to come across as refined and like you have no faults.

It feels almost fake in a way because the other person is doing the same thing and you both know, in all actuality, you don't act like that in normal day-to-day life. It's exhausting and hard to know for sure if the person you're with is actually there because they like you or if they just want to be seen dating you.

Yes, that's happened multiple times since I became police chief.

This whole night with Quinn I have never felt more like myself. It's the best feeling I've ever experienced.

I'm not saying I haven't been trying to impress Quinn. God knows I've done everything I can to make sure I don't do something stupid, but even though I'm trying to impress her, I still feel like I'm being my full authentic self. It proves to me that whatever is happening between us is something real and has the potential to be life-changing.

Despite how terrified I am, I'm all in.

12

COOPER

I pull into the parking lot of Jones's Diner and park the truck. The diner is a trailer with the classic silver siding and red and white booths inside. They have the best burgers and milkshakes in town. In the summer, they open up the side windows and you can walk right up and order ice cream without having to go in.

The temperature isn't too stifling since the sun has gone down, so there are quite a few people milling about. The six picnic tables set up next to the walk-up window are mostly filled with families and teenagers tonight.

I jump out of the truck and run around to help Quinn down. I'm only noticing now how tall she is because at six-two, I'm pretty tall, but Quinn comes up to my chin. She's the perfect height so that I'd have to lean down a little to kiss her, but I won't have to bend in half to reach her.

I realize I'm staring at her mouth, and as I glance back at her eyes, I see she was looking at my lips too. We make eye contact, and it's like a punch to the gut. I feel winded when her ocean blue eyes link to mine. It's so powerful I have to look away before I do something stupid like kiss the hell out of her in front of everyone.

As I break eye contact, I see Quinn shake her head like she's snapping out of a trance too. Knowing she's just as caught up as I am helps to boost my confidence.

I grab her hand as we walk over to the counter because I can't hold back any longer, and she quickly links her fingers with mine. She gives my hand a squeeze, and the shock of the connection goes straight up my arm.

If my body lights up at the slightest touch from her, I wonder what it would feel like to have her whole body pressed up against me. Sliding and moving against each other.

Let's pause those thoughts before they get out of hand.

"What are you feeling? Shake, sundae, something with a little candy?" I ask her to distract myself. I keep my fingers linked with hers as we step in line to order. Now that I've got her, I don't want to let go.

"There are so many choices. I'm not even sure where to start," Quinn says with wide eyes as she takes in the menu.

"Well, let's start with the basics. Chocolate, vanilla, or strawberry?"

"I'm feeling vanilla. Is that boring?"

"Depends on if you get anything in it."

"I definitely want something in it."

"Okay, well that takes out the shakes. How do you feel about marshmallows?"

"I love marshmallows," Quinn says with a smile.

"Then I highly recommend the Rice Krispie treat blend. It's vanilla ice cream, marshmallows, and rice cereal all blended together."

"Oh, yum! I'll get that one," she says as we step up to the counter. I place her order and get myself a chocolate shake, even though I did eat those three snack cakes. I couldn't stop myself.

We don't have to wait long before our order gets called, so after I pick it up, we go find a picnic table. Quinn sits on one side and I sit on the other so we're directly opposite each other, leaning in close over the table. "I heard you talking at Megan and Todd's about all of the places you've lived. What was it like, living in different places all of the time?"

"For the most part, it was great. I enjoyed getting to be a part of so many different cultures, and I learned so much about the world through each experience, but to be honest, it was hard sometimes."

"What made it hard for you?"

Quinn takes a bite of her ice cream as she thinks about her answer.

"Well, to start, we never stayed in one place for more than a few years at a time, so I was never able to get comfortable with my surroundings. My parents would work with the hospitals or universities—sometimes both—to guest lecture or establish the best practice for diagnosing and treating the genetic disorder they discovered.

"Sometimes the clinics would already be set up and my parents would help with additional needs. Other times, the clinics would be starting from scratch, so we'd stay longer to make sure the place was stable. Once we knew they were settled and running smoothly, we'd move on to the next place."

"Did you have a home base to return to or anything?" I ask, trying to wrap my head around moving so frequently.

"I guess New York could be considered home base, but the longest they stay is about six months and only if necessary. We didn't stay there much when I was growing up.

"The only constant was my grandparents' house. I would get here at the beginning of June, stay through September, then fly back to wherever my parents were. I had a nanny/tutor combo, so I wasn't dictated by normal school sessions."

"So, your grandparents' house was home growing up."

"Yes, exactly, and despite all of the places we traveled to, their house was always my favorite." Quinn gets this faraway look in her eye as she tells me about her grandparents. I can tell she misses them a lot, and on top of that, she loves this town. Inside, I'm pumping my fist because this means she's here to stay. If there is a small chance she might move back to New York, I'm going to do my best to make sure it doesn't happen.

We may not have spent a lot of time together, but this girl is different than any other I've ever encountered. She's special, and I know deep in my gut, I need to do whatever it takes to hold on to her.

As we talk, I see Rachel walking by the diner. I catch her eye and wave her over to say hello.

"Hey, Rachel," I say as she gets closer to where Quinn and I are sitting. "Quinn, this is Rachel, my saving grace of a secretary. Rachel, this is Quinn Lawson."

"It's nice to meet you, Rachel," Quinn says, holding her hand out to shake Rachel's.

"Yeah, it's nice to meet you too, Quinn. Are you new to Sonoma? I don't think I've seen you around before."

"I just moved here from New York, actually. My grandparents, Dan and Carla Johnson, lived here, and I inherited their house when they died. One day, I got the harebrained idea to get out of the city and come home, so here I am," Quinn says, and it sounds like a spiel she's given several times since she's moved here. I can't imagine how many times she's had to tell it to all of the nosy townspeople.

"Oh, interesting, New York is quite a long way from here," Rachel says.

"We are very lucky to have Quinn here. She's an artist and is working on a painting of the lake," I tell Rachel.

"I don't know about lucky, but I am working on a painting of the lake. It's my favorite place here, and Cooper was kind enough to show me around," Quinn says, blushing at my praise. It seems like she may not believe we're lucky she's here. Maybe I'm just lucky she's giving me the time of day.

"That's interesting. Well, I should get going. See you tomorrow, Cooper, and good luck on your painting."

"Oh, sure! See you tomorrow, Rachel," I say.

"It was nice to meet you."

"Yeah, you too," Rachel says with a half-wave.

As we watch her walk away, I tell Quinn, "Rachel was a huge help to me when I was transitioning from deputy chief to chief of police a couple of years ago. She's been my secretary for over four years now, I think."

"I bet it's nice to have someone solid like her to rely on. What's it like to be the police chief? What does a normal day look like for you?" Quinn asks.

"Well, most of the time, it's a lot of paperwork, but I take calls from dispatch and still get to be out on the street a lot. We've recently had a string of break-ins in the next town over we've been helping out with. That's taken up quite a bit of my time, lately."

"I like that the neighboring towns work with each other on this kind of stuff. It doesn't seem like the area has much crime," Quinn says.

I feel a little guilty about downplaying the seriousness of the B and Es, but I also don't want to scare Quinn when I'm not sure if she should be scared. Besides, it's not like I have a lot of information I can tell her anyway.

"Yeah, it's been a lot of extra work, but we're happy to be able to help Westlake." It's starting to get late, and as much as I don't want this night to end, I need to get home to Piper. "You ready to head out? It's starting to get late and, unfortunately, I have to work tomorrow," I say as I gather up our trash.

"Oh wow, yeah, I had no idea what time it was," Quinn says as she gets up from the table. After dumping our trash, I hold my hand out and she slides her hand in mine, fitting together like a puzzle piece. I hold on tight as we walk to the truck and reluctantly let go so she can get in.

"Okay, most embarrassing moment of all time?" I ask Quinn once I'm in the truck. I turn the key, and the rumble of the engine fills the space.

"Oh, yikes! You're really digging in there," Quinn says, and if it wasn't dark, I bet her cheeks would be pink. "Ugh, I don't want to tell you this but I'm going to anyway. One time, in New York, I was walking with Hailey, not paying any attention to where I was going, and walked straight into a trashcan, falling face-first into the trash."

"Oh no," I say, feeling awful for her but also really wanting to laugh.

"I smelled awful the entire day, even after showering and scrubbing my skin until it was raw," Quinn says.

I'm silent while I try to hold in my laughter when Quinn says, "It's okay, you can laugh. It wasn't at the time, but it's pretty funny now." Not being able to stop it, a chuckle burst from my chest at the visual I have.

"I'm sorry, I just have this visual of your long legs sticking up out of a trash can, and I can't keep it in," I tell her as she starts to giggle.

"You're not far off," she says. "Tell me your most embarrassing story."

I sigh, "Okay, here goes. Todd and I were goofing around one night when we were teens and got the big idea to jump the fence around the baseball fields. We wanted to race the bases to see who was the fastest.

"Now, Todd has been tall since the minute he hit puberty, so he cleared the fence with no problem. Me, on the other hand, not so much... So, instead of clearing it, my pants got stuck at the top, and instead of ripping like you think they would, they got hooked, and I was stuck there hanging from the top of the fence by the back of my pants."

"Oh my god," Quinn says with the cutest giggle. I glance

over at her and see that her eyes are wide and she has the biggest grin on her face. "How did you get down?"

"Well, Todd tried to lift me up, but he wasn't strong enough, so he ended up having to call my dad. When he got there, I thought he was going to be so pissed at us, but he stood there and laughed at me for a solid minute before he helped me down. He then proceeded to tell everyone we saw afterward. I think that was my punishment, and it was worse than a grounding would have been."

"I think I would agree. If Hailey ever talked about my trashcan mishap, I would be mortified," Quinn says as I pull into her driveway and park the truck.

The porch light is on, but the house seems quiet. Hailey must already be in bed because most of the lights are off inside. I look over at Quinn to see she's already looking at me.

"I had a great time tonight," I say to her.

"I did too, Cooper. It was one of the best nights I've had in a long time," Quinn says with a smile. Hearing my name fall from her lips makes my blood heat. I want to hear her scream it as I'm driving deep into her.

Jesus, where did that come from? I mentally shake away my dirty thoughts before they get any more out of hand.

"Could I take you out to dinner soon? I'd like to see you again," I ask.

"Definitely." Quinn's smile lights up her whole face.

"Great, I'll walk you to the door," I say, getting out and walking around to help her down. I hold on to her hand as we walk up the sidewalk. The evening breeze is cool but gentle, making everything feel calm and quiet. It's late, so the street is empty and still. The only light comes from the porch and a few lamps along the street.

We get to the front door and Quinn looks up at me. "Thanks for walking me to the door and for the perfect evening. I can't wait to start painting." Excitement shines in her eyes.

I want to kiss her goodnight, but I'm not sure if it would be welcome. I don't want to screw this up by moving too fast, but I also feel so comfortable with her that it just feels right.

"You're welcome. I'm excited to see what you create." My eyes drop down to her lips again. They're plump, and she has this perfect bow shape on her top lip. I look back up to her eyes and see she's looking at my lips too. I lean forward a little, hoping she picks up on my intentions before I make a fool of myself. Her eyes draw up and meet mine. "I really want to kiss you," I say quietly.

A small smile pulls at the corner of her mouth, and she nods her head. Taking that as a green light, I lean forward and brush my lips lightly against hers. I press down a little harder and take her full mouth with mine. Electricity runs through me all the way to my toes, and my body ignites like it might burst into flames.

I deepen the kiss, needing more of her. My tongue lightly traces the outside of her mouth, teasing her to open up for me. She makes the sexiest noise in the back of her throat as she lets me in. I cup the back of her head as her fists clench onto my button-down.

Her mouth is velvet soft, and I can't get enough of her. My fingers dig into her hip as I pull her closer to me so her body is pressed tightly against mine.

Our tongues duel in a sensual dance that I never want to end as Quinn meets and matches me thrust for thrust, taking and giving just as much as I am.

I know she can feel the effect this kiss is having on me, but she doesn't seem to mind because she pushes harder against me, making me groan as I feel her grind against me.

I pull back a little, not wanting to end the perfect kiss but needing to in order to breathe.

Both of my hands are tightly fisted in her hair, and her

fingers are twisted in the strands on the back of my head. I lean my forehead against hers while we catch our breath. I've never experienced anything so intense in my life. What is it about this woman that makes her so different from anything I've ever had before?

"Wow," Quinn whispers, her eyes are still closed, and she seems as dazed as I feel.

"I was thinking the same thing."

I pull my head away as she opens her ocean blue eyes. Everything I'm feeling right now is reflecting back at me. It feels like she's staring deep into my soul, and I finally know for sure I'm not alone in this whirlwind of emotion. "I should go before I get too carried away with you."

Quinn grins up at me. "I don't mind being carried away."

"Good to know," I say, smiling as I lean in to kiss her again because I can't get enough of her. I try to keep this one shorter than the first, but I still end up falling far too deep.

I pull back from her before I sweep her into my arms and take her upstairs. The feeling of her body pressed up against mine will be playing in my mind until I get my hands on her again.

"Goodnight, Quinn. I'll call you tomorrow," I say as I reluctantly step back from her.

"Goodnight, Cooper," she says, turning to unlock her front door and stepping inside.

I step down off her porch once I hear the deadbolt slide closed indicating she's safe inside. I've never felt as good as I do right now. I can't wait to see her again, and I already know that no matter how many times I see her or touch her or kiss her, it will never be enough.

QUINN

Did that actually happen? I lift my hand up to my mouth and touch my lips. They feel swollen and tingly and amazing. It might all be in my head, but I swear I can physically feel them tingling.

I'm standing in my entryway, leaning against my front door. I can feel how flushed my face is, and my heart is still beating insanely fast. I hear a door open down the hallway and a second later, "Quinn, are you home?"

Hailey comes walking down the hallway towards me. She's wearing her sleep shorts and a tank top, but I doubt she was sleeping. Being a night owl, it's still early for her.

"Look at you getting in at eleven at night. Are you flushed? What have you been up to, Quinn?" Hailey teases with a big grin on her face. I blush even more despite knowing all we did was kiss. Even if that kiss was one of the most passionate encounters I've ever experienced.

"Tell me everything." She squeals as she grabs my hand and drags me to the living room. She turns on the table lamp as we plop down on the couch. It's dark in the house except for the lamp Hailey turned on and the light over the sink in the kitchen.

It's also incredibly quiet. Something I'm starting to love but haven't quite adjusted to.

After living in New York for so long, I got used to the noise at night. Here, there is a certain level of calm that blankets the town when the sun goes down. The streets are still, the stars shine bright, and the world seems to take a collective deep breath to settle in for the night.

"It was amazing, Hailey. Like World Series level great," I say with a huge smile and a contented sigh. I tuck my feet up under me and get comfortable on the couch. Knowing Hailey, we'll be here until she's satisfied with the amount of detail I give her, which could be a while.

"I need more details. What did you do, where did you go, how many times did you have sex?"

"Hailey, oh my god, we did not have sex." My face is flaming.

"Well, I wouldn't judge you for jumping into those hot pants on the first date. Can you say yummy?" Hailey winks at me.

"You are being ridiculous." I laugh, her outlandish quips still surprise me sometimes. "But Hailey, he's wonderful. He took me out on his boat to get the pictures, and he was so patient the whole time, even though I barely spoke to him. You know how I get when I'm in the zone. I think I spent more time looking at my camera than talking to him. He brought along a picnic dinner, which was really thoughtful, and the sunset was beautiful. I can't wait to start painting."

"Yeah, the sunset is great and all but get to the good stuff," Hailey pushes, and it makes me grin. Replaying the whole evening in my head is almost as good as the night itself. Oh, who am I kidding? It's not even close. I can't wait to see him again.

"After the sun went down and we got back to the marina, he asked if I was ready to go home, and instead of being my normal shy self, I went for it and told him I didn't want him to take me home. He said he wasn't ready either which, of course, made me as giddy as a middle school girl, so we went and got ice cream. We talked the whole time about basically everything, and it was perfect. I've never connected with anyone so quickly. It feels like I've known him my whole life."

"I love that so much. It's one thing to be drop-dead gorgeous. It's another to also be able to hold a conversation," Hailey says with a nod of her head.

"Exactly! We never ran out of things to talk about, and if there was ever a silence or pause, it wasn't an awkward one. It was comfortable."

"This makes me so happy. Okay, continue with the rest of the evening because I know your face didn't get flushed because of conversation."

"Well, he walked me up to the door when we got home and asked me to go to dinner with him, and of course, I agreed because I'm not an idiot. Then he kissed me good-night, and holy hell, can he kiss. It was soft at first but quickly turned passionate and consuming. I don't even feel like I can describe it very well." I wish he was still here and I could kiss him some more. Possibly horizontally, on my bed, with no clothes on.

"Wow, I don't think I've ever been kissed like that," Hailey says dreamily.

"I definitely hadn't either until tonight. It was the best first date ever."

"Oh my god!" Hailey gasps. "You guys are so going to get married."

"What?" I screech. "Are you crazy? We've had one date."

"I'm calling it now. You two are most definitely going to get married, and when you do, I'll say I told you so," Hailey says with a smirk, making me roll my eyes at her.

"So how did he leave it?" Hailey asks, thankfully changing the subject.

"He said he'd call me tomorrow. Is it bad that I don't want to wait that long to talk to him again?"

Tonight unequivocally beat all other dates. All of the guys I've dated before—granted there haven't been many—have never made me feel like this. Like the girl in the rom-com who finally gets the guy she's always dreamed about. I think Cooper has the potential to be that guy. We still have so much to learn about each other but the fact that I felt so comfortable with him tells me all I need to know.

I didn't come to Sonoma looking for a relationship. I wanted to find somewhere to call home. A place I can count on and trust to know will always be there for me. New York was just the place I lived. And maybe I didn't try very hard to make it my home, but I also think in the back of my mind, I knew I'd end up here.

My grandparents' house always felt like home growing up, and that's what I need surrounding my life now. Adding Cooper into the mix is a huge risk but at the same time, I feel like I'm in a place where I'm finally ready to dive in headfirst. No matter the consequences.

"If I got kissed like you did, I wouldn't want to wait for the next chance either, but we both know he'd already be in my bed," Hailey jokes.

We sit in the quiet of the house for a minute, and it's only then I remember Hailey is leaving tomorrow. She won't be around to fill the silence or make me laugh with her crazy antics.

I lean over and wrap my arms around her shoulders. "I'm not ready for you to leave tomorrow," I say. "Have you decided what time you're going to head out?"

"Not yet, but probably pretty early. I need to go into the office and catch up on the stuff I've missed before I start on Monday," Hailey says as she hugs me back.

"You are going to be phenomenal in this role. I'm so proud of you," I tell her. She has worked so hard for everything she has, and as much as I wish she would stay here with me, I know this promotion is a huge opportunity for her and will put her on the map for bigger and better things.

"Thanks, Quinn. You know I wouldn't be where I am if it wasn't for you. You entrusted me with things a normal assistant wouldn't get to do, and I am so grateful for that. You're my best friend, and I'm going to miss you so much."

"Stop, you're going to make me cry," I tell her while my eyes fill, and I blink a few times to keep them from falling. We give each other another big squeeze and separate from our hug.

"As much as I'd like to continue this cuddle session, I have a ton of packing to finish. I love you, girl, and I can already tell this place is going to do wonders for your soul," Hailey says as we both get up off of the couch and start walking to our rooms.

"I think so too, Hailey."

After showering and getting my PJs on, I'm lying in bed, hovering in the space right before you fall asleep where you let go of all the things that happened in your day and you're about to fall asleep when I hear my phone vibrate on my nightstand.

Cooper: I just wanted to tell you that I had an amazing time tonight, and I am really glad you decided to move here.

Holy shit, Cooper texted me. Squealing, I sit up in bed and read his text again. If I didn't already think Cooper was different from any other guy before, this confirms my thoughts. He didn't even let a day pass before reaching out to me about our date, and I'm so happy he's on the same page as me. I take a minute to put my thoughts together before I respond.

Me: I'm pretty glad I moved here too. Especially after tonight.

Cooper: What happened tonight?

I love that he's teasing me right now because without the levity, being honest about my feelings is a lot more difficult.

Me: I went out on a date with a very handsome man who can kiss like no other.

Cooper: Who was he? I hope he was a gentleman.

Me: There was a moment there where he was a little less than gentlemanly.

Me: But I didn't want him to be.

Cooper: Whew, I was a little worried there for a second.

Cooper: So... you liked the kiss, huh?
Me: I loved the kiss.

Cooper: Good, so did I. The best I've ever had to be honest.

Me: Me too...

Cooper: I'm happy to hear that.

Me: Good night, Cooper.

Cooper: Good night, Quinn.

I put my phone back on the nightstand. The best kiss he's ever had? That's a little hard to believe. I'm sure he's had hundreds of kisses before me, so there's no way mine was the best. Then again, what was the point of saying it unless he meant it? Cooper doesn't seem like the kind of guy to say anything he doesn't mean. He's so sweet and kind, not to mention sexy as hell, which makes it hard to believe he would feel that way about me.

The kiss was definitely the best I've ever had, and to be fair, I've had a decent amount of first kisses. None of them even compare to the one I shared with Cooper tonight. He dominated the kiss but was so gentle at the same time. It was addicting, and I don't think I could ever get enough.

If we end up going out to dinner, I'm not sure how I'll make it through the whole night without jumping him. I don't think he'd mind. From what I could tell, the kiss affected him just as much as it did me, so maybe we could skip dinner and go straight to the kissing part. A little shiver runs through me as I imagine it.

I roll over and try to calm my racing thoughts, which isn't easy when every single thought I have is about Cooper. All I can hope for is that my dreams will be filled with those golden amber eyes and passionate kisses.

14

COOPER

Instead of having the laid-back day I originally had lined out, I've spent most of the afternoon out on the highway aiding in a big semi-truck crash. Some hot shot decided tailgating a semi would be a good idea, and when the truck had to stop suddenly, the hot shot slammed into the back of it, causing the truck to career off the side of the road taking about six other cars with it.

It's been absolute chaos trying to get ambulances and firetrucks in while redirecting traffic. Luckily there weren't any casualties, but a few of the drivers caught in this mess have some pretty serious injuries.

Captain Tucker James, of Sonoma's fire department, comes striding over as I'm talking with one of my deputies. He's a few inches taller than I am and built like a tank. He's also got this dark and brooding look to him that, without having known him for a good portion of my life, would be seriously intimidating.

"Hey, Chief, we're just about finished here. We've checked all of the vehicles to make sure they're safe for transport, and any passenger needing a bus is in one headed to John Francis," Tucker says, referring to the town's hospital named after one of the founders of Sonoma.

"Okay, great. The wreckers are on their way, so I'll have them start loading up the totaled cars. The other drivers are prepared to move along once statements are done. Thanks for the help, Tucker," I feel like I can finally relax after this ridiculously long day. What's worse is it's not even close to over. I'll have a bunch of reports to file and paperwork to finish when we get back to the station.

I shake Tucker's hand, and he heads back to his SUV. The two fire engines follow quickly behind Tucker, and all we're left with is the four wrecked cars, the semi, and a few police cruisers.

I walk back to my truck and wait on the wreckers to get here. While I'm taking a break, I message Quinn letting her know I'm still thinking about her and will call her tonight after I finish up the mountain of work I'll have waiting for me.

It's been a few days since we went to the lake, and we've texted or talked on the phone every day since. She responds saying she's looking forward to it, and then she tells me to be safe.

That thought makes me stop for a moment. If I get into a relationship with Quinn, I won't just be looking out for myself anymore. There will be a second person in my life to take care of and worry about. Someone who will be worried about me when I leave for my job. While being the police chief of a small town doesn't usually come with many risks, there is still a chance I could get hurt on the job. It comes with the territory.

It's not often I have to deal with violence, but I have had to deal with it, and there is always a chance of a call going south. It's happened to many others before, and it could happen to me.

What would happen to Quinn if I got hurt on the job? I'm not sure how I would handle that situation. I know she is incredibly independent and can take care of herself, but if she were mine, I'd want to be the one taking care of her. Maybe that's a little caveman of me, but it's what I've always wanted in a relationship.

I know I'm thinking about things so far into the future it shouldn't matter right now, but she matters to me, and I want her safe. Plus, the thought of Quinn being mine makes my chest puff out in pride.

I want her to be mine in every way, which makes me think about our first kiss, and just remembering it has my body heating up. I wanted to whisk her upstairs and have my way with her. That kiss was everything. The way she felt pressed against me, the sounds she made, god she's something else.

Okay, time to halt those thoughts while I'm at work. I do not need a hard-on while I'm trying to do my job.

I take a deep breath to calm my raging body and jump out of the car when I see the wreckers pull up to the scene. I give them the green light to load up the cars, and after another hour, we finally get the whole mess cleaned up and traffic back to normal.

I GET BACK to the station a little later and on my desk is a cup of coffee I have been desperately needing. I take a huge welcome sip and see Rachel poke her head into my office.

"I thought you might need a pick me up," Rachel says as she comes in and sits down in one of the chairs across from my desk.

"Thank you. Anything come in I need to know about?" I ask as I take another long pull from the to-go cup.

"Nope, you haven't missed anything."

"Great. I'll be here late tonight, but if nothing else comes in, you can head out early if you want to," I tell Rachel. Her mom was diagnosed with lymphoma a while back, so she's been having a tough time. Since she's the sole caretaker for her mom, I try to give her some extra time off whenever I can.

"Oh, thanks, Cooper. I may take you up on that offer. But first, you wanna tell me about the girl I met the other night?" she asks, wiggling her eyebrows up and down, making me chuckle.

"There are so many things I could say. Quinn is something else. She's unlike any girl I've dated before. She's amazing." It's probably too much to share with her, but Rachel is like a sister and has always supported me.

"Those are big words coming from the most eligible bachelor in town," Rachel says sardonically.

"Oh, whatever." I roll my eyes at her.

"You like this girl, don't you?" Rachel asks, turning a little more serious.

"Yeah, I really do." I don't want to reveal all of my feelings since I'm only just coming to terms with them myself. Besides, Quinn should be the first one I tell anyway.

"She better be good to you." Rachel narrows her eyes.

"I think it's more on me not to screw it up," I say jokingly, but Rachel shakes her head.

She stands up to leave and says, "Don't stay too late doing paperwork. Some of it will keep until tomorrow."

"I will do my best," I tell her even though we both know I can't leave something for the next day if it's on my desk today.

* * *

By the time I wrap up the paperwork, it's about seven in the evening. Mom invited me to their house for dinner earlier in the week, so I quickly call to let her know I'm on my way to their house.

After I get off the phone with Mom, I call Quinn. I hope she's available for dinner tomorrow night because I don't want to wait any longer than I already have to see her again.

After what feels like forever, she finally picks up. "Hey there," Quinn answers with a soft voice, the sound instantly relaxing me. I think I could listen to her talk for hours and it would still have the same effect on me.

"Hi. I'm sorry I'm calling so late. I had a bunch of paperwork to finish after the accident today."

"That's okay. Did you get everything done?"

"Yeah, for the most part. I've got a few things I'll need to do tomorrow."

"I'm sorry you had such a long day."

"It happens. I'm done now though and headed to my mom and dad's for dinner. What are you up to tonight?"

"I am hanging out with Megan, Lucy, and Sara right now," Quinn says. I can hear the smile in her voice, and I am so glad she's hanging out with the girls. They've been good friends of mine for a long time, and it makes me happy they're bringing Quinn into the group.

"You are? That's great. I'm glad you're spending time with them. What about tomorrow? Would you be interested in going out to dinner with me?"

"I would definitely be interested."

"Great. How does six work for you?"

"Six works perfectly."

"Awesome, I'll see you tomorrow then."

"See you tomorrow. Bye, Cooper."

"Bye, Quinn."

I pull into my mom and dad's driveway as I'm hanging up

the phone. I'm feeling much better after having talked to Quinn. It's amazing the effect she has on me, and now I'm not sure I'll be able to wait until tomorrow night to see her. I might have to change that.

15

QUINN

I hang up my phone after talking to Cooper, and I can feel how big my smile is on my face. We didn't even talk for very long, and I feel lighter than I did before I talked to him. He makes me happy, and now I get to see him tomorrow. I also make a mental note to thank Hailey for convincing me to buy that dress.

I walk back into the living room where Megan, Sara, and Lucy are curled up on the couch. Our wine glasses sit on the coffee table and music plays quietly in the background.

Instead of continuing to sit on my couch being sad that Hailey wasn't there, I texted Megan to see if she was busy tonight. Luckily for me, she wasn't, and neither were Lucy and Sara. Natalie was having dinner with her mom tonight, otherwise, she would've been here too.

We've been hanging out for a while now, and I don't think I've ever had this much fun with a group of girls.

Hailey would invite me along when she would go out with her friends from college, but I never fit in with them. They were always really nice to me, but I still felt outside of the group. I'm sure it was of my own making, but I never felt like I could open up and join in.

Growing up constantly on the move made it hard to make friends. I learned quickly that goodbyes were always harder the closer you got to the people around you, so I stopped trying to get close to people. I think the habit continued while I was in New York, and it's one of the reasons I never felt like it was home.

Tonight though, I haven't felt for a single moment like I was on the outside looking in. The girls have included me in every joke, retold several stories so I could join the conversation, and have been unbelievably kind to me. I've opened up a lot more with these girls too, and it's been amazing to finally feel like I can be a part of a group.

"Do you think that grin could get any bigger?" Lucy asks as I sit down on the couch next to Megan. Lucy and Sara are on the other side of the sectional.

"Definitely not. She looks like the Cheshire cat right now," Megan says teasingly. It takes me a minute, but I realize they are talking about me, and I can feel a blush creep up my face.

"Aw, she's blushing. She so likes him, you guys," Lucy says in a valley girl accent, which sets off the other two girls.

"Come on, spill it. What did he say to make you smile like that?" Sara asks.

Having felt so comfortable, I opened up and told them about my date with Cooper. I shared everything that happened from ignoring him while I took photos to the hot as hell kiss. These girls know him so well I thought I could gain some insight into the man that has swept me off my feet.

Megan let it slip that Cooper texted Todd after our date, so she already knew we went out. Cooper told Todd it was an amazing date, and I totally squealed like a little girl after she told me.

"He asked me to go to dinner with him tomorrow night." I can't help but feel my smile grow even wider.

"Yay! This is the best thing ever. Quinn, I am all for this," Megan says while clapping her hands. "This calls for one more glass of wine, I think." She grabs the bottle sitting on the coffee table and pours all of us another glass, emptying the bottle into mine.

"To Quinn, for landing the most eligible bachelor in Sonoma and making every woman in town jealous." Lucy winks while holding up her glass of wine.

"Oh, that's ridiculous," I say, shaking my head, but I still clink my glass against theirs and take a drink.

"Seriously though, Cooper is an amazing guy, and he needs someone like you who is down to earth and doesn't care about his job title," Megan says on a more sober note.

"Why would I care that he's the police chief? Other than being worried about him, I don't know why it would make a difference." I'm a little confused as to why it matters. What he does for a living doesn't change who he is as a person. I mean, I know I'll worry about him when he's at work. I was worried today when I got the text saying he was having a busy day. A busy day as a police officer is never a good thing.

Megan looks at the other girls, silently communicating something I don't understand. She turns back to me and says, "Look, Cooper doesn't date very often. I think the last date he went on was several months ago, and the last serious relationship he had was years ago." As Megan talks, I can feel my eyes getting wide. His last date was months ago?

"His last girlfriend died in an accident, and while they'd only been dating a couple of months, it still rocked him," Lucy adds. Oh, my poor Cooper. I can't even fathom how hard that must have been for him.

Megan continues, "On top of that, several women in town started blatantly propositioning him after he became police chief." I feel my jaw drop.

"They were seriously only interested in him because he's the police chief?" I ask incredulously. How does a title make that big of a difference for people?

"Yes, they were. Having a position of power in this town

means a whole lot more to some than it does others," Sara says. This must have caused some issues because I can feel the resentment coming from all three of them.

It's unfathomable that someone could use a person as wonderful as Cooper to get ahead. It's like these women took advantage of his heart, and honestly, it makes me irrationally angry.

"The thing you have to understand is, Cooper feels things so deeply. He's incredibly kind to everyone, but you have to show him you can be trusted before he'll open up his heart. I think he's halfway there with you already though." Megan smiles, attempting to make me feel better.

"I can't believe someone could use Cooper like that." My fists clench as my anger rises. "How could they be so selfish and not take his feelings into account? I don't understand the depravity you'd have to have to hurt a man like him. He's so good and gentle and kind."

As I'm ranting, Megan reaches over and squeezes my hand. The gesture is so welcome and comforting, but it doesn't dispel my ire towards the women who would take advantage of such a remarkable man.

"I think we can all agree it's horrible, and it goes a long way for us to see you get so upset on his behalf. We can see how much you care for him already," Sara says as she drinks the rest of her wine.

"I am angry, and it honestly scares me a little just how much I do care for him. Is it possible to feel this deeply about someone when you haven't spent much time together?" I ask the group.

I feel so out of my depth here. This is far beyond anything I've ever experienced, and I have no idea what feelings are rational and what are certifiably insane. At the same time though, how can something that feels this good be bad?

"I definitely think it's possible, and I can only hope I'll feel the same way someday," Sara longingly says. Megan and Lucy nod their heads and agree.

I wish I could see Cooper tonight. Talking about him makes me want to see him, but I guess I'll have to wait until tomorrow.

The conversation flows into other topics, and as we're chatting, Todd comes in through their kitchen. He looks so dark and almost menacing, but when his eyes land on Megan, his smile grows and love shines through, softening his features.

I hope to have a relationship like theirs one day. A relationship where no matter how much time passes, we still look at each other with the same amount of love Megan and Todd seem to have.

Having given the wine enough time to lose its effect, I get ready to head home. I say my goodbyes and head to my car, and as I'm getting in, my phone starts ringing. I feel my heart rate pick up, hoping it's Cooper calling.

I try not to feel too much disappointment when I see it's my mother instead. I take a deep breath and prepare myself to answer. My parents have always had big dreams for me, and because they set the bar so high, I've spent my entire life never quite reaching it. It gets exhausting hearing the tinge of disappointment in my mother's voice when we talk.

"Hi, Mom."

"Hello, darling. I hope I'm not calling too late. Your father and I just landed in New York and wanted to check in with you since we are in the same time zone," she says.

"No, it's not too late. What are you doing back in New York?" It's highly irregular for my parents to be back in the states this time of year. The last I knew, they were in London.

"Well, I don't want to worry you, but your father has been having some health issues, and we decided it would be best to spend some time resting in the city," my mother says with an air of casualty I know is fake. This must be a bigger deal than she's making it out to be for them to take time off and stay in the city.

"What kind of health issues? Is everything okay?"

"Oh yes, darling, your father's having some stomach pains, and the doctors say the stress is making it worse."

"Do I need to come to the city? Is he going to be okay?"

"You're always welcome to come to the flat, dear, but he will be fine. He just needs rest is all. We have done plenty of tests, and it's nothing serious."

"Okay, well, please keep me updated," I tell her. I wish she would've told me sooner, but I shouldn't be surprised. It's pretty typical for them to update me only after something major has happened.

"How is Sonoma?" my mother asks with a hint of disdain. My grandparents moved here after my mom went to college, and she has only visited a handful of times. Small town living was not her idea of a fulfilling life.

"It's really great, Mom. I've made a few friends and am settled into the house. I'm happy." I definitely will not be telling her about Cooper. She was not happy with my decision to move here in the first place, believing I was throwing my life away. Telling her about Cooper will let her know I'm serious about staying a good long while, and that's not a fight I want to have right now.

"Are you going to start practicing again? I'm sure they could use a good lawyer down there," she says haughtily as if the people here are all criminals. I sigh into the phone, knowing no matter my answer, she won't be happy with it.

"Not right now, Mom," I say, trying to placate her. I have no desire to practice here at all, but I will not be sharing that additional detail either.

"Well, you're going to have to do something, Quinn Elizabeth. You can't live like a bum forever," she says, scolding what she considers my lack of drive. Little does she know, I talked to Trish, and she wants to sell both my paintings and photographs in her store.

But, "painting is not a career, it's a hobby" as my mother has always said, so it's not like that would make her feel better.

"I know, Mother, and I will. Look, I have to go. Please keep me updated on how Dad is doing." Preferably before you make any other decisions as drastic as moving back to New York.

"Yes, yes, I will." She sighs.

"Goodbye, Mom," I say, hanging up after she responds.

I take a deep, cleansing breath and start my car. I decided it would be safer to stay parked while talking with my mother, knowing it would take every ounce of concentration so I wouldn't slip up and tell her something she didn't need to know about.

I pull out of Megan and Todd's driveway and head home. Working to dispel my morose mood, I think about Cooper and our date tomorrow. I can't wait to see him. After hearing how big of a heart Cooper has, I make myself a vow to do everything in my power to protect it with all that I have. It's the least I can do to show him how much I care.

16

COOPER

"What do we know about the B and Es?" my dad asks, breaking the silence with his gruff voice. We've been banished to the back deck while mom finishes up dinner. She refuses to let us help her and has always hated us being underfoot while she cooked.

"Honestly, not a whole lot. We can't get any evidence from the crime scenes and there doesn't seem to be much of a pattern to them either. We're at a total loss, and we haven't been able to catch a break." I feel Piper nosing my hand, begging for attention. I picked her up when I got back from the highway accident, knowing I wasn't going to be home at a decent hour.

"Man, Westlake is getting hit one after the other. I'm glad Roberts has let you guys in though. He's a tough old bastard, but he's damn good at his job," my dad says.

He was the police chief before me and has been someone I've looked up to since I was little. He's always been my sounding board, even when I was a teenager, and now that I've taken over as chief, he's become pivotal in my success.

I knew I could bring a problem to my dad and he would be able to help me work it out. Most of the time, he didn't even need to say anything. Once I laid it all out there, I could figure out the solution on my own.

Unfortunately, the problem with the B and Es seems to elude both of us, which is concerning and really uncommon.

Eventually, Mom pokes her head out of the door, telling us we can come back inside. We dutifully follow her and set the table for dinner. It's been this way since Levi and I were little. Mom would cook—usually kicking the boys out of the kitchen—and then Levi, Dad, and I would clean up afterward.

"Where's Levi at tonight?" I ask after we get everything on the table and we're all sitting down. The wooden table has been laid out with a light blue runner and some sort of pillared centerpiece Dad and I moved to the end, out of the way.

The table is big enough to hold six, so Mom and I are facing each other on opposite sides with Dad at the head of the table. Our plates are laid out in front of us, and the serving dishes are arranged in the middle.

"He is working late because some disaster happened. You know how he gets. He said he'd come over if it wasn't too late when he finished," Mom says, rolling her eyes.

Levi works with Max building and renovating houses. Max is the architect and designs the houses, Levi is the contractor and makes the designs happen. Usually, when Levi says there's been a disaster, it's an exaggeration, but he can't let it go, so he ends up working insane hours. It's paid off though because their business has taken off in the last few years.

"I hope he can make it. I haven't seen him much lately with everything going on at work," I say as Dad starts to dig into his plate. Mom made spaghetti and meatballs tonight, and I'm starving.

I try to come over regularly for dinner, but being so caught up in work, I haven't been able to see them recently.

They still live in the same house I grew up in, and—with the exception of a few renovations here and there—it's stayed pretty much the same.

"So, I heard a rumor today about you," my mom says, her eyebrow arched as she looks at me. There are so many things this could be about, but I have a feeling I know exactly what —or better yet, who—she's talking about.

Luckily for me, Levi comes bounding into the room like his tail's on fire.

"Sorry I'm late. The shipment of tile came in later than expected today, and I wanted to have it on the floor before the day was done," Levi says as he kisses Mom on the cheek and pats Dad on the shoulder. He sits next to Mom and starts digging in like he's been starving for a week.

"What's the rush, son? Food's not going anywhere," Dad says with a chuckle. Levi has always been this way. Constantly on the go, never able to sit down for too long, and has a wit as quick as he moves.

"I'm starving, and Mom told me she was making spaghetti, so I knew I needed to dig in before fatty over there ate it all," Levi says.

"We both know I'm stronger than you are. It's okay to be jealous," I taunt. Which is only slightly true. I've always had a bigger frame than Levi, and between the police academy and my workout routine, I've buffed up over the past ten years. Levi was always a little smaller in both height and size, but since he's been doing construction, he's quickly gained on me.

"Boys, no fighting at the table tonight. I finally have you both here at the same time, and I won't have you ruining it," Mom says with a look that says you may be over thirty, but I can still take you down.

"How's the house coming along?" Dad asks Levi, and I mentally breathe a sigh of relief. With Levi's interruption, I don't have to talk about Quinn, but I know it's coming, so I need to be prepared when it does.

It's not that I don't want to talk about her with my parents because I do. I would love to share how incredible she is, but I need more time to understand what's happening between us before I talk about it.

I want to explore everything she is to me and everything she could be before I share exactly how quickly this girl has knocked me off my feet. Hopefully, I can keep the information to a minimum and it will be enough to satisfy Mom.

Who am I kidding, it won't even come close.

As has become normal, my thoughts continue to drift, thinking about Quinn. I hope she's having fun tonight with the girls. Maybe I'll text her when I get home and see how her night went.

"Do you think he knows we've been talking about him this whole time?" I hear Levi say to my mom as I come out of my thoughts, noticing everyone is staring at me.

"Doesn't seem like it," my dad says in response.

"What?" I ask, realizing I missed most of the conversation.

"We were discussing the Johnsons' granddaughter and the rumor going around about you and her being seen together," my mom says with a knowing look. Levi is smirking at me because he knows I'm about to get the third degree.

"Oh right, um, yeah. She likes to paint, so I took her to the lake to get some pictures, and since it was warm, we got ice cream." I shrug my shoulders and try to come off as nonchalant.

"You two seemed to hit it off at Megan and Todd's the other night," Levi adds, making me glare at him. Fanning the flames of this already precarious situation will only encourage my mother, and I do not need her sticking her nose in and scaring off Quinn.

It would be nice to feel settled with her before I introduce her to my crazy family.

"We're just getting to know each other right now," I say with a pointed look at Levi. He's enjoying this way too much, but it seems like he's going to back off the topic.

"Am I going to get to meet this girl?" Mom asks.

I roll my eyes at her because what else am I supposed to do? I've barely gotten a chance to get to know Quinn, and Mom is already wanting to meet her.

"One day perhaps, if you don't butt in." I wink at her so she knows I'm teasing.

She huffs at me. "I would not butt in, I just want to know if she's good enough for my son, that's all."

"Now, Alice, we all know that's not completely true. You're the queen of butting in," my dad says, chuckling at her.

"Oh, you hush over there." Mom glares but luckily lets the conversation go. I think I skated by okay for now, but I know it won't last too long. You can't stop the Alice Jackson inquisition, you can only postpone it.

The conversation finally drifts away from me and on to other gossip around town. A new flower shop opened up downtown, and the owner is a bit of a mystery. No one has been able to get much out of her or her backstory, but mom is determined to bring her out of her shell.

I follow along for the most part, but my mind is all over the place. Between Quinn and the B and Es, there's a lot going through my head. After dinner, Levi and I clean up and head out quickly afterward. I'm ready for this long ass day to be over.

17

QUINN

I pull into my driveway feeling the tug of exhaustion pulling me towards my bed. It's been a great day of painting and socializing, but I am beyond ready to crash. Getting out of my car, I grab my stuff and walk into the kitchen, closing the garage door with a push of the button.

Now that Hailey isn't here, the house feels a little emptier and a lot quieter, but it's starting to feel like home. I haven't gotten all of my decorations put up, but that will come soon. Maybe I can convince Cooper to help me hang up some of my paintings. I walk over to my studio to check on how my recent painting is drying. Sometimes colors can change as they dry, so I want to double-check it's still looking okay.

As I walk into the room, something feels off. Like the tranquility of my favorite place has been disrupted, but I don't understand why. I look around and realize my paint-brushes have been switched around, and my storage bins aren't as tidy as they were when I left.

I usually clean up and organize after I have a paint session so it's ready to go anytime I get an itch to paint. I know it's a little anal-retentive, but everything has its place so that while

111

I'm painting I can quickly grab whatever I need without spending time searching for it.

My brain starts moving on overdrive trying to rationalize what I'm seeing. Maybe I didn't clean up quite as well as I thought. I did lose track of time earlier and had to hurry to make it over to Megan's. I walk over to look at my bins and realize my paints have been mixed up as well, and that chaos confirms my fears.

Someone else did this.

I feel the panic rise in my chest as I try to figure out what to do now. I back out of my studio and walk into my kitchen to get my phone, taking deep breaths the whole way to stop my panic from overwhelming me. My hands shake as I call Cooper because he's the first person who came to mind, and I know he'd both help me and make me feel better.

"Hey there. I was just thinking about you," Cooper says softly. In any other circumstance, I would be melting at his words, but this is not a normal situation. I take a deep breath so I don't lose it over the phone.

"Cooper, I think someone was in my house."

Cooper's tone immediately turns serious, "What do you mean?"

"I just got home from Megan's and wanted to check on my painting, but when I walked in, I noticed my studio had been rearranged. My paintbrushes and bins of paint had all been moved."

"And you're sure you didn't leave it like that before you left?" Cooper asks.

"No, I have a system I stick to, and I have never ended a session with my studio looking like this. Cooper, what do I do?" I feel myself starting to get hysterical.

Someone I don't know was in my house. Someone I don't know touched my things.

I feel a tingle in my spine like I'm being watched, and I

look around the half-lit rooms of my house, making sure no one is there.

"Take a deep breath, Quinn, it's going to be fine. Go get in your car with the garage door open, and don't go anywhere until I get there. Okay?"

"Okay, I'm going now," I respond as I walk back through my kitchen and out to my garage.

"I'll be there in a minute," Cooper says in a soft voice.

"Thank you," I say quietly once I'm sitting in the driver's seat of my car.

"Stay on the phone with me, honey. Tell me about your night. How were Megan and the girls?" I take a deep breath feeling incredibly grateful for Cooper and his ability to know I need to think about something else right now.

"The girls were great. Natalie couldn't be there, but we still had a good time."

"I'm glad you were able to hang out with them. We've all been close since we were in school together."

"I heard all about it. They have some pretty funny stories from your school days," I say, giggling at all the hilarious stories the girls shared with me.

"Whatever they told you was exaggerated," Cooper says emphatically, which only makes me laugh harder.

"So, you and Todd didn't throw up on each other after riding a rollercoaster at the fair?" I tease him since he so easily teases me.

"That was food poisoning, not the rollercoaster," Cooper says sullenly.

"I'm sure it was."

I see his truck pull into the driveway, so I hang up the phone. Once he's parked, I get out of my car and walk towards him as he opens his door and gracefully slides out.

I immediately wrap my arms around him, needing to be surrounded by his comforting arms. All of the tension I was feeling a few minutes ago drains away as he holds me tight against him.

Suddenly I feel something wet on my arm, and I lean back, peeking my head around Cooper. There, sitting in the driver's seat is the sweetest little dog I've ever seen. Although to call her little isn't entirely accurate. She's fully grown and has the tan coloring of a lab, but her ears stand up tall so I don't think she's a full lab.

Cooper turns to see what I'm looking at and chuckles. "Quinn, this is Piper. My nosy best friend," he says as he gives her a pat on the head. I hold my hand out for Piper to smell.

"Hi, Piper. Aren't you a pretty girl?" I say as I gently rub her head. She leans into my hand as I'm petting her, making me smile. It's then I notice Cooper never let me go. His arm is still wrapped around my back, and his hand is curled around my hip.

The way his fingers are digging into my side makes everything female in me stand up at attention. His cologne wafts into my nose, and the feel of his strong body pressed up against me plays into all of the delicious fantasies running through my head.

The reason he's here unbiddenly pops into my head, effectively acting like a bucket of cold water dousing my raging hormones. I take a deep breath to refocus my mind.

"Should we head inside so you can see what's going on?" I ask, not wanting to end the moment but knowing this needs to get done.

"We probably should. I'm going to leave her in the truck while we're inside." Cooper says with another pat to Piper's head while telling her to stay there. We step back and he closes the door.

Walking in through the garage, Cooper holds my hand, giving it a squeeze. Before we get inside, Cooper turns to me, "Let me do a quick walkthrough to make sure no one is inside, and then I'll come get you when it's clear." I feel a whole-body shudder move through me at the thought of someone still being inside. I don't have the capacity to say anything at this moment, so I nod my head and wait.

A few minutes go by and Cooper comes back, giving me the all-clear. A deep breath I didn't know I was holding flows out of me.

"Besides your studio, did you notice anything else out of place?" Cooper asks as we enter the kitchen.

"Not really, but I honestly wasn't paying much attention. After I realized what happened, I just wanted to get out." I look around the room, cataloging my belongings. Being back inside makes my skin prickle with the knowledge that a stranger was in my house without me being here.

"Let's look at your studio first, and then we can check the other rooms."

Cooper guides me across the living room and into my studio. The doors are still open from when I was in there earlier, so we walk right in and, automatically, my gaze goes to something I missed before.

The painting I did of Cooper's eyes is facing outward and leaning against the leg of my easel. Now I know for sure someone was in my studio. I had that painting tucked away with other canvases, and only by going through those canvases would you have been able to find it and pull it out.

I'm just unsure as to why that one painting was pulled out.

Cooper looks around the room, seeming to take in every detail. "Without touching anything, can you show me what has been moved or changed?" Cooper asks.

"I first noticed my paintbrushes were all out of order. I keep them organized by size so when I need a specific brush, I can quickly grab the one I need without having to search for it.

"I thought it was weird, and normally I do a better job of cleaning up but figured I was in a rush or something. Then I noticed the baskets holding my paints were a little askew, and when I opened one, the paints that are normally in each drawer were switched around." I point to each item as I tell him about my system.

"I know it seems a little obsessive, but I keep each basket organized by color, and when I opened them, they were all mixed up. I'm sure I sound crazy but this system helps my imagination have room to flow and not get hindered by mess," I tell Cooper, hoping he doesn't think I'm insane. In every other aspect of my life, I don't need organization, but when it comes to my studio, it's the one place I need it so my mind can focus.

"If it was just my paintbrushes, I would have brushed it off and moved on, but my brushes combined with the paints makes me sure this wasn't an issue of time management or distraction. On top of all of that, when we walked in, I noticed this painting on the floor," I say, pointing to the canvas I never wanted Cooper to see. "I had it tucked in with the canvases over there. Someone had to have gone through them and pulled this one out."

"Okay, I'm going to run out to the truck and grab my kit. Do you want to take a look around and see if anything else is out of place?" he asks.

"Sure," I respond, nodding my head. I don't want to be left alone in the house, but I summon all of my courage and follow Cooper out of my studio and back into the living room. As he heads back out to his truck through the garage door, I start walking around downstairs, trying to find anything out of place.

Cooper comes back inside with a grey briefcase-type box in his hand and heads into the studio. Since everything seems to be fine, I continue my search upstairs.

I walk through all the rooms, not seeing anything out of place until I walk into my bedroom and immediately freeze.

18

QUINN

M y stomach turns as I take in the scene before me. Where the subtle mess of my studio would have gone unnoticed by most, the chaos of my bedroom would be missed by no one.

Every item that was once sitting on a surface, is now on the floor. My bedside table lamps, picture frames, and knick-knacks are all spread across the carpet in no obvious order. It's the most bizarre and unnerving thing I think I've ever seen. It makes absolutely no sense and has effectively scared the hell out of me.

I slowly back out of the room and walk downstairs to get Cooper. "If I wasn't already sure someone had been in my house, my bedroom would have confirmed it," I say as I enter the room.

Cooper looks up at me, and I can see a tightness in his eyes that wasn't there before. I hate that this is causing him more stress after an already exhausting day.

"Let's go take a look." Cooper sets down the fingerprint brush and stands up.

We silently walk upstairs, and I lead him down the

hallway to the master. I stand aside so he can get the full effect as he walks through the doorway.

Cooper quietly curses as he takes a look around. "Those were my sentiments exactly," I say as I step into my bedroom behind him.

"Is anything broken?" he asks, walking a little further into the room.

"It doesn't look like it."

Cooper sighs, "I'm so sorry this happened, Quinn. I'm going to call in Todd and Derek to help me dust for prints, but if it's anything like your studio, I doubt we get anything solid." He runs his hand down my arm and then pulls out his phone, heading downstairs to call Todd and finish up dusting the studio.

I stand in the doorway of my room, trying to wrap my head around the war of emotions swirling inside me. The most prominent being unease. The sense of safety that surrounded me has been disrupted, and I'm furious by how easily they were able to breach my carefully constructed bubble.

Your home is supposed to be your sanctuary. The place where you can fully be yourself without judgment or ridicule. It's supposed to be a place where love can be found and should be cherished, but this violation makes a mockery of that.

I hear Cooper coming back up the stairs, his presence instantly calming my frayed nerves. His hands land on my shoulders, and I lean back into him, drawing from his strength to fortify my own.

His arms surround me, seeming to understand I'm in desperate need of his support. I feel him brush his nose on the top of my head and kiss my hair. "Thank you for being here," I say, trying to convey all of my gratitude for this amazing man.

"I wouldn't want to be anywhere else." Cooper presses

another kiss to my head. "Todd and Derek will be here in a few minutes, and it shouldn't take us too long to dust everything." All I can do is nod my head to acknowledge him. This has turned into a surprisingly emotional evening.

Cooper releases me from his embrace and steps around me to start dusting all of the disturbed items. Soon after, I hear a knock on my door and walk downstairs to let in Todd and Derek.

"Thanks for coming, guys. I'm sorry you have to be here so late," I say as I let them in and introduce myself to Derek.

"It's nice to meet you, Quinn. I just wish it was under different circumstances," Derek says as he shakes my hand.

"It's nice to meet you too, and I completely agree. I'll show you upstairs. Cooper's already started, so hopefully, you won't have to be here too long." I turn toward the stairs and lead them to my bedroom.

"Don't worry about it, Quinn. I'm sorry this happened to you," Todd says as he and Derek walk into the room. Cooper gives them an update, and they get started dusting everything.

I don't want to watch them go through my things, so I go back downstairs to have a minute alone. I can't get over that someone was in my house. Every time I think about it, a shiver runs through me.

I'm not sure what I'll do when the guys leave. Imagining trying to sleep in my bedroom after knowing someone else was in there... I don't think I can do it.

When Cooper and the guys are done, I'll pack a bag and see if the hotel or bed and breakfast in town has any rooms because I do not want to sleep here tonight.

Thinking about someone in my house makes me wonder how they got inside in the first place. I already checked the lock on the front door, and the garage door was closed when I got home, but I guess there's a possibility they could've gotten the code somehow.

That leaves the back door, which is one I don't use very often. I haven't had a chance to put any furniture in my back-yard, so I don't spend much time there.

As I step into the kitchen, I hear the guys coming down the stairs. They're talking about something, but I can't make out what they're saying, so I continue to the back door and it is unlocked. I'm not sure if having the answer to my question helped or made me feel worse.

Cooper comes around the corner, his eyes searching for mine. When they land, it feels like all the air gets knocked out of my lungs. I watch him take inventory of my face, searching my features to make sure I'm still doing okay.

Seeming satisfied with what he finds, he says, "I think we're done upstairs. I'm going to double-check I covered everything in the studio, but we should be done after that."

"Okay, I was just checking the back door and I think that's how they got into the house. I guess I left it unlocked at some point, but I'm not sure when. I don't ever use this door."

"I was wondering," Cooper says, putting his arm around me to pull me into a hug. "It's going to be okay, sweetheart," he whispers into my hair, comforting me. His affection in front of Todd and Derek surprises me a little, but I'm also happy about it at the same time.

"We're going to head out. You good, Coop?" Todd asks from behind us.

Cooper turns with me still in his arms. "Yeah, I think we're good."

Todd smirks and nods his head. "I'll write up the report tomorrow when I get to the station."

"Thanks, you've got my notes and her statement, but I've got some stuff to catch up on, so I'll be there if you need anything else," Cooper says.

"See you guys tomorrow." Todd and Derek turn to walk out the front door leaving Cooper and me by ourselves.

"Let's see if we can get any prints from the door," Cooper says, grabbing the case he left at the bottom of the stairs.

"Is it okay for me to touch things in my room?" I ask.

"Yeah, should be fine. We've searched through everything, and it should be good to clean up now," he says. I nod my head and walk upstairs to pack my bag.

Pulling together my toiletries and enough clothes for a couple of days, I get myself ready to go. Once that's done, I pick up a little so it's not such a mess when I get home. Cooper comes in while I'm cleaning up and helps me get some of my stuff put away.

"This may be a little forward, and feel free to say no, but I don't feel super comfortable leaving you here alone, so would you want to come and stay with me for a little while?" Cooper asks hesitantly.

"You want me to come and stay with you? I mean, I didn't feel comfortable staying here either but I was just going to get a hotel room or something." I wholeheartedly would rather stay with him than in a hotel room.

"Yes, I really do," Cooper says with his million-dollar smile. Despite my nerves being shot, that smile still makes my knees weak.

"Well then, I would love to come and stay with you. I'm already packed, so I'm ready to leave whenever."

"Perfect. Let me do a quick walkthrough of the house and see if we missed anything, and then I think we can head out.

* * *

COOPER FINISHED up his checks and we're driving to his house now. At my own insistence, I'm driving my car, following closely behind him.

When I first agreed to stay with Cooper I was really excited about getting to spend more time with him. Now that I'm on my way to his house I'm sort of freaking out.

What if I do something silly or embarrassing? I can be a pretty awkward person, so there's a good chance I will make things weird.

Needing some moral support, I call Hailey. It's late, but being the night owl she is, I know she'll still be up.

"Hey, is everything okay? It's late for you," she answers.

"Everything is fine. Sort of. Long story short, someone broke into my house and rearranged some of my stuff, and now I am on my way to Cooper's house to spend the night."

"Holy shit. We'll get back to the break-in in a minute. Did you say you're on your way to Cooper's house?"

"Yes, and I'm freaking out. I didn't think things through when I first said yes, and now I think I might be losing it."

"First of all, take a breath because a panic attack would not be helpful right now. Secondly, you go girl. I am all for this." I do as directed and take a deep breath which helps more than I expected. "Good, now I know you, and I know what you're thinking. You're worried you're going to do something embarrassing and he'll run for the hills. Am I right?"

"That's pretty accurate, actually," I reply, feeling a little dumb now that she's said it out loud.

"You do realize that if you did something embarrassing and he actually kicked you out, that would make him an epic douche canoe, right?"

"When you say it out loud, I realize how silly it is." I sigh.

"You also wouldn't be going out with him if you thought there was even a chance for him to act that way," Hailey points out.

"Also true. You have officially talked me off the ledge. Thank you," I say, feeling grateful for my friend.

"You are very welcome. Now, go jump his bones and don't do anything I wouldn't do," Hailey demands, which makes me laugh.

"There isn't much on that list," I say teasingly.

Hailey snorts. "Exactly, so go get 'em, tiger, and call me tomorrow with details." And then hangs up, not letting me respond, which oddly makes me miss her.

A few minutes after I get off the phone with Hailey, Cooper pulls into the driveway of a two-story traditional house. I think it might be grey, but it's hard to tell at this time of night.

I pull in next to Cooper and take another deep breath to calm my nerves. I watch him get out of his truck, and Piper jumps out behind him. After getting out of my own car, I grab my suitcase from the backseat as Cooper walks over to me with Piper at his heels. He grabs my suitcase and then takes my hand to lead me inside.

As soon as we walk through the door, Piper takes off through the kitchen and into the living room, grabbing a toy from the floor and bringing it back to where Cooper and I are standing, making us both laugh.

Everything is open and windows line the back wall. I can't wait to see it in the daytime.

"I think someone is excited to have a guest over," Cooper says, chuckling at Piper's antics and easing some of the awkwardness surrounding us. He picks up the toy and throws it into the living room for her to chase.

Turning to me he asks, "Ready for the tour?" I smile and nod my head. I think all of my words went out the window to make room for my nerves.

Cooper points out the open kitchen, living room, and sliding glass doors that, I'm guessing, lead to his backyard. He leads me down a hallway to a half bathroom and then shows me upstairs where there is a guest bedroom and a room made into a home gym.

"...and lastly, here is my room," Cooper says as he leads me into the master. A king bed dominates the room and is covered in a grey comforter that looks insanely fluffy and soft. I have this sudden urge to jump face-first onto the bed.

A bench seat sits at the end of the bed, and a dresser stands against the opposite wall.

"The guest room is ready if you want to sleep in there, but I'd also be happy to share my bed if you wanted," Cooper says with a grin.

"Oh, you would, huh?" I ask, the playfulness making my nerves dissipate, helping me relax a little.

"Yes, I'm nothing if not hospitable to my guests' needs," he says with mock seriousness.

"Do all of your guests get to share your bed then?" My eyebrow lifts in accusation.

Cooper grabs me and pulls me close to him. One hand holds the side of my face while the other wraps around my waist.

"No, only you," he says seriously. I don't have time to decipher what that means before he leans in to brush his lips on mine. What starts as a slow-burning kiss quickly turns into an erotic experience as our tongues duel and our bodies align, fitting against each other perfectly.

My hands fist in his hair while his slide around my waist to cup my ass and pull me into him. I am completely consumed. The break-in feels like a distant memory while I'm in this moment with him.

My whole body lights up from this kiss, and I need so much more.

19

COOPER

If I thought our first kiss was hot, it doesn't even come close to the intensity of this one. I have never lost control quite like this. Having her pressed up against me is unlike anything I've ever felt before. I feel like I'm drowning in it, and I never want to come up for air.

Suddenly, Quinn pulls back from the kiss. Confused, and a little worried I pushed my luck with the ass grab, I pull back to see what's going on and notice Piper is at our feet with a toy in her mouth. The sight of her sitting there, staring at us, patiently waiting to play makes me want to laugh. Smiling, I look back at Quinn and she looks at me. As soon as our eyes meet, we both burst out laughing.

Bending over, I give Piper some love. I'd be mad at her for interrupting us but she's so dang cute I just can't. I stand back up and pull Quinn into my arms to give her another kiss.

"You never answered my question," I whisper against her lips.

"I got a little distracted. What was the question again?" Her face is flushed, and her hair is a little wild from my hands. She's absolutely gorgeous.

"Which bedroom would you like to sleep in tonight?" I ask, running my nose up the column of her neck. She smells fantastic. Like wildflowers and sunshine. Quinn tips her head to the side to give me better access, and I kiss her from below her ear down to where her neck meets her shoulder, earning a moan.

"If I can have more of this, then I pick your bed," Quinn sighs. I kiss my way back up her neck and then down the line of her jaw.

"You can have whatever you want if you're in my bed," I tell her, ending my exploration at her lips.

"Then let's go to bed," Quinn says, making me smile. I kiss her again, just because I can, and tell her I'm going to grab her suitcase and lock up downstairs.

Taking a deep breath, I try to calm my raging body. I don't want Quinn to think I asked her to stay with me just to have sex, granted, that would be fucking amazing. I honestly did not want her to be in her house by herself after the break-in. I wanted to keep her safe, and even if all I get tonight is one perfect kiss, I'll be happy.

I double-check all of the locks to make sure everything is as it should be. After going through what she did tonight, I don't want Quinn to be worried about safety. Grabbing her suitcase and making sure Piper is following, I head back upstairs.

Piper goes to her bed and lays down, knowing we're in for the night. I don't see Quinn at first but find her in my bathroom. It's good sized with a double vanity, a huge soaker tub I've never used, and a walk-in shower.

I watch her for a few moments as she looks around. Her long legs are on display in the cutoff shorts I love, and a tight t-shirt shows off her curves. I want to explore every inch of her with my hands and lips.

My cock stands up at the idea, making my pants tight. I quickly adjust and step into the bathroom.

"Think you can make this work for you?" I ask teasingly, accidentally startling Quinn.

"Geez. I didn't hear you come back up," Quinn says with her hand over her chest.

"Sorry, I didn't mean to sneak up on you." A sheepish grin pulls at my lips. I don't want to push my luck, so instead of pouncing on her like I want to, I bring her suitcase in and place it on a chair in the corner.

"Mind if I brush my teeth, and then the bathroom can be all yours?" I ask, walking over to my side of the vanity. I don't have much sitting out besides my deodorant, toothbrush, and aftershave.

"Not at all," Quinn says, turning to grab something from her suitcase. I start brushing my teeth and look over to see Quinn doing the same at the other sink. It's a little odd to have someone else here in my space, but at the same time, she fits so perfectly. Like she's always been there getting ready for bed with me.

I finish up and walk over to her as she also finishes. "I like having you here," I tell her.

Quinn smiles at me, "I like being here."

"Good, I'm done, so it's all yours." I quickly kiss her forehead and walk out of the room to get ready for bed.

Normally, I sleep in my boxers, but I don't want to make Quinn uncomfortable, so I find some gym shorts to put on instead. Turning the overhead lights off and the bedside lamp on, I get in bed and pick up the mystery novel I've been reading. I'm hoping this will take my mind off the fact that Quinn is in my bathroom changing her clothes. The thought has my dick standing up to take notice.

Jesus, I'm like a middle schooler who can't control himself at the mere thought of a naked girl.

Shaking my head at my wayward body, I try to focus on the characters in my book. Quinn comes out of the bathroom, and I look up to see she's wearing a pair of boy shorts and a tank top that shows off the tops of her breasts. Christ, she's fucking sexy.

I tear my gaze from her body and notice she's staring at my chest. Her eyes are wide and she's biting her lip which sends a bolt of lust all the way through me.

"Come here," I say, my voice deep and husky. Seeming to snap out of the trance she was in, she walks over to the other side of the bed and crawls in.

I grab her around her waist and haul her onto my lap. Her knees settle on each side of my hips, and her center pushes against my cock.

When her hands land on my chest, she asks, "Can we go back to what we were doing before we were interrupted?"

I grin at her. "Absolutely."

She leans in, placing her lips on mine, and her eagerness only adds fuel to the fire. The kiss quickly turns ravenous as we explore each other. Our tongues sliding and teasing.

Her hands roam my chest and shoulders sending streaks of fire across my skin. I need to feel all of her, so I slide my hands up her rib cage, stopping just below her breasts, my thumbs barely brushing the underside.

"Touch me, Cooper, please," Quinn says, pushing her chest closer and leaning in to continue kissing me. Not needing her to tell me twice, I slide my hands up to cup her perfect breasts. She's not wearing a bra, and I can feel her nipples through the tank top. I run my thumbs across the peaks, pinching and pulling as Quinn grinds down on me in response.

Needing more, I wrap my arm around her waist and flip us so she's under me. Quinn lets out a little squeak in surprise. Pulling back, I ask, "This okay?"

"More than okay. Just surprised me a little," Quinn says with a bright smile. She tightens her hands in my hair and pulls me down to continue kissing her. Leaning on one elbow so I don't crush her, I use my other hand to continue

128

my explorations. My palm slides up under the hem of her shirt. The feel of her skin is so soft as I work my way back up to her breasts.

Quinn's hands move from my hair to the hem of her tank as she starts to pull it up over her head. More than willing to help, I lean back a little bit and pull it off. I toss it on the floor and get my first look at her. "You are so beautiful," I say in awe, my hand traveling from her collarbone down between the valley of her breasts.

I can't get over the fact that this extraordinary woman is here with me right now. She makes everything so much brighter when I didn't think it was possible.

"Back at you. I walked out of the bathroom and almost swallowed my tongue," Quinn says, giggling while running her hands down my chest, her fingers tracing the outline of my abs. The feel of her hands on my body almost makes me combust.

"You almost swallowed your tongue? What about me when you came out in these teeny tiny shorts?" I ask, grinning at her. I love that we're still able to laugh with each other, despite being half-naked.

"Well, if you don't like them, I can always take them off," she says with a lascivious grin.

"Then I absolutely hate them. Take them off." I wink. Quinn giggles again, and the sound does something funny to my insides. Wanting to make sure she knows where I stand, I say, "Quinn, I want you to know that I did not ask you to stay here because this is what I was after." I press my rigid cock against her so she gets my drift. "I genuinely wanted you here to keep you safe and for my own peace of mind, so if we don't go any farther than this, it will still be one of the best nights I've had in a long time. Minus the break-in portion."

Quinn smiles up at me which releases some of the tension I was feeling. "I know, Cooper, and I appreciate you telling me. I never once thought you were asking me to stay for

129

this," Quinn says, lifting her hips to rub against my cock, making me groan at how good it feels.

"I want this. More than I've wanted anything in a long time, and at the risk of freaking you out, I'm going to be honest, I feel so much for you already, and I want to see where this could go. For the first time in a really long time, I'm genuinely happy, and you and this town, and even Megan and the girls, are all the reason why."

Quinn's honesty floors me. She's incredible, and I know deep down she is going to change my life for the better. "I feel the exact same way, Quinn. You have completely knocked me on my ass, and I am so lucky to have you here. Not only in my arms right now but in my life as well."

I run my hand down her face, brushing her silky brown hair off her cheek. Her blue eyes, so open and vulnerable, absolutely slay me. I lean down to kiss her, keeping one hand on her face. Where our other kisses have been fast and full of passion, this one is slow and sensual, fitting the mood after our confessions.

Quinn's hands run down my back, her fingers digging into my muscles, pulling me closer to her as our tongues glide together and the kiss deepens. Her hips lift, grinding against me, so I push harder into her. The friction, even through our clothes, is intense.

I feel her hands dip into the waistband of my shorts to cup my ass, setting off a firestorm inside me. I do everything in my power to hold back, not wanting to completely lose it with Quinn. She deserves to be worshipped, so I set out to achieve that goal.

I kiss around her right breast, never quite reaching the peak, while using my fingers to play with the other. Her skin is so silky, and the feel of it under my hands is incredible.

Quinn digs her fingers into my hair, trying to direct me, but I won't be rushed. I run my nose around the underside and finally up over the peak. Pulling her nipple into my mouth, I tease and lick, garnering a moan from Quinn.

Using my teeth, tongue, and mouth, I worship both breasts and then start to work my way down her stomach and across her hips. I run my fingers under the waistband of her shorts and look up at her to see if she's still with me. She nods her head in silent approval, so with my fingers hooked around the waistband, I slowly pull her shorts down her lean legs.

My cock aches at the sight of her completely bare to me. She's stunning.

I run my hands up the inside of her thighs, letting my thumbs skim across the outside of her sex. I lean down, spreading her legs with the expanse of my shoulders, opening her up to my tongue as I get my first taste. She's sweet as honey and highly addicting, just like I knew she would be.

I explore her, getting to know what she likes, what makes her moan, and what doesn't. I focus my attention on her clit, building her up higher and higher as Quinn's fingers knot in my hair almost to the point of pain.

I know she's getting close, so I add my fingers, sliding one in and then another soon after. I feel her detonate, her inner walls squeezing my fingers tightly. I can't wait to feel her wrapped around my cock.

20

QUINN

A m I dead? If I'm not dead, then I'm in pieces scattered around the room. The power of that orgasm shattered me. I've never felt anything like it before. As I float back down to Earth, I feel Cooper kissing his way back up my stomach.

"No, you're not dead, but what a way to go." Cooper chuckles. Oh god, I said that out loud? That's embarrassing.

"Don't be embarrassed. I take it as a compliment," Cooper says as he comes into view over top of me with a cocky grin on his face.

"I'm going to stop talking now because I can't seem to keep my thoughts inside." I cover my face with my hands. Cooper grabs them and holds them above my head.

"I'd rather you didn't keep your thoughts inside. I will always want you to share them with me," Cooper says with a gentle kiss to my nose and then my lips, making me smile. My taste is still on his tongue, making my core tighten and my body beg for more.

I run my hands down Cooper's back, finding that at some point, while I was dead to the world, Cooper removed his shorts and rolled on a condom.

I take in the beautiful man before me and want to pinch myself to make sure I'm not dreaming. His sculpted chest leads down to toned abs and a V-line points to his rigid cock. Stretching up almost to his belly button, it's thick and slightly intimidating in its size. It's been so long since I've done this I'm not quite sure it'll fit, but it will be so worth it to try.

"Keep looking at me like that and you'll unman me," Cooper says.

"I apologize for ogling, but you are one seriously sexy man," I say, making Cooper laugh. I pull him down to kiss me again, not giving him the chance to respond. Cooper positions himself at my entrance and slowly enters me, making me moan.

"Christ, you feel so good. Better than I ever imagined and I did, frequently," Cooper says, fully seating himself inside me.

"I'm going to want you to share those fantasies with me soon," I tell him as I adjust to his size. The stretch and pull of my inner muscles edge into a painful pleasure I love.

Needing him to move, I lift my hips, grinding myself on him. A deep growl rumbles through Cooper's chest, and he starts to move. He picks up his pace, rolling his hips with every thrust.

The feel of him sliding in and out of me is like nothing I've ever felt before. Every push and pull of his hips sends me higher and higher until I'm sure I won't survive the fall. Cooper hooks his arm under my knee, opening me further to him, allowing him to drive deeper.

"Oh god, don't stop. Please don't stop," I moan as my body tightens and quivers.

"Never," he says, and I feel myself tipping over the edge, my hips lifting to meet every thrust. The pleasure he's creating is so intense I'm not sure I'll survive the explosion.

"That's it, baby. Come for me," Cooper growls, and his

words send me soaring as my orgasm crashes through me. I thought the first one shattered me, but this one obliterates everything I thought I knew before. Wave after wave pulses through me, and I know I will be forever changed.

Cooper quickens his pace, chasing his own orgasm as aftershocks ripple through me. With one final thrust, Cooper groans, and I feel him pulse inside me as he comes. His body shudders, and his arms give out as he falls down on top of me.

"Fuck, that was incredible," Cooper says, nuzzling into my neck as we both try and catch our breath.

"More than incredible. Mind-blowing," I say, wrapping my arms around him, enjoying his weight on top of me.

"Mind-blowing, huh?" Cooper asks, grinning as he lifts his head to look at me. I smile and take in his beautiful face. His amber eyes shine with emotion as they look back at me.

"Definitely."

"I'll be right back," Cooper says, kissing me quickly and heading into the bathroom to clean up. While he's in there, I take a mental assessment of how I'm feeling. I'm over-whelmed with the riot of emotions coursing through me, and at the same time, completely and utterly content. This is what I've been missing in my life, and now that I have it, I'm going to do my damnedest to never let it go.

Cooper walks out of the bathroom, and I finally get a full look at him. He is the epitome of sex on a stick, and I don't think I'll ever get my fill of him. The muscles in his toned chest and abdomen flex as he stalks back over to the bed. I lick my lips, worried I might be drooling, and watch Cooper's eyes darken as he follows the path of my tongue.

"You are seriously the sexiest thing, laying in my bed right now," he says, turning off the lamp and getting into bed. He pulls me in close to him so we're laying on our sides face-to-face. "How are you?" Cooper asks once we're settled.

"Forgetting about the break-in, pretty fantastic. Thank you for taking my mind off of it."

"It was a hardship, but I'm glad I could help."

"Hey," I say in mock outrage.

"I'm only teasing. This has been one of the best nights I've had in a while." Cooper runs his thumb across my cheekbone. His fingers slide into my hair, continuously playing with the strands. It feels heavenly as all of the exhaustion I've been pushing aside is catching up to me.

"Thank you for coming when I called. I don't know what I would have done without you there."

"I'll always be there, no matter what," Cooper says. We're silent for a moment, holding on to each other as we lay in the darkness.

"You painted my eyes," Cooper whispers, breaking the silence surrounding us.

"I was kind of hoping you'd forgotten about that," I say, cringing.

"Not quite. Why did you paint them?" Cooper asks.

"I know it seems creepy, and I promise I didn't set out to paint them, but after I met you, I couldn't get them out of my head. I couldn't get *you* out of my head, so it just sort of happened."

"I get it, actually. I couldn't get you out of my head after the barbecue either. I had to talk myself out of going to your house a million times so I wouldn't freak you out," Cooper says, making me laugh. The idea of him struggling just as much as I was is hugely comforting.

"So, are we officially together?" I ask because I need to know for sure. I need to hear the words from Cooper confirming that I haven't built all of this up in my head.

"Yes, I want you to be mine, Quinn. I've wanted you since the first day I met you, and I want to be yours if you'll have me."

"There's never been anything I want more," I say, leaning

in to kiss him because I've finally found what I've been searching for, and it's better than I could ever have dreamed.

Instead of the gentle, easy kiss I planned, it quickly turns passionate and frenzied. It's like a spark ignites when we kiss, and it burns hot and wild every time. I roll over on top of Cooper, straddling him, needing more and knowing that no matter how much he gives me, it will never be enough to satiate this need.

Cooper grabs another condom from his bedside table, and I quickly roll it over him. Knowing I'm more than ready for him, I lift up and position him at my entrance, sliding down until he's fully seated, making us both moan from the extraordinary feeling.

Working to adjust to the fullness, I slowly lift up and slide back down, rotating my hips in the process. Cooper grabs onto my hips, digging his fingers in so hard I'm pretty sure there will be marks tomorrow.

"So fucking good," Cooper grates out as I pick up speed. He sits up to take my nipple into his mouth, sucking and biting both breasts while guiding my hips up and down his length. I feel my insides start to quiver, and I know I'm about to crest over the edge and into oblivion.

Cooper seems to notice too and reaches down to push on my clit, sending me into a screaming orgasm that also triggers his. We fall back down onto the bed, breathing heavily. My entire body is dead weight right now. I have no hope of trying to move.

"I think you sexed me into a coma," I say to Cooper once I get much needed oxygen into my lungs. I feel his chest move as he chuckles, and his lips press against the top of my head as he kisses me. I move to look at him and, even in the darkness, I can still make out his handsome face. "In all seriousness though, it's never felt like that before," I say, trying to convey the impact this is having on me.

"It's never felt like that for me either. I don't think I'll ever

136

get enough of you. You've got me hooked," Cooper says, running his hands through my hair.

"I'm just as addicted to you, so we'll have to help each other," I say with a smile. I roll off of Cooper so we can clean up, and as soon as we're back in bed, he pulls me up against him so my back is to his front. My whole life I've only ever slept alone but the feeling of Cooper behind me makes me wish I could've been sleeping with him instead.

21

UNKNOWN

I run the back of my hand down the side of her face. She's beautiful. Hair as soft as silk, skin like porcelain, body built like a magazine cover. Most girls would kill to look like her.

It's a pity she won't stay that way for long.

Lessons need to be learned. Consequences put in place.

I give her a little slap on the cheek to wake her from her peaceful slumber. I need her alive and aware, otherwise, what's the point?

Her eyes start to flutter open. Awareness slowly sinking in. Her gaze locks with mine, and in that moment, her fear pours out. Power surges through me because I made that happen.

I am no longer unknown. I am no longer unseen.

She tries to scream, but the gag in her mouth prevents any sound from escaping. No one would likely hear her at this time of night, deep in the woods that surround the lake. The silence of the trees blanketing us as the moon overhead shines through just enough to light up the beautiful canvas laid out before me.

Naked, bound, and spread across the ground, her skin is pale and luminous. To most, it would be obscene, but to me, she is a little plaything to do with what I want. A little whore that deserves nothing less.

The toughest part now is deciding how I want to start. Which cut am I going to place first? Starting with the legs prolongs my fun, but the chest gives me more space to work.

Tonight, I think I'll start with her stomach.

The sounds she makes as I slide my knife across her skin. Oh, what I wouldn't give to be able to hear those sounds uncovered.

The sensation of her flesh under my knife is addicting. I have complete control over everything. Where my knife goes across her body, how deep I want to make the cut. It paints the picture I've always wanted to showcase.

My destruction has never been this contained, and yet the ripple of what I've done will create more chaos than ever before.

I am omnipotent.

I will be feared and I will be seen.

22

COOPER

A noise pulls me from the deepest sleep I've had in a long time. Quinn's scent surrounds me as I slowly wake up. Her back is to my front, and my arms are wrapped around her, holding her as close as I can. Waking up with her in my arms is indescribable and gives me this feeling of utter contentment I've never experienced before.

I've always slept alone. I haven't felt comfortable enough to spend all night with a woman in a long time, but waking up with Quinn feels so completely right.

After last night, I know I will never get enough of her. She has infiltrated every wall and barrier I've erected to keep my heart safe, and I'm terrified by how easily she could destroy me. I've been hurt before but I know that if she walks out of my life, it'll be a whole lot worse.

All I can do is hope she feels the same way and that she'll guard my heart like it's her own.

I realize the noise that woke me up is my ringing cell phone, so I gently extricate myself from the warm cocoon that is Quinn's body. I do my best to not wake her up, but we're so entwined it's nearly impossible and she stirs. "Is that mine or yours?" she asks in a sexy, sleepy, voice. I kiss her head and tell her it's mine and to go back to sleep.

Looking at the clock, I see it's six in the morning, and this overwhelming feeling of dread washes over me.

"Chief Jackson," I answer without looking at the caller ID.

"Hey, Coop. You need to get over to the lake. We've found a body." Todd's voice comes through the phone, haunted and strained.

"I'll be there in forty-five minutes," I say, hanging up the phone.

"What is it?" Quinn asks, sitting up with the sheet wrapped around her.

"That was Todd. They need my help at the lake," I tell her, getting out of bed and heading into the shower.

My thoughts are spinning around and around, trying to figure out what's happening. If it was a drowning or boating accident they wouldn't need me. My guys have seen those enough times now they could handle it on their own. This is much bigger, and I know deep down this was not an accident, but maybe if I don't let my thoughts go in the direction they're headed, it won't be true. I also realize how ridiculous that is.

I finish up my shower and quickly brush my teeth as Quinn comes in wearing my t-shirt from last night. It barely covers her, and I wish this morning was starting a million other ways than it is right now.

She walks up behind me and wraps her arms around my waist, and it's exactly what I need right now. I'm all spun up inside, and as soon as her arms tighten around me, I feel myself relax into the embrace. I turn around in her arms and bring her in close to me.

"I'm sorry this morning isn't going quite like I planned," I say into her hair.

"What did you have in mind instead?" she asks, looking up at me with a smile.

"Well, for starters, it would involve some breakfast, and then maybe a little of this." I lean down, giving her a quick kiss.

"Mmm, well that'll give us something to look forward to." Quinn steps back to let me finish getting ready. "Do you want me to take Piper? She can hang with me for the day while you do what you need to." At the sound of her name, Piper jumps up from her bed and comes over to say hello.

"Are you sure? That would be great, but I can also take her to my mom and dad's if you don't want to deal with her." I give Piper's head a pat. Quinn leans down to pet Piper too and says, "I wouldn't have offered if I didn't want to hang with her."

"Thank you. I need to head out, but please stay and make breakfast or whatever." My mind is racing with every thought about what I'm going to be walking into at the lake as I head downstairs with Quinn and Piper following behind me. Quinn lets Piper out into the backyard and comes back into the kitchen as I'm rummaging around.

When I find what I'm looking for, I turn to Quinn. "I wish I could spend the morning with you, but I want you to know that last night was incredible, and I really, really like you," I tell her, handing over the spare key to my house. If I had more time, I would contemplate how comfortable I am handing over a key to my house to this woman but I don't, so I'm giving it to her anyway.

"It's your job, Cooper, but I understand what you're saying. I'm glad you enjoyed last night because I definitely did too. We can talk more later," Quinn says, her eyes heating while a blush creeps into her cheeks. I want to throw her over my shoulder and take her back upstairs, but I can't, and it's killing me.

I cup her face and lean in to kiss her, making sure she knows exactly how I feel right now and how much I want her.

142

"I'm not sure how long I'll be today, but I would like it if you stayed here again tonight instead of going home." There are a million things I want to say to her but right now is not the time.

"Okay, call me when you can, and I'll be here when you get back," Quinn says. I nod at her and walk out the door before I lose all of my control.

Once I'm in my truck and headed to the lake, my mind immediately shifts to what's waiting for me there. Despite my efforts, my thoughts go straight to the worst-case scenario.

If my gut is correct, this will be a first for Sonoma. Our town has always been safe. The only crimes that ever happen here are underage drinking, bar fights, and every now and then some stolen property. Although, if I'm being honest with myself, I feel like this has been headed our way since the very first B and E in Westlake.

A feeling of disquiet has blanketed the town since the first report, and that sensation has only amplified since then. With each new case being more aggressive than the last, our sense of safety has diminished and weakened. Knowing that my town feels unsafe and distressed has been a much larger weight on my shoulders than even I realized.

It's my job to protect these people, and if they feel scared or uncertain then that's on me. Protecting them should be my number one priority, but how do I protect them from something we've never encountered before? Something so unknown and feared yet so well studied there are textbooks on the subject.

It's foreign and uncharted territory which, in turn, makes me feel out of control, and that is the crux of the issue. I do not have control of this situation and without it, I am unsure of how to lead.

I pull into the parking lot of the lake for a much different reason than the last time I was here. I hope Quinn is

143

comfortable at my house. I feel bad having to leave her there, but I didn't have any other options, and I definitely do not want her to go back to her house without me. With what I'm about to walk into, I'm not convinced it is safe anymore.

Looking around, I see a myriad of activities happening all at the same time. There are police cruisers and an ambulance parked as close to the beach as they can get. The lights on a few of the cruisers are flashing from red to blue, scattering their light across the other cars. A couple of deputies are standing back watching the parking lot, and I nod in their direction as I walk towards Todd who is standing by the building.

"What have we got?" I ask him when I get close enough. He turns and starts to lead me behind the tackle shop and into the woods.

"Female victim, early twenties. Tom was doing his normal checks of the grounds before opening up the marina and called it in." He stops walking for a minute and turns to me. "Cooper," he pauses and looks at me. It's then I know this is going to be worse than any worst-case scenario I could've dreamed up. I see turmoil and revulsion swirling in his eyes. "It's bad."

Not in the least bit prepared for what I'm about to see, I nod my head for him to continue on, and it's then I see the caution tape wrapped around the trees. Our deputies stand silently on the outer fringes as the medical examiner works in the middle.

As we get closer, the scene becomes clearer, and I almost wish I could stay on the edges with my deputies. I don't want to go in there, but I owe it to the victim to do my job.

Ducking under the tape, I see her fully now. A sheet covers her body to give her some dignity. Her hands and feet are bound to stakes in the ground and spread out like a star. Her skin is so pale it has almost a bluish tint. The earth around her is stained dark from her blood, telling me she was brought here alive.

Everything about this scene points to one hard truth.

This was murder.

23

QUINN

I watch as Cooper pulls out of the driveway from the
window over the kitchen sink. His tail lights fade down
the road until I can't see them anymore, and the silence of
the house fills the room. I turn around and take in my
surroundings. His kitchen is a U-shape and pretty modern
with dark cabinets and countertops, masculine but still nice
all the same.

My eyes catch the lone key on the counter and the signifi-
cance of this morning wraps around me like a cherished
blanket. I pull the edges of those feelings closer as I pick the
key up and hold it in my hand.

When I woke up this morning, cuddled in Cooper's arms,
I knew things between us had shifted. This was no longer
just a crush, testing the waters of our feelings. This was a
real, vulnerable relationship. A connection surmounting on a
whole other level than I've ever had with anyone else.

Throughout my life, I never allowed myself to connect
with anyone. There was too much potential for loss
because nothing was ever permanent. Hailey was the first
person to ever break through the steely walls I'd built up,
and while I am incredibly grateful for her friendship, what

146

I'm building with Cooper has the potential to be so much bigger.

I don't know if I'm ready for bigger. I don't even know if I'll be good at it. In college, I had a couple of boyfriends, but once I got into law school, I didn't have time for relationships. I dated here and there but no one ever stuck, and I didn't try very hard to make them stick. It was just so much easier to be my own independent person.

I didn't have to tell anyone what my plans were. I could go out with Hailey when I wanted, or I could stay at home in my sweatpants and eat ice cream for dinner. It was the perfect setup for me. However, being in this town and surrounded by people who genuinely care about me, I'm realizing I was pretty lonely.

Imagining my life filled with Cooper and his adorable puppy brings the biggest smile to my lips. It would be a life full of color and vibrancy. One where I would no longer be lonely, and that alone is worth exploring what bigger could mean for us.

Thinking about Piper makes me remember where I am, so I walk to the back door and peek outside to see she is standing on the patio ready to come back in. "Piper girl, should we try and find some coffee and then go on a walk?" I ask her out loud. Piper barks at the word walk, so I take that to mean she is happy with the plan.

Being in Cooper's house alone is a little strange, but as I snoop around and find what I need for coffee, I begin to get more comfortable. I also find the stuff to make peanut butter toast for breakfast, but I want to get dressed before I eat, so while my coffee is brewing, I head back upstairs.

I quickly clean up in Cooper's beautiful stone-tiled walk-in shower and change into clean clothes. With Piper at my heels, I head back to the kitchen to gather my breakfast and walk out to the patio.

Cooper's backyard is nicely manicured with a patio table

and four chairs under a navy blue umbrella. I sit at the table while Piper runs off into the yard chasing the butterflies fluttering around the flowers planted against the privacy fence. A light breeze floats in the air as I sip my coffee and enjoy the sunshine. I'm realizing how much I've missed out on by not having any patio furniture in my backyard.

Thinking about my house reminds me of the mess I walked into last night. All of my thoughts have been so focused on my amazing night with Cooper that I haven't given much thought to the break-in.

In all honesty, I haven't wanted to give it much thought. I was so afraid yesterday, and thinking about other things kept the fear at bay but ignoring the issue will only allow it to fester, so I need to buck up and decide what to do next.

I don't know what to do next.

Ugh, why can't I just say, *fuck you, you bastard. You don't control me!* while shaking my fist and then go home? If it were Hailey, that's exactly what she would say. She wouldn't allow this guy to push her out of her home, but unfortunately, I'm not as strong-willed as Hailey. This break-in has affected me profoundly, and I'm going to need more time to take back the space.

I should go back to the house and see how I feel in the light of day. Now that I've had time to calm down and the incident isn't quite so fresh, I may feel differently.

With a brewing to-do list in mind, I finish my coffee and call Piper to come back inside with me. I clean up my breakfast mess in the kitchen, and Piper and I head out on a walk as I promised.

We only manage a couple of miles, and as we walk back into the house, my phone starts ringing. Looking at the screen, I see it's Megan calling, so I quickly accept the call while taking Piper off of the leash.

"Good morning," I answer.

"Hey, I hope I'm not calling too early. Todd told me about

the break-in, so I wanted to check on you. How are you?" Megan asks.

"I am doing surprisingly well, all things considered. They didn't steal anything and there wasn't any damage. Things were just out of place and in super-creepy ways."

"Oh god, I can't even imagine how unnerving that was. Did you stay there last night? If you're not comfortable at home, you are more than welcome to stay with us," Megan offers.

I have no idea what to tell her. Cooper and I haven't had a chance to discuss our relationship much ourselves, let alone discussing it with others. Do I come right out and say I stayed with Cooper? I mean, I don't want to lie to her, and with how she and the girls reacted the other night, I think she'd be happy for us. Plus, I'm going to need some perspective on navigating this, and who better to ask than one of Cooper's oldest friends.

"Thank you for offering, but I am staying with Cooper for a couple of days," I say as nonchalantly as possible. I don't want to make a big deal of it since this wouldn't have happened in any other circumstance.

Suddenly, I hear high-pitched squealing on the other end of the phone, and I have to pull my phone away from my ear.

"Oh my god, oh my god! This is amazing!" Megan shouts. "You're staying with Cooper? Like right now, you're at his house? I can't believe this. I am so excited," she says all in a rush of words I can barely keep up with.

Chuckling, I confirm her questions which causes more squealing, making me laugh harder.

"Okay, I need details, and to get details, I'm going to need some backup," Megan says almost to herself. "Oh, there's a new spa over in Westlake. We could do a girls' day tomorrow. I'm thinking manis, pedis, and maybe even a facial? We can dish on Cooper and keep you distracted from the break-in."

"That sounds amazing and exactly what I could use right now," I say, feeling a little overwhelmed at the realization that for the first time in my entire life, I am a part of a girl tribe. A group of women lifting each other up so each one knows they are strong and capable of getting through both the good and bad things life throws at them.

I finally have a group I can lean on when I'm struggling, and that is something to be celebrated. Even though I'm going to get interrogated about my relationship with Cooper, I am beyond excited.

"Okay, I'll call the girls and the spa and set it up. I'm sorry you're having to deal with the break-in, but I am so excited for you and Cooper," Megan says.

We say our goodbyes, and I hang up the phone, placing it on the kitchen counter. Mentally running through my to-do list, I realize I'm going to have to buck up and go to my house today. Trish asked me to bring in a few more paintings because she only had one left, and I forgot to pack them last night.

Maybe in the light of day, it won't be so bad. Then I can move on from this whole episode. That would also mean I no longer need to stay at Cooper's, and the thought makes me irrationally sad.

24

QUINN

I've always prided myself on being calm, cool, and collected. There are very few instances where I've not been able to maintain that state. Meeting Cooper for one and, apparently, walking back into my house after the break-in.

Sitting in my driveway, staring up at the beautiful house I now call home, I feel tears prick my eyes. I hate that this person has reduced me to a sniveling joke. They've obliterated my ability to stay cool under pressure, and that is the most frustrating part of this situation. Not only were they in my house and messed with my things, but they also messed with my mind. It's wholly unacceptable that they've disrupted my ability to remain steady in the face of chaos.

Through a burst of anger, I get out of my car and head inside. I'm determined to put this episode behind me, and in order to do that, I have to buck up and take back my space.

Once I'm inside, I do a quick scan of my kitchen and living room, inventorying everything I see. Nothing appears out of order, and as the silence surrounds me, I'm comforted knowing it still feels like home. It's still the place that has always welcomed me into its loving arms. The place my heart has held close since I was a little girl.

I walk through the house towards my studio with a little more confidence than I did when I first got into the house. I just have to keep remembering that this place is mine and no matter what happens it will always be mine.

Easier said than done, though, when I feel uneasiness snake down my spine walking into my studio.

My paintbrushes are still disorganized, and the drawers holding my paints are still askew. The uneasiness grows when I look down and see the gold flecks of Cooper's eyes staring back at me. I never moved the painting back to its storage place, and it feels almost as if whoever did this is mocking me with the painting.

It sends a message saying, *I see you. I've discovered your secrets and know who you are.*

Shaking off the tendrils of fear, I take a deep breath and start reorganizing my things, putting away Cooper's painting, fixing my brushes, and righting all of the wrongs I come across. It's cathartic and aids me in making the space mine again.

Once everything is back in its place, I flip through some of my finished pieces, picking out my favorites to give to Trish. Before now, I'd never had the urge to sell my paintings. I created them for myself because I enjoyed doing it. It was never a hobby I wanted to make money on, so I never did anything with them.

Being in this place has inspired me to want to share them. After seeing the other artists' work in Trish's store, I decided it might be fun to see if anyone would want my paintings too. If they didn't buy them, I would've been okay and found another way to earn money, but much to my delight— and Trish's too, I'm sure— they've become really popular.

I choose three paintings to take with me and make a mental note to finish up a few more since my selection is dwindling. I love that I have a reason to spend all day painting now.

I walk back out of my studio after packaging up my work, and my gaze lands on the stairs. I didn't finish cleaning after Cooper invited me over, and I know there's still a mess up there. Having already spent an hour cleaning up my studio, I don't have it in me to clean my bedroom too.

I know I would feel even worse while cleaning up there since it's is supposed to be the place you feel the safest. The one place in your home that no one goes into without your permission. It's where you have the most intimate moments, and knowing a stranger was in there, going through all of my things, just about sends me over the edge of panic.

Shaking my head, I walk past the stairs and back into the kitchen. Despite feeling like a chicken, I'm pretty proud of myself for coming back here alone in the first place. I completed the tasks I set for myself and plan to tackle the rest another day.

Once I'm outside and walking to my car, I feel the weight of that daunting task slide off my shoulders. I take another cleansing breath while I secure my paintings in the trunk of my car and then jump into the driver's seat.

My drive to Trish's store is short, and I score a parking spot right in front. I grab my paintings and head inside, causing the bell over the door to ring. The store is pretty busy this afternoon which is nice to see.

I don't see Trish anywhere, so I walk to the back where she keeps her inventory, set my paintings down, and head to her office. Peeking in, I see her sitting behind her desk reading over some paperwork.

The office is small but cheery, decorated in warm greys and blues. A leafy green plant sits in the corner, and a bookcase takes up part of another wall. I give a quick tap on her door, and she looks up and smiles at me.

"Hey there. Just dropping off some more paintings. How's it going?" I ask.

"Hey, things are good. I sold your last one today, so perfect timing."

"That's great to hear. I should have a few more for you next week."

"Perfect! Hey, do you have a minute to chat?" Trish asks.

"Of course," I respond, walking into her office to sit.

"I have an opportunity I want to discuss with you," she starts, and I nod my head for her to continue. "I bought the store next door and want to open it specifically for art. I've got several suppliers now and want to showcase their work better than how I'm currently able to. I'm wondering if you'd be interested in helping me out with both getting the store up and running and then managing it when it's finished. I can't run the whole project by myself, and you're the only person in town I'd trust to do it justice."

I try to take in what Trish said through my shock. Is she really asking me to run her gallery? That would be an absolute dream. I already know she has a fantastic collection of artwork, and I could work with the local artists in the area. I'd have a stable income and wouldn't have to rely on only my commissions. I don't think I could've thought of anything more perfect for me.

"Really? You want me to help you run the store?" I ask, just to double-check I didn't mishear her in my excitement.

"Absolutely. With your background and eye for art, you're perfect," she responds.

"Wow, I would be honored to help you with the store. What does the timeline look like?" Trish gives me a huge excited smile and claps her hands together. Over the course of the next hour, she gives me all of the details, and we make a game plan for what she'll need my help with, which is quite a bit more than I expected.

In the beginning, my job will be overseeing construction

and ensuring the space is built to enhance the art. When we're satisfied with that portion, I'll basically be working with the artists to keep inventory up and then selling the artwork.

I am ecstatic and ready to jump in right now. Trish told me Levi and Max's construction company are going to be working on the remodel and can't get started for a couple of weeks, but that will give us time to plan out the store and be ready to hit the ground running when they begin.

Trish and I set up a time to meet again, and I head out afterward. I go grocery shopping to get some stuff for dinner even though I'm not sure what time Cooper will be home. I figure whatever I make, I can reheat if he's home late.

I hope he's doing okay and that the call he got this morning isn't anything serious. I guess if it wasn't, he wouldn't have been called at six in the morning.

Who would've thought something so serious would happen in such a small town? I guess no matter where you go, bad things can happen.

25

COOPER

"Anybody got an update?" I ask, looking around at my guys.

This has been one fucked up day, and it still isn't over. We spent most of it at the lake and are now back at the station trying to identify our Jane Doe. She doesn't match anyone on the missing persons list, and no one has come forward asking about her.

We're running her DNA but that can take a few days, and if she's not in the system already, it won't do any good. Without an ID, we don't have many leads to run down until the evidence from the scene gets processed.

"We've still got guys out canvassing but so far, nothing, Chief," Derek says from his desk. In normal circumstances, the guys share desks with each other, and we've never had any issues with space, but as the extra guys trickle in from canvassing, our small bullpen is rapidly filling up.

"Okay, come find me when everyone's back. I'd like to lay out everything we know before calling it a day," I respond, making my way out of the bullpen and back to my office.

As I sit down at my desk, I take a deep breath to try and calm my racing thoughts. There are too many questions and scenarios running through my mind to make sense of what was discovered today.

A murder.

Done so cruelly, I wouldn't even wish it on my worst enemy.

It's hard to fathom it actually happening here, in my sleepy little town.

When I signed on as chief, I knew there would be some tough days. Having seen my dad go through the ups and downs of being chief, I thought I was pretty well prepared, but this is a whole new ball game.

How do I help my guys overcome the horrors of that crime scene? How do I help them stay grounded when all I want to do is rip the bastard who did this to shreds? For the first time since joining the force, I wish I'd done something different. Something that would never have allowed me to see what I did today.

I shake my head to clear my pointless thoughts. While I may not have wanted to see what I did today, the fact of the matter is, I did see it, and that Jane Doe needs me to find out who hurt her. No matter what happens on the job, I know I was born to be a police officer, and maybe fate led this girl to me because I'll stop at nothing to get her justice.

A knock on my door interrupts my inner monologue. Looking up, I see it's Rachel.

"Hey, can I get you anything? Something to drink or eat?" she asks me, a small empathetic smile on her face.

"No, not right now, but would you order some sand-wiches for the guys?"

"Sure, I'll call Sal's and have them bring it by. Any updates?"

"Not yet, unfortunately, but we've still got a few more guys out canvassing."

"Okay, well let me know if you need anything. I'm here to help you any way I can."

"Thanks, Rachel, I appreciate it." She gives me a quick nod and then leaves my office.

Taking advantage of this little break, I check my phone to see if I've missed anything. I've missed a call from my mom, and I have a text message from Quinn. I open the message and, for the first time all day, a huge grin stretches across my face. She sent me a picture of her and Piper. They're lying on the floor of the living room, and Piper's head is on Quinn's shoulder. Piper has a toy rope in her mouth and Quinn is sticking her tongue out at the camera.

The text says, *We're missing you.*

I quickly dial her phone number and wait for her to answer. I've missed her terribly today. Especially knowing she's been at my house hanging with Piper.

Her voice carries through the phone after a couple of rings, and instantly I feel the tension in my shoulders lessen.

"Hi, handsome. How are you?"

"I'm doing okay. Thank you for the picture. It made me smile. How are things there?"

"I'm glad you got it. Things are great here. I'm making some lasagna for dinner if you're home on time. If not, it'll keep, and I can reheat it for you when you get home."

"That sounds so good. I'm hoping we can wrap things up here in a bit."

"Okay, no worries, just stay safe, please," Quinn says.

"I will. I've got to go, but I'll text you when I'm on my way home." I hang up the phone after Quinn says goodbye. The thought of going home to Quinn fills me with a happiness I've never felt before. How is it that I've only known this girl for a couple of weeks and she's already one of the most important people in my life? I guess after all I've been through, it's easy to know when you've found the real thing.

I make it through most of the paperwork on my desk before Todd lets me know all the guys are back.

The noise walking back into the bullpen is loud with all

158

of the deputies working through the sandwiches Rachel brought in. Seeing the camaraderie between my guys makes me feel like, despite the gruesome scene this morning, we'll all be able to move on and get our Jane Doe justice.

"Okay, guys, I've heard from most of you but let's go over everything again so we're all on the same page," I say, walking over to the whiteboard to make notes. I nod at Todd for him to start.

"Our Jane Doe is a twenty-five-year-old female. So far, we've got no identification, and she doesn't match any of the missing person reports. The ME's initial observations indicate she was killed sometime between midnight and four AM. Cause of death was blood loss due to the lacerations across her body.

"From what we can tell, she was taken into the woods alive and killed there. We should have complete lab results in the next few days." As Todd continues his update, I start putting up the photos we got from the scene and making notes.

Each group of canvassers gave an update on who they talked to and what was said. They all report the same thing. No one knows who she is nor had they seen her before.

"Thanks, everyone," I say once all of the updates are done. "Until we have the ME's report, I know we don't have much to go on right now, but someone knows this girl, and we need to find out who. I want our next shift canvassing any gas stations or diners along the highway. If no one around Sonoma knows her, she may not be from here. I'm going to send out her info to Westlake and Denton as well as others around the area. Hopefully, we'll get a hit from something soon."

I look around at the grim faces of all of my deputies. Having never had to deal with something like this, it's going to affect them all profoundly. "Before we let the evening shift have their bullpen back, I want you guys to know that it's okay to struggle with what we saw today. It was brutal and not something you could ever prepare yourself for.

"If it becomes something you can no longer deal with on your own, please come and talk to me. I'm not going to judge you or think any less of you for needing to talk it out. Honestly, I'll see you as less of a man if you don't come and talk to me, so just remember my door is always open and my cell is always on." All of my guys nod their heads, and I know my message got through. I got lucky with a great group of officers, which makes my job a lot easier.

"Keep on this, guys, this is our number one priority right now, so let's continue our search, turn over every stone until we find him." Everyone nods their head in understanding and disperses. The guys who aren't on evening shift head home while those who are either head out on patrols or sit down at desks to work.

I hate that everything else is going to go on the back burner, but I know we won't have the resources to solve this murder and help with the B and Es.

By the time I'm out of the station and headed home, it's past seven, and I'm exhausted from both the physical and emotional toll of today. Pulling into my driveway and seeing Quinn's car there helps to release some of the stress.

I walk inside to the smell of pasta sauce and garlic. It's quiet, so I know Piper and Quinn aren't downstairs. I take off my boots and quickly put everything away so I can go find my girls. That thought makes me smile and has me walking quickly up to my room.

The bedside lamp is the only light on, and Piper is laying in her bed. Her head pops up when I walk in, and she quickly jumps up and comes to give me some love. Quinn isn't in the room, so I'm guessing she's in the bathroom, although I don't hear any sounds of movement in there. I look around the corner and what I see stops me dead in my tracks.

There are candles around the bathtub, and the room

smells like vanilla. Quinn is lying back in the tub with headphones in her ears and her eyes closed. Her hair is piled on top of her head, the long line of her neck is exposed and tempting, and the tops of her breasts peek out above the bubbles in the water.

Fuck me, this is it. She's it. What I've been searching for my whole life and could never find. I feel my heart lurch in my chest as the realization pulses through me. I always hoped, one day, I'd find the right girl to settle down with and maybe have a family but as time went on, I started to give up on the idea.

I thought I might've been close with Rissa but after she died I just stopped hoping for the right one to come along. None of the women in town wanted me for me. They liked the title I hold or the face I carry, but none of them came around because they liked who I am as a person.

The moment I met Quinn, I knew she was different. She had something inside of her that I longed for and knew I needed in my life. Now she's here, in my house, in my bathtub, looking like a goddess who deserves to be worshipped. As I walk towards her, I vow to be that guy. The one who shows her every day how much she's worth and how special she really is.

26

QUINN

Waking up with Cooper for the second morning in a row seems absolutely decadent and something I could seriously get used to. After he came home last night, I could see in his eyes that something terrible happened and knew it wouldn't help him to talk about it right then. I talked him into getting in the tub with me where we promptly flooded the bathroom floor and had to use all of his spare towels to clean up.

The mess was worth it to see some of the lightness come back into his eyes as we laughed and teased each other. We spent the rest of the evening talking and getting to know each other better both mentally and physically.

We talked about anything and everything from Cooper's girlfriend who died to my strained relationship with my parents. We even talked about what we wanted for our futures, and knowing we're on the same page made me fall even harder for Cooper.

We also managed to christen several of the surfaces around the house. I'm deliciously sore this morning, and that revelation puts a smile on my face.

I slowly try to untangle myself from Cooper's hold on me so I don't wake him. He looks so peaceful right now with his lashes splayed across his cheeks and the frown lines from last night smoothed out. I know as soon as he wakes up, those lines will be back, so I want him to stay asleep for as long as possible. He also has to be back on duty today, and two late nights in a row are not going to help him stay on his game.

I'm still not exactly sure what happened yesterday, and Cooper didn't provide any details. I don't know how much he's allowed to tell me about the investigation, but I figure if he can or needs to talk it out he will, and I'll be here to support him either way.

After I quietly brush my teeth, I sneak downstairs with Piper at my heels and let her out into the backyard. I love watching her run around back there, so carefree and playful. I would've wanted a dog just like her growing up if I were allowed.

I start a pot of coffee and root around in the kitchen to see what options we have for breakfast. My cooking experience is pretty minimal. I have the basics down because how else was I going to survive living alone, but I also spent so much time at the office that cooking was never something I had time to do.

Now that I have the time, I think I'd like to learn more. Maybe try out some more difficult recipes and see what happens. It'll probably turn into a mess, but I think I'll enjoy trying. I wonder what else I could try that I never got to do before. I should start making a list of things I want to learn how to do. I could even try and get the girls in on it too.

I love that I finally have a group of girls to do things with. I know I always had Hailey but she had her own group of friends she hung out with, and that was okay with me. I never felt left out because I never had the desire to join in, but now, I have both the desire and the time to cultivate these friendships, and I'm grateful they've included me in their group.

Cooper has all of the ingredients for pancakes—and by ingredients, I mean the box of prepared mix—so I start putting that together and find some bacon in the fridge that doesn't look expired. I let Piper back in while the oven preheats, and she and I dance around in the kitchen while we wait.

Out of the corner of my eye, I see Cooper leaning against the wall, watching us with a little smirk on his face. He's only wearing his running shorts, and I feel my cheeks heat up as embarrassment floods through me at being caught dancing.

"Don't stop on my account," Cooper says with a little chuckle. "I was definitely enjoying the show." His eyes scan me up and down, and I realize I only have his t-shirt on and nothing else. His heated gaze sends a bolt of lust straight through me, and I can't control the little shiver that runs down my spine while I check out his bare chest.

He stalks over to me and grabs me around the waist, pulling me in tight to his body. His head leans down and he kisses me thoroughly, our tongues, dancing and twining like we've been doing this with each other forever.

"Good morning," he says when we finally come up for air. "Good morning," I reply, completely and utterly smitten with this sexy man. My eyes rove over his face wanting to capture this moment forever. His golden eyes are shining with adoration, his features soft and happy, the stubble on his jaw is rough and shadowy. He's everything I've ever dreamed about and more.

The oven beeps, letting me know it's pre-heated, and we pull apart from each other. "I was going to make pancakes and bacon if that sounds okay," I tell him as I put the tray in the oven and heat up the griddle for pancakes.

"Sounds perfect, but you don't have to do that. We could

go to Jones's and get breakfast if you want." I look up at him, and while I know he would do that so I don't have to cook, I don't think he really wants to leave. I can see the tension building as if he's preparing to go out in public with the knowledge that something bad has happened and no one else knows.

"That's okay. I may not be the best cook in the world but I can manage, so let's stay here and relax until we both have to leave." I watch as the tightness he was gathering dissipates and his shoulders drop. All he does is nod his head, but I can see in his eyes he's relieved. He walks around the breakfast bar and sits at one of the stools.

"Oh, I forgot to tell you last night. Trish offered me a job!" I say, partly to distract him and partly because I want to share it with him.

"Really? That's great. What would you be doing for her?" he asks with genuine interest. I love that he listens when I talk and doesn't pretend to care.

"She bought the building next to her shop and is going to turn it into a gallery so she has more space to sell the art she brings in. She asked me to help her get it started and then run the gallery after we get the building ready." I'm still finding it hard to believe she wanted me to help her, but I'm beyond grateful and so excited.

"Sounds like it'll be perfect for you. I can't wait to see what you do with the place. When will you get started?" he asks.

As we talk, I finish up the pancakes and the bacon comes out at the same time. I tell him all about the job and what I'll be doing as we eat, and the longer I talk about it, the more animated I get. I can't wait to get started, and more than likely, the next couple of weeks are going to feel like they drag on.

"I also forgot to tell you I went by my house yesterday to

get a few paintings for Trish. It felt weird being there, but I think once I get everything back the way it was, it'll be fine."

Cooper's eyes snap to mine. "You went inside your house yesterday? Did someone go with you?" I can see fury building behind his eyes. I just don't understand why.

"No, I went by myself. I forgot to pack a few paintings in all of the craziness, so I went over there to grab them. I thought it was okay to be back in my house and put everything away," I say, my brow furrows in question to his anger.

Cooper stands up so quickly his chair almost falls over, and he takes his plate into the kitchen. All of his movements are jerky and stilted. I can tell he's trying not to yell at me right now.

"It wasn't safe for you to go in there. You should've waited for me. Someone could've been in there waiting for you to come back. They could've hurt you, and I wouldn't have been there to keep you safe." He's standing at the kitchen sink with his hands gripping the countertops so hard you can see the whites of his knuckles.

I open my mouth to respond, feeling my temper rising, ready to lash out at him. But then I look at Cooper, taking in his body language, his words, and suddenly I don't think this is about me anymore. It is about me, but the underlying issue isn't me going into the house, it's what happened yesterday, and I think Cooper is scared.

As that thought permeates my brain, I feel my anger drain and the tension coiling in my stomach starts to loosen.

"Cooper, honey, no one could've gotten in there. We made sure everything was locked before we left. I was safe the whole time I was there," I tell him as I walk up behind him and wrap my arms around his waist. "Tell me what's really going on."

He blows out a deep breath and turns around, wrapping his arms around me and squeezing tight while I run my hands up and down his back. I can feel his nose on the top of my head, and he breathes me in like I'm his lifeline.

"I don't want your world darkened by mine, Quinn. That isn't fair to you when you are the bright spot in my life. You are sunshine, lighting up the shadows of my life, and I can't have you dimmed." God, this man could seriously melt the snow in the middle of a New York winter.

"Well, maybe my light is strong enough to keep out this darkness too," I say, hoping he'll tell me what's going on. I'm not trying to be nosy because I honestly don't think I want to know, but by telling me, it will help ease the load on his shoulders, and that's all I want for him.

Cooper takes a deep breath and leans back, separating us like if he's not touching me then the darkness can't get to me either. I brace myself for the words. "A girl was murdered the other night. But, Quinn... it wasn't just that she was killed. That was horrible, but it's what the bastard did to her. He sliced her up. All over her body.

"I've never seen anything so cruel. We think she was alive while he did it, too, and I... I can't get the thought out of my head of how much pain she was in while she died. No one deserves that. And now, the town I swore an oath to protect, isn't safe anymore, and I'm not sure I know how to get us through this."

Cooper looks me dead in the eye as if he's preparing for me to run while imploring me to stay. He looks so unsure it brings tears to my eyes. That poor girl, going through something so terrible, and then for someone as kind-hearted as Cooper to have to see her like that. I can't imagine.

I move in closer and slide my arms back around Cooper. My heart is breaking for both the girl and this amazing man. "Oh, honey. I'm so sorry this happened. I'm sorry that poor girl had to go through something so terrifying, and I'm sorry you had to see it. But you know what?" I lean back and put my hands on his face to make sure he's listening. "She is also

167

lucky because she has you to find out who did this to her. You are the best person to get her justice, and you won't give up until you do." I look at Cooper a little longer to ensure he knows I mean what I say, and he nods at me, telling me he heard me.

He leans in and kisses me for all he's worth, and I know, in that moment, Cooper will have my heart forever.

27

COOPER

"Ben, I know you've had a bit of trouble recently, but it's time to move on, honey," I hear Quinn say as I walk through the door of what will be Paint and Paper, the gallery Quinn's helping to open. I'm not sure how I feel about her calling someone else "honey", but by the look on her face, she's not doing it out of love. The place is noisy with a few construction guys working and talking.

I watch as her eyes roll back so far into her head I'm afraid they may get stuck. "You went on one date, Ben, and while I know you're a romantic, that doesn't constitute a love connection," she says, making me chuckle. She finally sees me, and her face breaks out into a megawatt smile.

It's been a few weeks since the break-in, and I honestly can't remember what it was like to not have her in my life. Her laughter has brought me so much joy, and it feels as if we've been together for years instead of weeks.

She holds up a finger telling me it'll be another minute, so I go find Levi to keep me busy while I wait. The space has really come along in the week and a half that Levi and Max have been remodeling. They've hung the drywall and are in the middle of installing light oak floors. There are faux brick

169

columns evenly spaced to break up the room and what looks like a makeshift desk made out of sawhorses towards the back of the room.

I find Levi in the back room, putting together shelving units to house the inventory that won't fit on the walls or in display cases. His navy hat sits backward on his head, and his tool belt is slung around his hips. We look identical to each other with the exception of our eyes, his are hazel while mine are more brown.

"Hey, bro!" Levi says as I walk towards him.

"Hey man, it's looking good out there," I say, giving him a quick hug.

"Thanks. Yeah, it's coming together nicely. We've only got a few weeks to go, and we might be able to speed that up a bit if all goes well," he says.

Quinn comes around the corner and walks straight to me, lifting her chin so I can kiss her hello. Just like always, a quick peck isn't enough and we both fall in deeper. I'll never get enough of the way she kisses. She completely opens up for me, and every time it both humbles me and sets my blood on fire.

"Get a room," Levi huffs, making us laugh and, much to my dismay, pull away from each other.

"If you could kiss like that, you'd be more understanding, Levi," Quinn says with a wink. Throughout the renovation, they've been getting to know each other better and I love that they've bonded.

"Oh, sweetheart, I can kiss a helluva lot better than that, I just don't want to watch the two of you do it," he says with a cocky grin.

"Okay, we do not need any more information," I say, stopping Levi from going into any more detail about his "skills". He chuckles as Quinn and I turn and walk away, sending a wave over my head to say goodbye.

"So, what brings you by, handsome?" Quinn asks as we

walk back out into the main lobby.

"I wanted to see my girl and check in on how things were coming along. I haven't seen it since they ripped out the carpet and wallpaper."

She smiles up at me and grabs ahold of my waist. "I'm glad you stopped by today. We're getting so close to being done I can hardly believe it. Did Levi tell you they might be done sooner than we thought?"

"Yeah, he did. What will happen when they're done? Are you going to open right away or do you have to wait?" I ask her. I have no idea how any of this works, but watching Quinn jump into this venture with both feet has been amazing. I always knew she was smart, I mean, she was a lawyer for Christ's sake, but seeing her in action makes me so incredibly proud to be by her side through it all.

"Well, we already have an opening day party planned for the end of July when we thought the renovations would take longer. All of our marketing materials and stuff have the date on it, so we can't change that, but if the renovations are done early, I'll have more time to prepare for opening day, which will be helpful."

"Got it, quicker renovations mean not as many late nights for you. I'll tell Levi to get his ass in gear," I joke, making her laugh. "I wish I could stay and take you to lunch, but I've got to get back to the station."

"No worries. I've got several more artists to call to get an idea of what inventory we'll have."

"Can I come by tonight if it's not too late when I'm done?" I ask her. Despite my objections, Quinn decided to move back into her house after the break-in. I wanted her to stay with me, both to keep her safe and because I loved having her there, but she thought she'd look weak if she never went back to her house, and I couldn't blame her. She kept my house key though so I feel like that was a win.

"Of course you can, even if it's late when you get there. I

was going to order a pizza tonight so text me if you'll be there to eat, and I'll make sure to put olives only on half," she says with a mischievous glint in her eye. She knows I hate olives and even if they're on half, the whole pizza will still taste like them.

"Careful," I warn, lowering my voice so only she can hear me. "You're angling for a smack on that perfect little ass of yours." I can both hear and feel her intake of breath. She still has her hands on my hips, and I've wrapped my arms around her shoulders so I can speak directly in her ear. To anyone else, it would look as if I was hugging her.

She looks up at me, those blue eyes shining with lust and fake innocence as she says, "I'd happily take my punishment, Officer."

Fuck me. My cock is hard in an instant. Which is not comfortable in a police uniform, for the record.

"You'll be the death of me, you know that?" I ask her. She just smiles up at me, so I kiss her with all of the pent-up desire that's now coursing through me and make sure she knows how much I want her.

* * *

MY EYES ARE CROSSED. And blurry.

I look away from the computer screen I've been staring at for the last two hours to try and relieve the stress on my eyes. I wonder if they'll be stuck like this. Oh god, I'm going to have to get glasses.

And now I'm losing my mind.

I've been watching security footage of a parking lot where our victim was potentially last seen. We've got a four-hour window when it's likely she'd show up, and that's all we have to go on. We did finally get a hit on our Jane Doe who is now known as Ashley Delmont. Her mother reported her missing when she didn't hear from her for their weekly chat and didn't show up to work.

After we got the ID, we were able to get info on who she was, but most of our leads for how she might've gotten here have hit dead ends. Her phone pinged off a cell tower in the area of two rest stops, and that was the last place she was recorded being at. Derek is looking at one rest stop while I'm looking at the other, hoping for something to indicate what could've happened or who could've done this. Although with my eyesight shot to shit, I'm not sure how much I'll see now.

"Can you feel your eyes bleeding?" Derek asks, making me laugh.

"I was literally just wondering if I'd damaged my eyesight forever," I tell him, rubbing my eyes and looking around the bullpen again to see if it's any better. Luckily it is, but I'm not quite ready to get back into it. It's quiet right now with the other deputies out on patrol.

"Have you found anything?" I ask Derek.

"Nope, just some questionable behavior from some of the truck drivers, but that's pretty standard," he says, rubbing his eyes as well. I nod in response and stand up to grab some coffee. Even though it's late afternoon, I know I'll need a pick me up to finish the rest of the footage.

I sit back down in my chair and start watching the footage again. I get another thirty minutes through the feed when I hear Derek. "Chief, I think I may have something." I jump up from my chair and walk over to the desk where he's sitting.

"We're looking for a silver Toyota, right?" he asks, rewinding the footage.

"Yeah," I say and focus closely when he pushes play. There on the screen, a silver Toyota with matching plates pulls into the parking lot of a rest stop about fifteen miles north of Sonoma. We watch as she parks near the building, gets out of her car, and walks towards the bathroom. The cameras only cover the front of the building, and the bathrooms are off to the left side on the outside of the building.

She exits the frame once she's around the building, and we wait for her to come back out. Five minutes go by and she still hasn't returned, making my gut start to churn.

"She's not coming back out, is she?" Derek asks quietly.

"No, I don't think she is." I sigh. We let the video run for several more minutes to make sure she doesn't come back out, but she never does. "Let's get a unit out there to pick up her car."

"On it," Derek responds as he pulls out his phone to call the crime scene unit.

"Let me grab my stuff, and we'll head out there to meet them," I tell Derek, who nods in response.

I grab up everything I need from my office, and text Quinn to let her know I'll be late getting to her house. She responds saying she'll go pick up Piper and to be safe. God, I love this woman, and I intend to tell her very soon.

QUINN

The jingling of Piper's collar makes me sit up from the couch. A little buzz of nerves moves through me as I wonder what could've alerted her. Ever since the break-in, there's been this uneasiness sitting in the pit of my stomach like something is not quite right. I have no idea why I feel that way. There's been no sign of anything amiss and I have no reason to justify those feelings.

Usually, I just brush it off as lingering stress from the break-in. But sometimes, at night, I can't shake the feeling that maybe things aren't quite right.

I hear a key in my front door and look over at Piper with a smile on my face. It's amazing how quickly that pit disappears when he's so close. It's why I haven't told Cooper about my feelings. Anytime he's with me, which is regularly, I know I'm completely safe and have nothing to fear. Plus, he'd have me moved in with him in a heartbeat if I even hinted that I was worried about something.

As fast as we've moved, I'm not quite ready to take that next step with him. There's something holding me back, an awareness that's making me pause. I know we have deep feelings for each other, even though we haven't said the words. I know this thing we're doing means a great deal to both of us and will for a long time but there's something nagging me to not take that step.

I hear the door open and watch Piper race to the front door to see who's here. I look up at the sunburst clock in my living room, noting that it's nine o'clock, and get up off the couch to greet my man.

Walking around the couch and into the hallway, I watch as Cooper greets Piper on bended knee. Her tail swishes back and forth as he rubs her face and talks to her with the cutest puppy dog voice. I'm pretty sure my ovaries are bursting watching this hulk of a man in a police uniform cuddle with his dog.

As soon as I have that thought, Cooper looks up at me with a smolder hot enough to bake cookies with. Damn, I am one lucky woman. I feel like fanning my face.

"Keep lookin' at me like that, sweetheart, and you'll be over my shoulder and naked in about point two seconds."

Oof. I'm actually fanning my face now while a blush creeps up my chest and into my cheeks. Cooper stands up and comes to me. He places his hand on my face and gently rubs his thumb across my heated cheeks. "I love when you blush like this," he says in a soft voice. I'm never quite sure what to do when he looks at me like that, so I just smile and feel my heart grow even more full.

"Are you hungry? There's pizza left, and I promise there aren't any olives on it," I ask, making him laugh.

"I know it's still early, but I honestly just want to go to bed."

Scanning his face, I see the tightness behind his eyes, the lines marring his forehead, and I know tonight wasn't just a late night at work. Tonight affected him in a deep and more than likely lasting way.

I nod my head, "You go up, and I'll turn everything off down here." I reach up and kiss him with all of the love I feel but haven't said. Wanting him to know that I'll be here for him always.

As Cooper goes upstairs, I walk around locking the doors and turning off the lights. He hasn't been super open with details about the investigation, trying to protect me I'm sure, but on the nights he struggles, he usually opens up about some of it.

He once told me he sometimes sees my face as the victim because I look a little like her, and he worries it could be me one day. He's been a lot more concerned about my safety because of it, and as much as it can be annoying sometimes, I don't mind since I know it comes from a good place. There's also a healthy dose of fear in me knowing how she was murdered. The cruel things that happened would be a nightmare, so I don't mind when he puts extra cameras up at my house and the store.

I get everything turned off and locked and head upstairs into my bedroom. The lamp on my nightstand is on, and I can hear the shower in the bathroom running. I stand in the doorway for a bit and marvel at the sexiness standing before me.

If I thought Cooper loving on Piper was hot, that has nothing on a naked and wet Cooper. He's turned away from me, looking at the showerhead; the water sluices down the muscles in his shoulders and back, highlighting all of the bumps and ridges.

"You gonna join me or keep ogling?" Cooper asks without turning around, making me giggle.

"I'm seriously enjoying the view right now, but I'll happily join."

I quickly take off my clothes and open the doors to get in behind him. He looks over his shoulder, and I watch his eyes turn liquid gold with desire. Wrapping my arms around him, I put my face on his back and breathe. The scent of water and Cooper fills my lungs, and I let it run through me, shoring up the cracks I didn't know were there until he helped to fix them.

He turns around in my arms and grabs my face, lifting it to his mouth so he can explore me the way he always does no matter where we are or how long or short the kiss is. I feel myself ease into it and open myself to him. Giving everything I have so he knows I'm his and always will be.

He pushes me against the back wall of the shower, making me gasp at the chilliness. Cooper takes advantage, and his tongue darts into my mouth in a sensual slide. His hands are everywhere, stopping only for a few seconds until he moves on. A desperate noise escapes my throat, making Cooper chuckle.

"Are you torturing me on purpose?" I ask while his mouth traces my jaw, underneath the lobe of my ear, and down my neck. His tongue traces the path of my collarbone, and I'm pretty sure I've never been this turned on in my life.

"Not torturing, worshipping," he says against my skin, dragging his nose down between my breasts and across the peak of my left nipple. He sucks the taut bud into his mouth, and I think I levitate off the ground.

I feel him smile as he moves to the other nipple, again, never staying in one spot for too long. It's both maddening and so freaking hot. My hands go into his hair as he drops lower, running his tongue from one hip bone to the other and then up around my belly button. My hips move on their own, trying to direct him lower, but he's determined to go at his own pace.

Steam billows around us as one hand settles on my hip and the other throws my leg over his shoulder. His nose traces my sex, and I think I growl. I'm so completely out of my mind I'm not even sure what's happening right now.

His tongue swipes across my slit, and my hands tighten in his hair.

"Fuck, you taste good," he rasps.

He keeps the pressure on my clit, flicking and licking when I feel a finger sliding into my opening, and then quickly, a second joins the first. My orgasm is building, so close to the precipice, just waiting to fall over when he suddenly stops, ripping a disheartened moan from my lips.

I barely have time to open my eyes to figure out what's going on before I'm lifted into Cooper's arms and slammed down onto his cock.

"Oh fuck," he grits, while I scream, "Yes," simultaneously. After the first night, we decided to forego condoms since I'm on birth control and we were both clean.

His thrusts are hard, possessive, and rugged as we're both taken somewhere I'm not sure we've ever been over these past few weeks.

I can feel my insides quicken, and if I had my wits about me, I'd say something, but all I can focus on is the intense slide of his cock deep inside me. Pushing me higher and higher until I'm not sure I'm going to survive the fall.

"Go over, Quinn, I've got you," Cooper grates out, and his words remind me that even though this is the roughest he's ever been with me, he's still the man I love, and I'm sent over.

Everything in me tightens, exploding around his shaft so hard I'm not even sure how he stays inside me. I hear him groan and feel him expand and pulse as he comes just as hard as I did.

Our muscles slowly relax, and our ragged breathing slows as we come down from the high. My arms and legs are still wrapped around Cooper, and his hands squeeze my ass as I pull back to look at him. His eyes are shining, and a little cocky smile is pulling at the corners of his mouth. He looks so carefree right now, and I don't want to break the spell.

"Can we get out? The water is about to freeze my ass off." He grins, making me burst out laughing. I nod my head, smiling from ear to ear. Setting me down, he turns and shuts off the water. I grab towels for us both, and we quickly dry off and walk into the bedroom to get ready for bed.

I slide in on my side and braid my hair so it won't dry a crazy mess and watch Cooper as he putters around, hanging his uniform and sliding on some boxers. Despite our water escapades, I can see the tension in his shoulders coming back.

"Hey, come here and lay down for me," I say to him, pulling back the comforter and grabbing my lotion.

He walks over and, at my direction, lays down on his stomach, taking a deep breath once he's settled.

"You were so relaxed a minute ago, I don't want you to lose that," I tell him, straddling his hips. I squeeze some lotion onto my hands and then rub them together. The vanilla scent floats in the air and surrounds us as I start at the top of his back and work my hands into the muscles in his shoulders and neck. His groan, the only sound in the room, makes me smile as I continue to work through the knots in his back.

"That feels so good, Quinn," he moans, my name rolling off his tongue like an unintentional seduction.

I move my hands across his back until he's no longer tense, and he melts into the bed like I was hoping he would.

Suddenly, he grabs me around the waist and flips us over so quickly I squeak, and my eyes go wide with surprise, making him laugh. He smiles down at me so wide there's no way I couldn't smile back at him.

"You always know exactly what I need. A lot of the time better than I do," Cooper says with a seriousness in his eyes that tells me what he's about to say is important. "I don't know how I lived without you, Quinn, but I am beyond grateful to have you in my life now. You make every day brighter than the one before, and I want you to know how much you've come to mean to me." He swallows hard and looks me directly in the eye.

"I love you, Quinn. I love you with everything I am, and I can't imagine a day without you in it," he says. I feel tears gather in my eyes as I look at this incredible man. I run my hand across the side of his face as a smile bigger than any other breaks across mine.

"I love you so much, Cooper. I always thought I was fine on my own and didn't need anybody else besides myself, but these past few weeks with you have shown me that I was just waiting on you to come into my life. You're everything I've ever dreamed of, and I'm so glad you're mine," I tell him, meaning every word with my whole heart.

He leans down and kisses me with all of the love he just expressed and spends the rest of the night telling me how much he loves me in ways words could never express.

29

QUINN

"Cheers," we yell, clinking our glasses together and throwing back the shots as if we genuinely enjoy the fire that races down our throats. Each of us shivers once they're down, naturally making us laugh at our reactions. There are several shot glasses scattered across the sticky table along with other glasses filled with various mixed drinks.

"Why do we put ourselves through that so many times in one evening?" Natalie yells above the noise of the bar.

Donna's is packed tonight, the noise level matching the number of people vying for space over the pop music playing through the speakers. We decided a girls' night was in order for no other reason than we just wanted to spend time together, so we ditched our guys and came out on this Friday night.

"Because it makes us feel like this afterward," Sara replies, giving a little shimmy to emphasize her point. We're all pleasantly buzzed, possibly on the edge of drunk. We're also lucky enough to know that eventually, one or all of the boys will show up and make sure we all get home safely. Mostly because, if the girls are hanging out together, the boys are hanging out together as well.

It's been an adjustment, having a big group of friends like this. They know everything about each other, and I literally mean *everything*. There's no topic they don't talk about or information they don't share with each other, and while that concept is foreign to me and has been difficult to participate in, I absolutely love it.

There's a genuineness to the circle of trust these women have with each other, and I feel incredibly lucky to have been invited into it. Even when they tease me about how easily I get embarrassed.

"Okay, okay, okay. Time for Quinn to dish on why she looks like she's floating on air," Megan says as the girls all nod in agreement. I giggle, feeling my face turn red, and a smile stretches across my face.

"Sometimes I hate how easily you guys can read me," I say as the girls all laugh at me. I let out a deep breath and share the most incredible moment of my life with the girls that mean the world to me. "Cooper told me he loved me the other day," I say, and immediately a chorus of squeals springs from the girls making me laugh.

"Finally! I've been waiting since you guys went on your first date. I can't believe it took this long," Lucy says.

"Seriously, me too," Megan chimes in.

"I mean, it hasn't been that long since we started dating, but it's also because we've both been crazy busy and when we are able to carve out some time together, we don't do too much talking," I say, wiggling my eyebrows despite how red my cheeks get.

"Ah, Quinn, I'm so proud of you," Natalie squeals. "We'll have you giving us the dirty details in no time," she laughs, making me roll my eyes despite the smile that stretches across my face. "But in all seriousness, this is the best thing. You both deserve the world, and I am so happy for you guys."

"Ditto," Sara says, lifting her glass. "To love, and the hope we can all find a soul mate as hot as Cooper Jackson."

"To sexy soul mates!" Natalie responds, and we all clink our glasses together in agreement.

"Speaking of sexy, Tucker James just walked in," Lucy says, looking directly at Natalie as the rest of us look around the room to spot him. Based on where everyone is looking, I find him over by the door. He's definitely good looking if not a little intimidating. He's huge, somewhere close to six-five if I had to guess. He's got a ball cap on, so I can't quite make out his face, but his shoulders are wide and look like they might bust out of the t-shirt he's wearing. It seems like we aren't the only ones to notice his entrance as I look around spotting every female, and even some of the men, staring at him.

"Isn't he like the fire chief or something?" I ask, looking back at the girls.

"He's a captain. His uncle is the chief," Sara says.

"Natalie could probably tell you everything you'd ever want to know," Megan says with a teasing grin on her face.

"Did you date him?" I ask Natalie.

"God, I wish," she responds.

"She's been in love with him since before high school and, unfortunately, he hasn't ever noticed, which is his loss," Sara says, rubbing Natalie's shoulder, giving her both comfort and encouragement. "He doesn't date much at all, actually."

"Is he gay?" I ask, making the girls bust out laughing. I shrug my shoulders. "Well, what else am I supposed to think if he hasn't noticed Natalie? She's smart as a whip and genuinely kind, not to mention completely smoking. You're the whole package, so maybe he wants a different sort of package, which would be completely fine if that's the case."

Natalie smiles at me. "Thanks, Quinn. It's not that he wants a different package. I don't even think it has anything to do with me exactly. I think it's more he's not looking at anyone like that."

"Ah, I can understand that."

"You could always go up to him and see if he might be interested," Lucy suggests.

"And risk the potential for rejection? Absolutely not," Natalie says quickly. "I'll stick with my fantasies and continue pretending we have a future."

"You could have a future with me if you want, Natalie. Or at least for the night if you catch my drift," a guy says from behind her. His dark hair is slicked back, and he's got a cocky grin on his face. He reminds me a little of Peter from the firm in New York. Not in looks but in his arrogance.

"Not happening, Brad. You should just move on from our table," Natalie replies.

"I don't know, I'm seeing something very interesting here," he says, his eyes roam down my body and then come back to my face. He smirks as if his assessment and obvious interest would be a turn-on for me. It takes everything in me not to roll my eyes.

"What makes you say I'm interesting?" I ask, making sure confusion is written all over my face. Naturally, he takes that as an invitation and walks closer to me, placing a hand on my shoulder.

"Babe, you're the most interesting thing I've seen in a long time," he says, squeezing my shoulder. None of the girls say anything as they watch the interaction.

"So, if I tell you I'm a lawyer and could sue you for harassing me, would that be interesting to you?" I ask with a saccharine smile on my face and a glance at his hand on my shoulder.

"Whoa, whoa, whoa. Let's slow down there," Brad says, lifting his hand off my shoulder and taking a step back from me. "I'm not doing anything."

"Hmm. I'd beg to differ. I'd also suggest you fix whatever is happening down there," I say with a lift of my eyebrow and pointing to his open fly. "Or really, the lack of what's happening down there." Brad looks down and hastily does up his fly. "Your loss," he says sullenly and turns around and walks away.

There's a beat of silence as I turn my head and look back at the girls around the table. They're all looking at me with wide eyes and mouths slightly agape, and then we all burst out laughing at the same time.

"That was the best thing I've ever witnessed," Sara says in between bouts of giggles. None of us are able to get control of ourselves because we keep looking at each other and start all over again.

"Where did you learn to deal with guys like that? He is the smarmiest guy in town," Lucy asks as we slowly get a hold of ourselves.

"Law school, actually. In a male-dominated field, you have to learn how to not get trampled very quickly," I say. "I've never had to use my skills in a setting quite like this, but guys like that are all the same, so it wasn't much different from a courtroom or office."

"Brad's face when you told him his fly was open will forever be my favorite thing," Natalie says.

"Could you really sue him?" Megan asks

"Probably not, but he doesn't need to know that," I say laughing.

I feel a pair of hands land on my shoulders, and I instantly know they're the ones that belong there. Smiling, I turn my head and see gorgeous amber eyes looking down at me. "Hi, handsome."

"Hi there," Cooper says, leaning down to give me a kiss. When we surface, I see Todd, Max, and Levi pulling up chairs around the table. There's not really room, but we make it work. Instead of getting a chair for himself, Cooper lifts me up and plops me onto his lap. I raise my eyebrow at him and he just shrugs his shoulders and pulls me closer to him making me smile.

"What were you guys laughing about?" Levi asks once we're all settled.

"Quinn put Brad Hughes in his place, and it was one of the best moments of the night," Megan responds.

I feel Cooper's eyes on me as my cheeks heat up. It's one thing to feel completely myself when I'm with the girls but my confidence around the whole group is still lacking.

"How'd you do that, Quinn?" Max asks. I look around at the girls as we all start giggling again.

"I just told him I was a lawyer, and if he didn't want to be sued he needed to stop showing off the minimal junk he had in his pants," I say with a shrug of my shoulders.

"Oh my god," Levi says laughing. "I so wish I could've been here to see his face when you said that."

"It was the best thing I've seen in a long time," Sara says.

"His fly was down, and it was really gross," I add.

The girls finish recounting the story, but I don't hear much as Cooper's hand slides up my bare thigh and under the hem of the navy dress I wore out tonight. I feel my breath whoosh out of my lungs, and heat rises in my cheeks. The alcohol I've consumed has me wishing he'd slide his hand up just a little further.

A shiver runs up my spine, making Cooper chuckle. He leans forward, running his nose on the outer shell of my ear. "I need you so bad," he breathes, pulling me down against his lap to feel his hard length. I look deep into his eyes so he can see the lust and love burning in mine. I want him to carry me out of here and take me home.

Nodding his head as if he knows exactly how I'm feeling, we start saying our goodbyes to our friends.

"Have fun," Natalie sing-songs, wiggling her eyebrows and making everyone laugh. Cooper wraps his arm around my shoulder and pulls me close as they rib us for leaving early.

People say hello to Cooper as we slowly make our way

towards the exit. Not surprisingly, it's mostly women vying for his attention, but he just nods his head and keeps his arm around my shoulders.

We push our way out of the bar, and the noise level falls drastically. My ears ring a little from the quiet, and I fill my lungs with the smell of fresh summer air and Cooper's cologne. My head spins as the alcohol moves through my system, and I'm finally noticing its effects.

We walk towards Cooper's truck, hearing the sounds of our feet crunching on the gravel parking lot and the muffled music coming from the bar. "I don't think I could be any happier," I say into the quiet evening.

"And why's that?" Cooper asks. I can hear the laughter in his voice as if he's humoring my drunken statement.

"Well, I'm pleasantly buzzed, have the best friends I could ever ask for, and have the arm of the man of my dreams wrapped around me. I don't think my life could get any better," I say, looking up into Cooper's face as we round the hood of his truck and he guides me to the passenger side.

He pushes me back against the door and tucks a piece of hair behind my ear. I lift my chin to look at him better, and at my invitation, he takes my lips in a deep, drugging kiss that both fills me with love and leaves me wanting more.

His tongue pushes deep into my mouth, and I moan around it as he guides my head into the position he needs to pull me under his spell. We kiss until we have to pull apart in order to breathe. Cooper presses his forehead against mine as we both catch our breath. "I love you," he says on a whisper.

"I love you more," I say, making him laugh and roll his eyes. He opens the door to his truck and helps me in. "Not possible, drunk girl," he says, kissing me quickly and then shutting the door. He pauses outside and looks around the parking lot as if he heard something and is trying to see what it is.

He shakes his head and walks around the truck getting inside. "Everything okay?" I ask.

"Fine, just had a weird feeling like someone was watching us. I didn't see anyone though, so it was probably my imagination," he says, starting the truck and pulling out of the parking lot. His hand on my thigh has me forgetting all about the weird moment and thinking instead about getting my man home and very, very dirty.

30

COOPER

The sun peeks through the curtains lighting the room in a soft morning glow. It's still early for a Saturday morning, but since I didn't drink last night, I'm waking up like I normally would. Quinn is completely wrapped around me, her body radiating a warmth I'd never be able to match with any number of blankets or fireplaces. Her legs are tangled with mine, arms around my waist, and head on my chest. My entire arm is asleep but her naked body pressed against mine is definitely worth it.

Last night, when Quinn said she couldn't be happier, I laughed because I thought she was being silly in her drunkenness but right now, I understand exactly what she was feeling. I'm not drunk but I definitely have never been this happy, and it's all because of a beautiful woman who's given me her heart.

I press a kiss to the top of Quinn's head and untangle my body from hers. She's still out of it as I head into the bathroom which makes me smile. She's going to be hurting when she wakes up, so I grab her some water and Advil and put it on the nightstand when I'm done getting dressed.

Piper follows behind me as I go downstairs, her nails

clicking on the wood floor as we walk to the patio door. I let her outside and head into the kitchen for some coffee. Despite the fact that it's a Saturday, I have to go to the station today. There are days when I feel so inadequate at my job. It's been a month since this girl was murdered, and we're still not any closer to knowing who did this. I wish it was as easy as they make it look on TV but it's not, and every day that we don't know anything, the farther we get from catching this guy.

Blowing out a breath, I do my best to stop my thoughts from going too low. Doesn't always work, but as I look out the back door and watch Piper chase the butterflies I'm reminded of the good things in life, and that makes me smile. I slide open the door and step out onto the back patio as my phone starts to ring. Reading the caller ID, I answer quickly.

"Hey, Mom."

"Hi, darling. Am I calling too early?"

"No, I've been up for a bit. What's going on?"

"Just checking in to see how you're holding up," she says.

"I'm doing fine. Things have been crazy with the investigation and all, but I'm doing okay."

"That's good to hear. I'm making a roast tomorrow night if you're able to come. Levi will be there, so I wanted to make sure you were invited."

"Thanks, Mom. Yeah, I actually think I can be there. We're still waiting on a few things from the lab, so there's not much we can do until then."

"Perfect, and you know, you can bring Quinn. It'd be nice to have more than a quick conversation in a grocery store," she says, laying on the guilt.

A couple of weeks after Quinn and I started dating, we ran into my mom at the store, and I moved everyone along very quickly. Quinn made fun of me for getting us out of there so fast, and my mom is still mad that I didn't let her talk to Quinn for longer than a couple of minutes.

I was so thrown off, I did not react well at all. Luckily for me, Quinn just laughed at my stress instead of taking it the wrong way. It wasn't that I didn't want them to meet, I just wasn't prepared for them to meet right then. She laughed even harder as I tried to explain it to her and kept talking in circles instead.

"Actually, that's a good idea. Let me double-check with Quinn first to make sure she isn't busy, and if not, we'll be there."

"Oh great. Just text me and let me know then," Mom says with an enthusiasm I haven't heard in a long time which makes me laugh out loud.

"I don't know why you're laughing at me, but I don't care. I'm so happy about this, Cooper. Please don't do something stupid and ruin this for me."

"Oh my god! Of all the people to say that to it should be Levi, not me," I say, rolling my eyes while laughing at my ridiculous mother.

"And don't think I won't tell him to be on his best behavior, but you're the one in the relationship, Cooper Daniel."

Doing my best to hold in my laughter, I respond, "Yes, ma'am."

"Good, now I've got to get to the flower shop and find some fresh flowers for the house."

"I'll talk to you later."

"Bye, son."

Still laughing at my mom, I call Piper to come inside with me and take my coffee cup into the kitchen for a refill. While I'm taking a sip, I hear Quinn coming down the stairs. I turn to watch her walk into the kitchen and have to bite my lip so I don't laugh at her.

Her dark hair is an absolute mess around her head, her shoulders are stooped, and her arms are crossed over her chest. Her face is all scrunched up like she can't stand to have her eyes all the way open but needs them to walk.

"Good morning," I say.

"Shhhhh," she responds, blindly grabbing my coffee out of my hands. Keeping her eyes closed, she takes a long drink. "Ack! Why doesn't this have any creamer in it?"

"Because it's mine," I say, laughing at her as she pouts down into the cup. I turn to the fridge, grab the creamer, and splash a little into my cup. "There, try that," I say as I grab another mug from the cabinet and fill it with coffee for myself.

"Mmm. Much better," she says, taking a bigger sip. Shaking my head at her, I pull down the cereal boxes and pour some into two bowls. There are times I wish I could do more for her, like cooking a massive breakfast, but even when I do small things like this, she still looks at me with so much love and gratitude that it stops my heart sometimes.

Putting a bowl of fruity cereal in front of her on the breakfast bar, she finally opens her eyes, and the impact of those blues hit me like a brick wall. "There she is," I say quietly, making her smile. I bring my bowl of shredded wheat around the counter and sit next to her while we quietly eat together. I love these moments, when we're both content in the silence, and there's no pressure to be people we aren't.

"Why did I drink that much?" Quinn asks as we finish up our breakfasts.

"Because you were having fun, and despite how awful you feel, it was worth it," I say, kissing the side of her head and grabbing our bowls, taking them to the sink.

"Yeah, it was," Quinn says, smiling.

"Hey, are you functioning enough for me to ask you something?"

"Um, I think so. I guess it depends on how serious it is."

Laughing, I tell her about my mom's offer for dinner tomorrow night. "She told me I wasn't allowed to mess it up

193

or she'd wallop me. I told her she should say that to Levi and not me."

"That's hilarious. Good to know you still want me to meet your mom," Quinn teases me. "But seriously, I'd love to go over there for dinner. Just let me know what time to be ready."

"Will do. What are you up to today?"

"Painting. I've gotten so behind since we started renovating the store. Plus, it doesn't take much brainpower, and hungover painting usually results in some interesting pieces. You're going into the station today, right?"

"Yeah, I've got some paperwork to catch up on myself. Shouldn't be but a few hours though."

She nods her head and holds her hand out for me to grab it. "Come shower with me, and then we can get on with our days." I grab her hand and pull her up the stairs as fast as I can, making her laugh all the way up.

* * *

WALKING INTO THE POLICE STATION, it's relatively quiet. Saturday afternoons don't tend to bring too much trouble. Anything from Friday night has usually been taken care of, and it's still too early for anything crazy to have happened.

I walk through the main doors and into my office. The piles of paperwork have me sighing, and I haven't even started. Putting it off for a moment longer, I walk down the hall and into the bullpen to see if any of the guys are around.

"What are you doing here?" I ask Rachel, who's standing by the whiteboard with the investigation photos up.

"Oh, hey there," she says, slowly turning around. "I had some stuff I didn't get to yesterday. This is pretty horrible, huh?" She jabs her thumb over her shoulder, pointing to the board.

"It is. We'll get our guy though, don't worry."

"Oh, I'm not," she says with a small smile. "What are you doing here on a Saturday?"

"The same as you. Trying to catch up on all of the stuff I've gotten behind on these past couple of weeks," I tell her. She nods her head in understanding.

"How's Quinn?"

"Amazing," I say. I can't keep the grin off my face. "She's heading up the new art gallery for Trish. The opening day is a couple of weeks away. You should definitely come. You don't have to buy anything, but there will be appetizers and drinks and stuff."

"Sounds interesting. I'll see if I can be there. Well, I better get back to it. Let me know if you need anything since we're both here."

"Will do. I may send an email if there's anything I need you to file. It's been so long I'm not sure what I even have on my desk right now."

Rachel laughs and nods her head as she walks out of the bullpen and back to her office, which is little more than a cubical. I blow out a deep breath and slowly make my way back to my office. I shouldn't complain, but this is the part of my job I hate the most.

I sit down at my desk as a ding from my phone signals a text.

Quinn: If you hurry up, you can make it in time to help me clean up.
Me: Typing furiously as we speak. Wait for me.

Smiling to myself, I get to work and do my absolute best to get done as quickly as possible.

31

QUINN

I look in the full-length mirror on my bathroom door for the umpteenth time, trying to decide if this is the right outfit for dinner with Cooper's parents. I have on the white dress I bought at Trish's when Hailey and I went shopping. Maroon flowers flow across the dress and it's fitted at the waist. It comes down to my ankles, but with the t-shirt style sleeves, it's pretty casual.

I'm worried it's either too casual or not casual enough. Really, I'm just nervous about meeting Cooper's parents in general. When we were first introduced at the grocery store, Cooper got us out of there so quickly, I didn't have time to properly meet her. Which, at the time, was hilarious, but now, I wish I could've spent a few more minutes with her to get a feel for how this is going to go.

I've never met someone's family before. I've never let a relationship get far enough to warrant meeting the family, so I am completely out of my wheelhouse. I don't know what the protocols are for this situation because it's not something I've ever experienced.

I'm in love with their son, and there's a lot of comfort in knowing that Cooper loves me back, but what if I'm an embarrassment to him? What if I say or do something idiotic? Worse still, what if his parents aren't impressed with me? They could think I'm some wandering, goalless tramp who will bring their beautiful son down into the muck.

Okay, that was a bit harsh. I shake my head because even I recognize that isn't going to happen, but they could still be unimpressed with my life goals. I had this amazing career that I was insanely good at, and I threw it all away. My mom's words ring through my head, *"Aren't you going to practice again? You can't live like a bum forever."* Is she right? Am I a bum because I'm not using the degree I worked so hard for?

Ugh, I hate that I let myself do this. Just because I am not following the exact plan laid out before me by my parents doesn't mean I am a flighty, insignificant child. I do have goals and dreams for my life, they just aren't what my parents would deem acceptable.

The future I see for myself is not one with a bunch of numbers in my bank account but one filled with joy and laughter, love and respect, and maybe even little feet padding down the hallway chasing dog paws. That is what I want for my life, and a man with golden eyes has already shown me I'm worthy of it.

Taking a deep, fortifying breath, I grab my strappy sandals and head downstairs to wait on Cooper to pick me up. Looking around my home, I know that out of all the decisions I've made in my life, the decision to move to Sonoma was, by far, the best one. Not only because of Cooper, although he's the best thing to happen to me, but because I finally feel like myself and not some manufactured version of me that only makes other people happy.

If I can remember that when I get to the Jacksons' house, I think I'll be okay.

I see Cooper's truck pull into the driveway from the living room window, so I grab my purse and head out the front door. Once I'm outside, I lock up and turn to walk towards the driveway. I stop in my tracks as I watch Cooper get out and come towards me. Even in jeans and a t-shirt, he's the sexiest man I've ever seen. His long legs eat up the distance between us, and I'm quickly swept up into his arms, his lips meeting mine.

The ball of anxiety that was wound so tightly a moment ago, relaxes and settles as his lips devour mine. It's a reminder that I'm his and he's mine, no matter where we go, what we do, or who we see.

He slowly pulls back from the kiss. "Hi, handsome."

"Hi. I missed you today, and you looked so beautiful standing here on your porch, I couldn't resist," he says, smiling down at me, making me smile back. "Are you ready to go?"

"Yes, I am," I say with a deep breath. I can feel the ball tighten back up a little as we walk towards Cooper's truck. He opens the passenger door but stops me before I get in.

"You have nothing to worry about tonight. They're going to love you because I love you. There's nothing you have to do or say because they already know you're special. Just be the girl I fell in love with, and it will all be okay."

I feel my shoulders drop, and the fear I've been carrying all day melts away. With just a few words, this amazing man has assuaged every worry I've had, and I don't think I could love him any more than I do right now.

"I love you." With my hand on his face, I kiss him quickly and turn to get into the truck with a smile on my face.

* * *

WE PULL up in front of a beautiful farmhouse that's a few minutes outside of town. The lights shine brightly from the windows almost saying, *please come in, there's food on the table and love aplenty.*

"It's so pretty out here. This is where you grew up?" I ask

Cooper as he parks the truck.

"Yeah, we moved into this house after Levi was born and have been here ever since. Not much has changed but for a few modern updates throughout the years."

I feel a little stab of jealousy towards Cooper right now, looking at the house he grew up in. He got to have all of the things I longed for right here in this house. I know it's ridiculous because he can't change how I grew up, but there are moments where I feel this envy towards people who had childhoods like I wanted.

Shaking my head to clear my silly thoughts, I jump out of the truck, unable to wait for Cooper to come around. He meets me on my side and grabs my hand to lead me up the sidewalk and to the front door. Instead of knocking, Cooper walks right in through the red front door.

The mouthwatering smell of food hits me as we step inside. We walk down the short hallway that has a staircase on the right and a wide entryway on the left leading to a comfortable living room that's open to a dining room.

"Anyone home?" Cooper yells out.

"In the kitchen," Cooper's mom, I'm assuming, yells back.

We walk towards the dining room and around the corner into a beautiful modern kitchen. A huge island with grey countertops and white cabinets dominates the room. Alice stands at the stove, stirring something in a massive pot as we walk closer.

"Hi, Mom," Cooper says.

Alice turns to look over her shoulder with a smile on her face. She grabs the dish towel next to her and wipes off her hands. "Hi there. I'm so glad you made it!" She hugs Cooper quickly and turns to me.

"Mom, as you already know, this is Quinn. Quinn, this is my mom, Alice."

"It's nice to meet you again without someone pushing you out the door," Alice says with a mock glare to her son, making me laugh. I reach my hand out, "It's nice to meet you again too, Mrs. Jackson." Instead of taking my hand, she comes in and hugs me tight, which makes me feel both cared for and super uncomfortable. "Please call me Alice. I was so mad at him for not letting me get to know you at the store," she says as she leans back from the hug.

"If it makes you feel any better, I teased him mercilessly about it," I tell her, making her laugh.

"I knew I'd like you."

"I'm standing right here you know," Cooper says.

"We know," Alice and I say at the same time, which only makes us giggle harder.

"You guys are mean. Let's go find Dad." He huffs but sends me a wink before grabbing my hand and walking us toward a door that must lead outside. I smile and wave at Alice as we step onto a large deck. Trees surround the entire back of the house, creating a natural privacy screen around the backyard. Cicadas sing their summer songs and a gentle breeze blows through the leaves.

Cooper's dad sits at an outdoor table on the wide deck with a beer and a citronella candle in front of him. He stands as we walk towards him, and Cooper leans in for a hug as he says hello.

"Dad, I want you to meet Quinn. Quinn, this is my dad, Robert, but everyone calls him Rob."

"Hi, Mr. Jackson, it's so nice to meet you," I say.

"It's nice to meet you too, Quinn. Please, call me Rob," he says as he leans in and gives me a hug just like Alice did, which makes me smile. I've never been around people who hug this much, and it's actually really great.

"How are you liking Sonoma? You've been here a month, right?"

"Yes, a little over a month now. It's exactly the same as when I was little but also completely different, now that I'm experiencing it as an adult. I love it."

"That's right. I forgot Dan and Carla were your grandparents. They were great people."

"Yes, they were. I miss them, and living in their house has made me feel even closer to them." Rob gestures towards a chair for me to sit in, and we all sit down around the table.

"I'd ask you to tell me more about yourself, but Alice would have my hide if you told me things and she wasn't here to listen," Rob says with a chuckle.

"I wouldn't want to get you in trouble. Why don't you tell me how you dealt with Levi as a kid? I've gotten to know him while he's been doing renovations at Paint and Paper, and he's a nut."

Rob and Cooper bust out laughing, which makes me smile because they look so similar. They have the same light brown hair, facial structure, and amber eye color. Even their smiles are similar. The only difference between them is Rob has a little grey streaked throughout his brown hair, making him look distinguished, and a few wrinkles around his mouth and eyes.

"God, that boy was a handful. One minute, he was tearing through his mama's flower garden, and the next, he had a fistful of flowers for Alice to make up for it," Rob says with a chuckle. "He always knew exactly what to say to get out of trouble, unlike this one." He jabs his thumb towards Cooper.

"Were you always in trouble?"

"No, Levi always got me in trouble because he'd convince me to do something stupid, and then I'd feel guilty and tell Mom or Dad," Cooper says.

"Hey, my ideas were always brilliant. You just couldn't handle breaking the rules," Levi says as he bursts through the back door and comes to sit at the table. He kisses me on the cheek, slaps Cooper on the shoulder, gives his dad a quick half-hug, and finally slings himself into the last chair. "You were such a goody-two-shoes."

"You're just mad I stopped taking the blame for you."

"You're damn right. I started getting into trouble when you didn't do stuff with me."

Rob rolls his eyes at the boys. "Quinn, do you have any siblings?"

"No, I don't, unfortunately."

"Robert Jackson, don't you dare ask her personal questions when I'm not around," Alice yells from the open door making her husband scrunch his shoulders and direct a sheepish grin towards me. Alice walks out onto the deck and towards the table with a little smirk on her face telling me she's not really mad. "Dinner is ready if you boys want to set the table while Quinn and I get drinks."

We all stand up with our marching orders and head inside. Alice and I fill water glasses while the guys put dishes onto the table. We all sit down with Rob at the head of the table, Cooper on his left, Alice on his right, me next to Cooper, and Levi next to Alice.

The whole scene is fascinating to me. We didn't do things like this when I was growing up. My parents were normally too busy to sit at a table for this long, so we either had quick meals together or I ate with my nanny while they went to dinner parties with colleagues.

I listen to the Jacksons banter back and forth with an ease that I'll never have with my parents. The oddest part is I never felt unloved by my parents. They maybe didn't make time for me in this way, but they never made me feel as if I was unwanted. They took me to their labs and shared their passions with me, but we didn't have the same type of familial bonding the Jacksons have.

I think that's part of why my parents don't understand my move to Sonoma. They raised me in the hopes I'd have a similar passion for science and medicine, and when I didn't, they graciously adjusted to my desire to be a lawyer, knowing I'd be able to support myself.

Now that I'm no longer a lawyer, I'm sure they worry that

I will have no way of earning a successful income, and I can only imagine how hard it could be for a parent to see their child move so far outside of what they hoped for them. It's something to consider the next time I talk to my mom.

"Quinn, I heard my husband ask you about siblings. You don't have any?"

"No, it was just me growing up."

"That must've been lonely sometimes."

"At times, yes, but my parents brought me with them to the universities or clinics they worked in, so I was always around other people."

"Are your parents still traveling?" Levi asks.

"Yes, they are, although right now they're staying in New York so my dad can rest. I guess he's had some trouble with stomach ulcers."

"We'd love to meet them the next time they're in town," Alice says.

"They don't venture down this way very often, but I'm sure they'd be happy to meet you, too, if they do," I respond, knowing the chances of them coming down here is slim to none. Cooper's phone starts ringing from his pocket, and we all glance at him.

He looks at the screen and frowns, "Sorry, this is the station." He gets up from the table and walks into the living room and around the corner. Chatter around the table continues as if this is a normal occurrence, but my mind is on Cooper. The station calling on a Sunday night is weird, and a little bubble of anxiety sits in my gut.

I watch as Cooper comes back around the corner, and I immediately know something is very wrong. The stricken look on his face and the tightness in his eyes tells me everything I need to know.

Someone else has been murdered.

32

COOPER

Flashing red and blue lights brighten the darkened sky, floodlights are set up like spotlights, and organized chaos spreads through the landfill. Officers move through the scene, taping off the area as the crime scene unit marks and collects anything they can find that could be evidence.

I stand here, looking at a second crime scene, and I can't quite wrap my head around how this happened in the quiet little town I grew up in. Shit like this isn't supposed to happen here, and yet, another girl has been murdered.

Chris, the medical examiner, walks up next to me, and we both stand in silence for a minute, taking in the activity around us.

"What do you have?"

"Not much until I get her back to the morgue. Decomp suggests she was killed sometime Saturday night, but because of where she was dumped I won't have a specific time for a bit. Same cause of death as the last girl except this one was quicker. Our killer chose major arteries and made deeper cuts this time, so our vic died faster than the last one."

I sigh, "I'm not sure if that's a good or bad thing at this point."

"Me either. I'll send you my report once I get her on my table," Chris says as he walks with the paramedics who will take the body back to the morgue.

Soon after Chris walks away, Liam comes up to me to give me an update on what the team has found so far.

"We're bagging up pretty much anything that was touched by or around the body right now. We don't have an ID yet and don't think we're going to find it either. We found her naked and sliced, just like the last girl."

"So, no place to hide any identification."

"No, and we haven't found any personal belongings either."

"Highly unlikely at this point. Do we know if she was killed here or dumped?"

"She was definitely killed here. There's so much blood, Chief. I've never seen anything like it." I look into Liam's face, and there's a hauntedness in his eyes that makes me rage. He's only in his twenties, he shouldn't have had to see something so horrific.

"Focus your energy on finding any evidence you can. One little stone could lead to the whole mess toppling over, and then we'll get our guy. It's not going to erase the images in your head, but it'll help take the burden from your shoulders."

Liam looks at me and nods, walking back into the fray to help. I wish my words could do more but there isn't much that will make this situation any better. Getting justice may feel good temporarily but it won't take away the heartache. The only thing that's been able to help me is Quinn, which makes me feel incredibly selfish.

She doesn't deserve the evil that's now in her head because of me. She doesn't deserve to have a man love her whose job is to deal with the dark and depraved. The worst part is I'm just selfish enough to bring it home to her every night and allow her to make me feel better.

She's been the balm to the rage and unrest that's been running through my system since we found the first body. As soon as her hands are on me, I feel the tension bleed from me, and I can't give that up no matter how much better it would be for her. She's laying in my bed waiting on me right now for God's sake, and I love her more every day for her ability to shine a light into my darkness.

I was blown away at how well she meshed with my family tonight, although I shouldn't have been surprised. She hung in there with Levi's teasing and my mother's deep inquisitive dive, and when I came back into the dining room after I got the call, she took one look at me and knew. She held her hand out to me, working to calm the storm that was brewing inside me with just her touch.

I didn't want to drop her off and drive to the scene but knowing she'd be home when I got there made it bearable.

I watch the crime scene unit pack up the gear scattered around the area and tell my guys to head home when they've got everything together. We'll meet back up tomorrow to go through what we know since we'll need time to put it all together. With it being after eleven, there's no point in trying to do it tonight.

I walk back to my truck and jump into the seat, but instead of turning on the engine, I sit in the quiet of the cab and watch the rest of the clean-up process. I don't know where to go from here. I want to go home and let Quinn calm my swirling thoughts but I can't keep doing that to her. Using her to remove the darkness clouding my mind.

The one person I know I can go to pops into my head, but instead of driving there, I pull out my phone to call. It's so late I don't know if he'll be up.

It only rings a couple of times when I hear, "Hi, son."

"Hey, Dad. I hope I didn't wake you up."

"Oh no, I'm still watching highlights from the games tonight. I had a feeling you might be calling."

"I don't even know where to start."

"From the beginning. Walk through it from the moment you got to the first scene," he says. And I do. I walk him through what it was like at the first scene, the position of the body, the cuts, even how she was kidnapped.

"Okay, now tell me what was different about tonight." I think about that for a minute. There are actually a lot of differences between the first and second murder. The location, the position of the body, the way she was cut.

"It was like he was in a hurry this time. He staked her down in the ground, but his cuts were to the point instead of unhurried." We sit quietly for a minute, and I stew on what I said. Something isn't sitting right about that. Why would he have been in a hurry this time compared to the last? The location is secluded just like the first, she was tied down so she couldn't get away.

"He was pissed off... And because of that, couldn't control the cuts this time. Instead of delaying the kill to enjoy it, his anger caused him to slice quickly. He took it out on her, which means these kills are likely surrogates for the person he's actually angry at."

"So there won't be a connection between the victims and the killer then because he's looking for a specific person and these girls just happen to look like her."

A little shiver runs down my spine. I told Quinn once that I sometimes see her face as the victims because they kind of look like her. I'll need to make sure all of the cameras and security measures are working to make sure she's safe.

"What's your next logical step?" my dad asks.

"Figure out if this girl was picked up the same way as the first. If she was, we might be able to match cars in both locations."

"That's what I'd do too." I take a deep breath for the first time since I got the call tonight.

"Thanks, Dad."

"Always. Now, let's talk about your Quinn," he says, and I can hear the smile in his voice. "Your mother is smitten with her, and I gotta tell you, she charmed me pretty quickly too."

"She's great, right?"

"Have you told her how you feel?"

"Of course, I have. I probably took too long in telling her, but I did."

"Good, good."

"Dad—" I pause, not entirely sure how I want to say what I'm worried about.

"You're worried about bringing the job home to her," he says with the insight he's always had into what I'm thinking.

"Yeah," I say, blowing out a breath. "I feel so selfish when I come home and use her to make me feel better. I know the ugliness I bring home affects her even though I try not to give her any details."

"Let me ask you something. How would you feel if Quinn came home and didn't lean on you when she'd had an awful day?"

"Not very good, I'd guess. A little left out and maybe hurt that she didn't feel like she could come to me."

"Exactly, and how do you think Quinn would feel if you didn't share your worries and frustrations with her?"

"Pretty hurt that I didn't confide in her, I'd imagine."

"You're damn right she would. It doesn't matter how many details you give or don't, what's important is her need to be there for you and to support you whenever you need it. Just like you are there to support her whenever she needs it. That's how you make this work."

"And it doesn't make me a terrible person for leaning on her right now? Showing her how dark the world can be?"

"No, son, it makes you human, and I bet if you asked Quinn, she would rather share the darkness with you than to have you go through it alone."

What he's saying makes sense. Everything I know about

Quinn tells me she wants to be here for me. She's never complained about the late nights or the excessive phone calls. She makes me laugh when she knows I'm on the edge of my sanity, and with just a touch, she can ease the pressure that builds so rapidly sometimes I don't even recognize it's happened.

Suddenly, I have an urgent need to get home and see my girl. "I need to go, Dad. Thank you, for everything."

"Go home to your girl, Coop."

After saying goodbye, I start the engine of my truck and head home. My dad's words sift through my mind on repeat and, for once, I don't feel like my mind is spinning. I have a game plan for the investigation, and I don't feel like such an asshole for leaning on Quinn.

For the first time in over a month, it feels like I finally have a handle on things.

33

QUINN

Holding my brush in my hand, the weight of the wood light in my grasp, I swish it onto the canvas, adding color where there was none before. Shades of orange are layered into the reds and yellows, attempting to portray a sunset that changed my life forever. I've been working on this painting for weeks, trying to get it right, and every brushstroke feels wrong.

The pictures I took of the lake hang next to my easel but they don't do the evening justice, and I'm struggling to capture the moment with my paints. Taking a step back I look once more at the colors and while they look nice, they just aren't quite meeting the mark.

I hear a muffled ringing sound and realize my phone must've fallen in the cushions of my reading chair. I dig around, finally finding it and answering at the last second. "Hello."

"Hey girl, how are you?" Hailey asks on the other end.

"Oh, I'm doing okay. Having some trouble with a painting but other than that, I'm fine."

"Are you still struggling with the sunset painting?"

"Yes, and it's driving me crazy. I never have this much

trouble." In all of the years I've been painting, I've never taken this long to complete a project. When inspiration strikes, it usually takes me a max of a couple of days to finish.

"Hmm. Do you think it's because all of your feelings for Cooper are wrapped up in this project, and you're so set on it being perfect that nothing you do feels right?"

I freeze where I am and stare at the little bit of paint I've gotten onto the canvas. "Holy shit, Hailey, that's it. I'm so consumed with trying to portray every emotion perfectly that nothing is coming out at all!"

"God, I love it when I'm right." I laugh out loud and shake my head even though she can't see it.

"Yes, yes. You're a genius," I say reluctantly.

"You're damn right I am." She laughs.

"How are you doing? How's the new job?"

"I'm pretty good. The job is insane, and I'm sorry I haven't called much recently. I've been running around like a psychopath trying to get a handle on everything. The learning curve has been a lot bigger than I thought it would be." I've been worried about that. When she first started, she was so excited but talked about how the workload was crazy. Now, she sounds tired and stressed.

"Are you still happy? If this isn't what you want anymore, I'm sure we could find you something else easily." I ask, just to make sure.

"Yes, this is absolutely what I want. It's just taking longer to find my rhythm than I thought it would," she says, sounding resolute.

"Okay, but say the word, and we'll work it out."

"Thanks, Quinn. I promise I'm good though."

"I miss you tons, you know?"

"I miss you too, but hearing how happy you are makes the distance worth it." A call is beeping in, and I see it's my mom.

"Hey, my mom is calling me. It could be about my dad, so I need to answer it. I'll talk to you later?"

"Of course, love ya!"

"You too." I hang up and quickly switch the call over to answer. Taking a deep breath, I say, "Hello."

"Hi, Quinn. How are you?"

"I'm doing pretty good. How are you? How's Dad doing?"

"We're both doing well. Your dad's ulcers are going away, and we're hoping to get back to our schedule in the next couple of weeks."

"That's great, Mom. I'm glad to hear he's doing better." Knowing my parents are able to get back to the norm makes me feel so much better about my dad's health. I don't have to worry about him taking a turn for the worse. "I'm glad you called. I have a few things I want to tell you about."

After our dinner with Cooper's parents, I realized that even though the way my parents show their love is a little backward, they do still love me and want what's best for me. What I need to help them understand is that what is best for me looks a lot different than what was best for them. I may not be able to get through to them on the first try, but I'm going to keep trying until they understand.

"Have you started practicing again?" I cringe, knowing she's not going to be happy with my answer.

"Um, no. I got a job managing an art gallery. I've been selling my paintings in a store here in town, and the owner asked if I would want to help her run the gallery she's open-ing." I hold my breath while the silence on the other end of the phone stretches on. Naturally, I continue talking because I hate disappointing them. "I know it's not exactly what you had in mind for me to do, but I'm really happy about this. It allows me to paint and be surrounded by art every day." I stop talking before I ramble on even more.

"So, you're staying there indefinitely then?" I can't tell by the tone of her voice if she's mad or just indifferent.

"Yeah, I am. I love it here, Mom, and I know there's nowhere else I'd want to be."

"Well, I guess that's your choice to make." I blow out a big breath to quell the little pinch of disappointment. I didn't expect her to jump for joy, but I thought maybe my happiness would be enough.

"Are you mad at me?" I ask before I can think better of it.

"No, Quinn," she says, sighing into the phone. "I guess I expected you to do more. I know being a doctor like your father and me wasn't for you, but you spent all this time getting your law degree and you were so talented. I just don't understand why you'd throw away an amazing career to work in an art store."

My first reaction is to snap at her, to tell her my job is more than selling art supplies but then I think about my revelation after dinner with the Jacksons. My parents have only ever wanted me to be successful so that they wouldn't need to worry about me. Having a lucrative career in New York meant that I'd be fine on my own, so when I "threw that away" for a life completely foreign to them, they were probably scared to death. How do I convey to them that being here gives me a passion for life like my parents have in their career?

"Mom, why do you and Dad do what you do?"

"Um... well, I'm not sure," she stutters, thrown off by my question. "I guess we do it because we know we can help people who might be suffering and make their lives easier. By researching and teaching, we're able to share our knowledge which could impact someone's care."

"That makes sense, and I've always admired yours and Dad's drive to help others. In New York, my life was made up of going into an office I didn't want to be in and doing a job that didn't fulfill me at all. At first, I thought it did, but really, I was just out to prove that I could do it, not that I wanted to do it.

"Being here, in Sonoma, I finally feel like I'm exactly where I'm supposed to be. I've never felt more myself here, and I'm genuinely happy." I take another breath, feeling a weight fall off my shoulders with my admission. "Not only am I doing something that drives me, but I also met someone who makes me happier than any career ever could."

"You met someone?"

"I did," I say, feeling a grin spread across my face. "His name is Cooper, and he's the police chief in town. He's such a good man, and I'm head over heels in love with him."

There's another long pause while my mother digests that information. "I guess we'll need to meet this man. Make sure he's good enough for you."

I bust out laughing in surprise while also rolling my eyes at the underhanded dig. "I think he would like to meet you too. Things are crazy right now. He's got a lot on his plate at the moment, but when everything calms down, we'll make a plan, okay?" I know I'm glossing over the murders but she already has a disdain for this town, I don't want to add to it when I think I'm making a little headway.

"That would be good."

"Okay. I should go, Mom, but I'm glad you called."

"We'll talk again, and you can give me more information about this Cooper."

"Sounds good. Talk to you later."

I hang up after she responds and feel an immense amount of relief course through my system. I think I'll get them to come around and that gives me so much hope for the future.

* * *

AFTER STARING at my painting with my newfound insight, thanks to Hailey, I knew exactly what I needed to do to get it done. I jumped in my car to put my plan in place, and now I'm pulling into the parking lot of the police station with a box of muffins from the cafe in hand.

While this isn't my first time walking into the station, I

still feel a sense of unease when I walk into the main lobby. I think it's similar to the feeling you get when you see a cop on the road and, even though you know you didn't do anything wrong, you feel like you're guilty of something.

My feelings always make me laugh because I told Cooper how I felt once, and he told me he'd be happy to use his handcuffs on me if it would make me feel better. I haven't taken him up on his offer yet, but I get a little thrill every time I think about it. I may have to let him do that soon.

I walk past the reception area and into the hallway leading toward Cooper's office. I texted him to make sure he was around before I got here, and he told me he was buried in paperwork and would love to have me as a distraction.

I step into the doorway and take a moment to watch my guy as he leans over his desk, focused solely on whatever he's looking at. His desk is an absolute mess, and his two mismatched visitor's chairs sit at an angle facing him. I gently knock on the open door causing his head to come up and his face to light up with the million-dollar smile I love.

I smile back, "Hi, handsome." He's in his uniform, and he looks absolutely yummy.

He waves me in, and I close the door until it's cracked. He told me he has an open-door policy so his deputies don't feel like he doesn't have time for them or that he has more important things to do than talk to them.

I walk over to him and give him a kiss and hold up the box in my hand. "I brought muffins for the guys. I figured I could put them in the bullpen later."

"Thanks, babe. They'll appreciate that, and they won't last but a few minutes, so I'm just going to…" He sneaks one out of the box and immediately starts eating it as if someone's going to steal it from him, which makes me laugh. I sit down on the edge of his desk and wait for him to finish. After he swallows the last bite, I tell him why I wanted to see him.

"You know how I've been having a hard time painting the

215

sunset pictures I got at the lake?" He nods in response. "Well, I talked to Hailey about it and she had a great point. I was feeling so many things that night I'm struggling to convey them all into the painting. I thought you could sit with me while I paint, and it may help me pinpoint the right feeling I want to go with."

"I'm not sure how much I can help, but I'd love to sit with you anyway. Hey, maybe I can watch you paint naked. That's a thing, right?"

"Oh my god, Cooper," I say laughing. "The models are the ones naked, not the painters. Although, if I were better at portraits, it would be kind of fun to have you model for me." I take a minute to imagine what it would be like, but I know I'd just want to jump him if he was naked instead of painting him.

"Just let me know what you need from me. Naked or not," he says with a grin.

"Thank you," I say, smiling.

"You got it. Now, it's my turn to ask you about something." A frown line appears between his brows which makes me a little nervous. "I've been thinking a lot lately and... well... what would you think about moving in with me?" I'm stunned and, at the same time, not surprised in the slightest that he's asking me this.

"You want me to live with you?" I ask just to make sure it's what he wants.

"Yeah, I really do. I want to wake up with you every morning and come home to you every night. I want to see your stuff mixed in with mine and create a space that's ours together. You're the love of my life, Quinn, and I don't want us to live separately anymore." I smile, and then I laugh because I'm so happy. I grab his face and kiss him with everything I have. He pulls back before I get too carried away and smiles at me. "So, is that a yes?" he asks, making me laugh even harder.

216

"Yes, I would love to live with you."

A knock on the door interrupts our moment but that's okay. We're both still smiling from ear to ear. "Hey, Rachel, what's up?"

"Sorry to interrupt. Hey, Quinn." I give her a little wave as she continues on, "I just wondered if you had those files finished up for me to put away."

"Yeah, sorry about that." Cooper grabs a few file folders from his desk and hands them over to Rachel. "Thanks."

"No problem," she says and then heads back out of the office.

"So, we're doing this?" I ask just in case he changed his mind. There's a part of me that's still a little worried something bad is going to happen, but I want to be with Cooper. I want to take the next step in building our life together.

"Hell yeah, we're doing this. You already said yes, so there's no going back now."

"Hmm. If I took it back, would you handcuff me to your bed and never let me leave?" I watch Cooper swallow hard and his eyes ignite with lust which only makes the inferno in me get hotter.

"You're damn right I would. In fact, I might do that later so you can't get away from me."

"I wouldn't want to be anywhere else," I say, leaning down to kiss him with all of the promises for later and forever.

34

UNKNOWN

The shadows of darkness surround me as I watch her, leaving her completely oblivious to the danger lurking so close. Power surges through me as I move even closer, pushing my limits, all while staying unseen. It's only a matter of time until she knows who I am, and I will relish the fear in her eyes when she sees me.

I've been so patient, watching her flaunt herself in front of me, and as hard as it is, I will continue to be patient. I need to be fully ready before I take her, and that takes time. It will be worth the wait once she's where I need her to be.

My eyes find the sunburst clock on the wall telling me I don't have much time before I need to be out. I take one last look at her and make my way back through the shadows while she remains completely unaware.

35

COOPER

"Hey, Levi. I wanted to check in to see how everything's going?" I say through the phone. The sound of power tools echoes in the background as Levi and his crew work on finishing my basement.

It's been a week since I asked Quinn to move in with me. Originally, I thought it would be a quick and easy process. Pack up some boxes and then we're done, but that's not how it's gone at all. Combining two separate lives into one house is a lot more complicated than I realized.

We both agreed that my house was the best option because it has more space, but we needed to finish the basement in order to make everything work. My gym equipment is going to move downstairs so Quinn can use the space as a studio, and we're also going to make a theatre and guest suite down there. Since Levi finished early at Paint and Paper, he's taking the extra time to make updates for me.

I'm ready for her to move her stuff over now, and then we'll figure everything else out afterward, and I've lamented on the subject repeatedly, but she won't budge. She keeps saying we've got all of the time in the world, but I have this feeling of urgency to get her in my house and with me full-time.

I realize how ridiculous that sounds, and I've tried not to push too hard knowing that I'm being overbearing, but I need her with me, and I'm tired of waiting. I hate that I sound like a toddler not getting his way, but it's how I feel.

"Things are good. We're working on the bathroom now and priming the walls to paint. Should be finished up in a day or two and be out of your hair."

"I wish we could just move everything in now and do all this later," I say mulishly while Levi laughs at me.

"Your girl's not going anywhere, so unknot your panties and relax. Plus, by doing this now, you won't have to move all your shit out to do the renovations and then move it all back in. It'll be done, and you can move forward."

"Yeah, yeah, I hear ya. Just get it done quickly so I can lock down my girl."

"Just put a ring on it, and you'll be fine," Levi says jokingly.

"That's next, so don't worry."

"Seriously?" Levi asks, his tone sobering.

"Yeah seriously, she's it, man."

"I'm happy for you, Coop. You got lucky with Quinn. I hope you don't do anything stupid and mess it up," he says, laughing because even when he's being serious, he can't help himself from making a joke.

"You're hilarious," I say dryly, "but thanks."

"I'll keep you updated on our progress."

"Thanks. Talk to you later."

After we hang up, I look around my office, thinking about all of the changes that have happened. If you would've told me three months ago I'd not only be moving in with a woman but ready to marry her, I'd have laughed in your face. But right now, I've never been happier.

She's everything I've ever wanted or could've ever

dreamed of, and the best part is, I know that when things get tough—and they will because that's life—she'll be there to work it out. Anytime we've had a miscommunication or disagreement, we've been able to openly discuss it without anger or resentment getting in the way. It's the same way I saw my parents interact growing up, and it's what I've always wanted in a partner.

I feel like I've been sitting around twiddling my thumbs the last couple of days, but we're still waiting on the reports for our Jane Doe, and no one's come forward identifying a missing person. We got lucky with the first victim and was able to identify her quickly, so I'm hoping we'll get lucky again.

I get through another couple of hours' worth of reports when Todd peaks his head into my office with a hopeful look, "We got something, Chief."

I immediately jump from my desk and follow him into the bullpen. The other deputies in the room are buzzing with the knowledge that something is happening.

"Liam, tell us what you found," Todd says.

"Okay, I was going over everything from the first murder again and nothing was jumping out at me, so I thought, what could it hurt to run the license plates of the cars that left the rest stop after the footage shows our girl going missing.

"I wasn't able to check all of them because of camera angles and whatnot, but there were ten I could run, and I had one pop. The sedan had been reported stolen by an impound lot the morning after our first vic was killed but was then later reported as being back in the lot with no damages, so they didn't pursue it any further."

"Are you thinking this could be the car our perp used to transport?"

"Maybe. None of the other plates came back with anything suspicious, including driving records."

"Okay, you and Nathan head over to the impound lot, see

if you can get any more info about the incident and if they have cameras. We might see something related to our investigation they weren't looking for. I'd also like to take a look at the footage and get an idea of when the car got to the rest stop and how long they stayed."

"I can get on that, Chief, since I've watched the footage before," Derek says. I nod my head in response.

"Great job, guys. Keep turning over stones."

Todd and I walk out of the bullpen and head towards my office. He sits down in one of the visitor's chairs as I sit in my desk chair.

"How are you holding up?" I ask Todd.

"All things considered, I'm doing okay. Megan's been my saving grace and has helped keep me from spiraling too deep. How are you holding up?"

"Pretty much the same. After going through all of this with Quinn, I can't imagine wanting anyone else by my side."

"How's the move going? Megan is fit to burst with how excited she is for you guys." Todd laughs, shaking his head.

"I've been so impatient. I would've been happier if she'd moved in the day I asked and we figured out logistics later, but Levi reminded me it's better this way so we don't have to deal with renovations later."

"They didn't have much they needed to do down there, right? It shouldn't be too much longer."

"No, just a couple of days, but it feels like two days too many. All this past week we've only been able to see each other off and on between the investigation and the remodel at both my house and Paint and Paper. I'm not sure why I have this urgency, but it's sitting in my gut, and I know it won't get better until she's officially moved in."

"I get it, man. You want to keep her safe, and if she's at your house, then you know she's safe. I'd hate it if Megan wasn't at the house all the time." A ping sounds from my computer telling me I got an email. I quickly check it and see it's the lab report.

"We got the lab report from Chris. Looks like our Jane Doe was in the system already," I say while printing out the report but continuing to scroll through and relaying the information to Todd. He grabs the papers off the printer when they're done and follows along.

"Brooklyn Lewis, twenty-seven, was a certified nanny for a national company which is why her prints are in the system. No record, permanent address listed in Denton, but it says here she traveled for the nannying company, so she could've been living anywhere."

"We should try and get cell phone records for this vic as well."

"I'll send out the request. There's not much else in this report to go on. Let's get some guys on her social media pages and figure out who she was and where she was going."

"On it."

I put the call into our tech guys so they'll get started on cell records, and then I start going over the autopsy report. There's something niggling in my gut that tells me we're going to get our guy, and soon.

* * *

I RUN my hands through my hair as frustration starts to set in. I stare at all of the evidence, notes, pictures, and reports we've laid out on the conference table, trying to make something jump out at me. We've been here for hours turning over every stone to find something to go on.

Liam and Nathan didn't come back with much from the manager at the impound lot, but they did get the surveillance video, so they're trying to find anything we can use from it. It's late now, past seven, but all of my guys are still here, working to keep the momentum going even if our progress is starting to stagnate.

I step back from the table and walk over to the box of cookies Quinn brought for the guys. We're both having to work late tonight, so she also brought dinner for the two of us to get a little extra time together. She's at Paint and Paper trying to put together her inventory list. I guess none of the crates had been labeled like they were supposed to be, so she's having to go through everything crate by crate to make sure it's all there.

Her opening night is a few days away and she is so excited. I couldn't be prouder of all of the work she's put into this. I hope it's a huge success for her because she's put so much of herself into the store that I want people to love it as much as she does. Thinking about her makes me want to see her, but since we've both got a lot to finish up tonight, it would be better if I call her.

Stepping out, I click her name and bring the phone to my ear. It rings and rings until it goes to voicemail. That's weird. I quickly shoot her a text asking her to call when she can and head back into the bullpen.

"Hey, Chief, I've got something a little weird over here." I walk over to where Liam is watching the footage from the impound lot. "Check this out," he says and plays the video for me. I watch as someone in a ball cap pulled low over their head walks up to the car, immediately gets in, and starts it up.

"That was easy."

"I thought the same thing. You can't start this type of car unless you insert the key into the ignition, so unless they hotwired it, they wouldn't have been able to drive it off the lot without the keys. The manager there said there wasn't any damage to it, so they had to have had a key to get in."

"So how did they get the key?" I ask.

"And why did the manager not say anything about it when we asked?"

I nod my head in response to Liam's fantastic question. "Let's pick him up tomorrow and bring him here." I walk back over to the conference table, checking my phone to see if Quinn's texted me back, but she hasn't.

"I've got some more info on Lewis," Derek says, carrying a few pages of notes in his hands. "It looks like, from her social media pages, she was nannying for a family in Greensboro but wasn't needed anymore and was heading back to Denton for some time off before starting another gig. Doesn't seem to have much in the way of family, but we called her high school earlier, and she was pretty well known and well-liked. Worked several odd jobs around town, and all of her previous bosses said she was a great employee. They all said she was a great person but kept to herself mostly."

"Any boyfriends or friends that stood out to them?"

"Nope, we asked if she was dating anyone, and they all said they'd never seen her go out with anyone. If she went to get dinner anywhere, she was usually by herself."

I blow out a breath. "Okay, thanks, Derek. Not exactly what we were hoping for, but all good information."

Another hour passes as we continue finding out more about our second victim, and I still haven't heard back from Quinn. Other than her phone dying, I'm not sure why she wouldn't have called me back by now, and it's starting to bother me a little. We're pretty much at a standstill until we can go interview some of our leads tomorrow, so I tell the guys who aren't on shift to head out and I go pack up my stuff.

I want to check on Quinn since she's not answering her phone, so I head towards Paint and Paper. I notice her car is still here when I pull into a spot in front of the store. I walk in the door and look around. There are only a few lights on, and it's quiet. "Quinn?" I yell so she knows I'm here and I don't scare her. Not hearing an answer, I walk to the back room where all of the inventory is stored and look around. She's not here either, and my gut continues to churn.

Something isn't right. "Quinn?"

Still no answer.

I find her purse and her phone on a shelf along with her computer and an unfinished mug of tea. I keep walking around the back room and see that the bathroom door is open and the light's out, so she's not in there. Running my hands through my hair, I call Megan to see if she might know where she is.

"Hey, Coop."

"Hey, Megan, I was wondering if you've heard from Quinn tonight."

"No, I haven't. Why?"

"I'm at Paint and Paper, and her car's still out front and her stuff is still here, but she's not. Just wondered if you might've heard from her or something.

"Sorry, Cooper, I haven't heard from her. Could she have gone to get a coffee or something?"

"I don't think so. Her wallet's still in her purse."

"Hmm. Didn't you put up security cameras a while back? Maybe you could see if she stepped out or something?"

"Yeah, I'll have to go back to the station and get on my computer. I can't access it from my phone."

"Maybe leave her a note just in case she comes back after you're gone. I can also text the girls and see if any of them have heard from her."

"Thanks, Megan."

"Keep me updated, and I'll let you know what I hear back."

"Will do." After I hang up, I quickly write Quinn a note saying I was there and head back to the station. Todd comes down the hallway as I walk towards my office.

"Hey, what are you doing back here?" he asks.

"I can't find Quinn. Her car and purse and stuff are still at the store, but she wasn't there when I stopped by. Something doesn't feel right, so I'm going to check the cameras I put up to see if anything weird happened."

"Did you ask Megan if she knew anything?" he asks as we walk into my office. I sit down in my chair and Todd sits in one of my visitor chairs.

"Yeah, and she hasn't heard from her either. She said she's going to ask the rest of the girls if they know anything."

I get into my computer and log onto the website that runs our security system. It takes a few minutes, but I find the feed and make sure she hasn't shown up since I got back to the station. The store is still empty, so I rewind the feed until I see Quinn and press play.

She's in the back room when her head lifts and she looks towards the front like something caught her attention. I switch the camera to the one in the lobby and watch as she walks to the front door and lets someone in. The angle doesn't quite catch who came in, but it's obvious she knows who it is. Quinn walks back into the view of the camera and so does the person she let in.

"What the fuck?" I look up at Todd as my heart drops.

36

QUINN

"Ouch," I say, rolling my shoulders back as I stand up from my stooped position. I am going to be so sore tomorrow. For the first time since we started renovations on the gallery, I am not liking my job so much.

The moving guys screwed up the art we had perfectly organized, and nothing is where it should be. We had every-thing sorted by artist and medium, and they were supposed to put each group into one crate, but instead, they just threw whatever would fit into each box, and now, it's all out of order.

I've been going through each one to figure out what's in there, check it off my inventory list, and then place it on the storage shelves where it should go. It's been a tedious process and, unfortunately, one I won't finish tonight. I was hoping I'd get it all done or at least get close, but it's a little past seven now, and I'm only a third of the way through the inventory.

Thank goodness Levi finished the renovations early, or this would've been a nightmare to deal with right before opening night. As it is, I only have a few days to go, but that's plenty of time to get things together. I may need one more late night to have it ready unless I can push through the exhaustion tonight. I have nothing displayed in the lobby yet, so once everything is inventoried, I'll have to make my selections of what pieces to put out. I'm making notes as I go through the crates, so that should help speed up the selection process.

I take a steadying drink of my tea and get back to work. If I can push through another hour, I'll be in good shape tomorrow and won't have to work late into the night again. As I go through the boxes, I think about all of the craziness that's happened over the past week. Cooper thought I could move right in with him, which made me laugh at the time but now, I kind of understand why he was so upset about me not moving in right away.

Between his schedule and mine, it hasn't been the easiest to see each other regularly, and if I had already moved in, it wouldn't have been as much of a problem. Thankfully the renovations should be finished soon, so we don't have to wait too much longer. We've got some amazing plans for the guest suite, and I'm hoping Mom and Dad might stay with us if they have their own space. They'll probably insist on staying at a hotel, which is fine, but it'll still be nice to have the space.

I know I'm going to miss my grandparents' house though. Living there has been such an amazing thing for my soul, but it wasn't the most ideal location for the long run. We are going to hold on to it for now and most likely rent it out. Without a mortgage to worry about, we've got time to decide what's best.

I hear a knock out front and have a small hope that it's Cooper. He's working late tonight too, so I doubt he'll have time to stop by, but a girl can dream.

I walk out to the front lobby area and quickly unlock the door.

"Hey, this is a surprise. What's going on? Is everything

okay?" I ask as I step back into the lobby. Before I get a response, everything goes black.

* * *

I GROAN, my head feeling like it was kicked by a horse. God, what the hell happened? Did I fall down or something? I go to move my hands to make sure I'm okay, but they won't budge. I blink my eyes open and look down. My hands are tied behind me, and I finally recognize the feeling of bark against my back.

My legs are also tied down, but they're spread wide and the ropes holding me are staked into the ground. Sticks and rocks poke at my bare skin where my shorts stop on my thigh.

I look around and realize I'm in the middle of the forest. It's dark, but the moon is shining, so I can somewhat see my surroundings. It's silent, no animals moving or owls hooting. Nothing.

I feel my heartbeat kick up as adrenaline courses through me with the realization that I am in serious danger right now. My fight or flight response makes me start wiggling to see if I can get out of my binds, but they're incredibly tight and only hurts me more as I struggle.

"There's no use," a voice says from the shadows, making me jump. I didn't even see them there when I first took in my surroundings. They start walking out from the shadows, and everything in me stills.

"Rachel?" I ask, not quite believing what I'm seeing.

"Surprise," she says, walking closer to me, and it's then I see she's waving a large butcher knife. The glint of the moon catches the blade a couple of times, making it seem even more sinister.

"I don't understand. What's going on right now?"

"Of course, you don't. You're a stupid little bitch who

doesn't know what's good for her, apparently," she says, rolling her eyes. "You know, after I first met you, I thought you'd be smart. I mean, you were from New York for God's sake. I figured you might have some street smarts in you but apparently not."

"What does that have to do with why you've tied me up out here?" I watch as she squats down in front of me, her dark hair swaying in the breeze as she moves. While the knife being pointed at me is scary, what's scarier is how calm she is. She's completely in control and comfortable right now, as if this is a normal occurrence for her. There's a gleam in her eyes I've never seen before, like she's never been happier than right here in this moment.

"Because you took what's mine," she says, and moves so quickly I don't quite realize she's done it. I gasp as the knife slices down my shirt from neckline to hemline, somehow only nicking my skin at my collarbone where the knife started. She pulls the shredded pieces apart and tucks them behind me.

Rachel stares at my chest, making me feel incredibly exposed, but I realize she's not looking at my breasts. She's looking at the cut from her knife. Blood has pooled at one end, and I flinch as her finger slides across the wound, making my skin burn. She drags her finger down my chest, and blood follows the path of her finger.

"I've been waiting a long time for this moment, you know," she says quietly. "I feel like we're going to enjoy this together, one artist to another. My canvas will just be your skin instead of woven fabric."

My heart is beating so hard I'm genuinely afraid it's going to explode out of my chest. I try to get my thoughts together to figure out how to keep her talking. If I can delay her from cutting me, I might be able to figure a way out of this. "If I took something from you, I didn't know it was yours to start with, and I'm sorry. Can you tell me what it was?"

She looks me dead in the eye. Slightly cocking her head to the side to see if the sincerity in my voice is real. "He was never yours, but you took him anyway." My inhale is quick in surprise, and I feel my eyes get wide.

"Cooper," I whisper.

"You know, I had everything planned out. It was working too, and then you decided to show up and ruin everything." At my confused face, she rolls her eyes again. "He was finally leaning on me because of the break-ins. He was stressed and tired, and I was one step away from getting him to see me as more than his secretary, and then you show up in town," she says, viciously jabbing the point of the knife into my sternum making me cry out in pain.

She moves the knife away and does an assessment of my face, her eyes tracking down my neck and chest. "I don't understand what he saw in you that he didn't see in me. We both have dark hair and similar builds; you're a little taller, but that's nothing." She shrugs as if it doesn't matter anymore.

All while she's been talking, I've been trying to loosen the knot around my wrists. My hands ache from the way I've contorted them, but the knot is starting to give, so I push through the pain and keep trying to untie my hands.

Rachel looks up at me and smiles, "I'll let you in on a little secret since you won't be alive much longer." The knifepoint drags up my leg like she's planning the best carving points. "It was me. I broke into all of those houses," she whispers and then lets out a deep exhale and giggles as if she's happy to finally share her secret with someone.

"God, it was invigorating being in those houses. I felt alive for the first time in a long time. My plan was for Cooper to come to me for comfort because of the stress, but he didn't, so I had to keep escalating, granted that had the added appeal of making me feel fantastic."

"It was you who broke into my house too, wasn't it?" The realization hitting me like a brick wall.

"Well, well, maybe you're not so dumb," she says, caressing the top of my breast with the tip of the knife, moving it down my chest. "Although, instead of being smart and leaving town like you were supposed to, you went and made it worse by staying the night with Cooper." She pushes the tip of the knife in harder and slices down the left side of my torso, making me scream out in pain. Her face takes on this serene look as she watches the blood run down my side.

"You know, it's your fault those women are dead too. If you hadn't gotten in the way, I wouldn't have had to kill them. I will say, though, I enjoyed it thoroughly." She gives me another smile that makes me shiver with fear. "Shall we get started now? I'm running out of time to make you my masterpiece."

37

COOPER

"Todd..." My voice is strained. He comes around my desk, rewinds the footage, and pushes play. I watch again as Quinn opens the door, stepping back to let Rachel in, and just as quickly, Rachel whacks Quinn over the head with something in her hand. She goes down so fast you know she's out cold. "Oh my god," Todd says quietly.

I feel my blood heat with rage as I try to figure out what's happened. You can see Rachel dragging Quinn out of the frame and, I'm assuming, out of the building. I stand up and start towards the door, but Todd's hand on my arm stops me in my tracks.

"We have to be smart about this, Cooper."

"Be smart? Someone I thought I could trust just abducted the love of my life. I have to find her," I plead, feeling myself get more hysterical by the minute.

"And we will, but first we need to go through everything logically, otherwise we'll be chasing our tails and that won't help Quinn." I just stare at him. I know he's right, but I'm strung so tight I don't know how to do anything logically right now. "Let's go grab Derek and Liam and have them watch the video too." I nod in response.

I pace the room while Todd goes and gets them because I'm pretty sure if I had to speak, I'd break down right there. I move away from the desk as the three men come into the room. "We need you to take a look at this," Todd says, queuing up the video. I watch their faces as their eyes get wide when they realize what they saw.

Liam looks up at me, "Did this happen tonight?" Again, all I can do is nod.

"We need you guys to go through her office and see if you can find anything that would indicate why she would do this. Coop and I are going to her house with Nathan and Chad. I highly doubt she's there, but there's a chance she could be, so we'll have the backup. Call the minute you find anything."

The four of us leave my office, Liam and Derek heading towards Rachel's cube, Todd and I towards the bullpen. I stay back, close to the door, and watch the guys gather their stuff and follow us outside to the cruisers. Todd must've told Nathan and Chad where we're going because they walk straight to their car, and I follow Todd to my truck. He gets in the driver's side, and I get in the passenger side.

What could've ever possessed Rachel to do something like this? Quinn has never once been hateful towards her, and Rachel hasn't been hateful towards Quinn. I know Quinn would've told me if she was. My head is a mess as I try to rationalize what Rachel's done. None of it makes any sense, but as we get closer to her house, I know I need to pull myself together in case she has Quinn here.

It's highly unlikely, as Todd said, that she would be there. I mean, she knows it'd be the first place we would look for her, but that doesn't mean we should go in expecting nothing to happen.

Todd pulls into the driveway with Nathan and Chad right behind us. The house is a one-story, brown brick ranch and seems to be completely dark. "Are you going to be okay to go in? We both know you shouldn't be here at all, but if it were me, no one would be able to keep me away," he says.

"I'm good. I've shut it down and can handle it." Todd nods in response and gets out of the truck.

We walk up to the door and knock, "Rachel? Mrs. Cassinelli?" Todd shouts through the door, but there's only silence. We knock again and still no answer, so we try the door, and it's surprisingly unlocked.

Todd opens the door a crack, and the smell that permeates out of the house tells us we have every right to go inside without a warrant. We quickly clear the house and walk to the back bedroom where the smell is the worst. Opening the door, the room is dark and the smell slaps us in the face. Nathan gags, Todd and I hold our shirts over our faces, and we see Mrs. Cassinelli in the bed, decomposing. We all quickly back out of the room and out of the house to get some fresh air.

I lean against my truck and force every feeling down so that I don't lose it outside of Rachel's house. Quinn needs me to be strong right now, and if I let myself break down, I'll be no good to her. Straightening from my position, I look around and see Chad on the phone calling in the body, Todd has both hands on the truck and his head dangling between his arms, and Nathan is bent over with his hands on his knees breathing deeply.

I may be dying on the inside but these guys need a leader, and that's my job. "Okay, guys, let's wrap up and see what we can find until CSU gets here." The guys straighten up, and we all find something to cover our noses and mouths. Nathan and I find bandanas, and Chad and Todd use t-shirts.

We make our way back into the house. I walk to the back bedroom and quickly close the door to keep the smell from permeating the entire house until we can get the body out. Each of us takes a room, and I start in Rachel's bedroom. Everything is coated in a pretty thick layer of dust which tells me she hasn't been here in a while. Makes me wonder where she's been living all this time.

I start going through her room, systematically cataloging everything I find. It feels a little weird going through my secretary's possessions. It feels like an invasion of privacy, but then I remember that she bashed in Quinn's head, and I don't feel too bad anymore.

I am learning so many things about Rachel, making me realize I never really knew her at all. She's only a few years younger than me, and apparently, we went to high school together. I was a senior and she was a freshman, so I don't remember her. I was focused on getting into the police academy and didn't care too much about my last year there.

She seemed to enjoy reading based on how many books are on her shelf, and what's even crazier is that I know a lot of the titles on her shelf, having read them myself. I wouldn't have pictured Rachel as a mystery reader, but that shows you what I know.

I'm not finding anything pertinent to why she would take Quinn, so I leave the room to go check on the other guys and get some fresh air. As I turn to walk out, something behind the door catches my eye. I lean down and grab it, almost dropping it in shock. It's the painting Quinn did of my eyes. How the hell did Rachel get it?

I walk out to the main living space to find Todd and show him what I found. "Look at this," I say, waiting for him to turn and look at me. When he does, I hold up the painting, "Quinn did this right after we first met. It was in her house and was pulled out by whoever broke into her house."

"Do you think Rachel could've been the one to break in?" Todd asks.

"How else would she have gotten this? Although she would've had to break in a second time in order to get this painting because it was still there when Quinn came home to find her stuff messed up."

"This is crazy, man. None of this is adding up. I mean, Rachel hasn't been here in weeks based on the smell of Mrs. Casinelli and the mound of dust on everything. She abducts Quinn, and now she's breaking and entering? None of this makes sense."

My phone starts ringing as Todd is talking, and I see it's Derek on the other end. I answer it quickly, telling Todd who it is.

"Have you found something?" I ask, walking outside to get away from the smell of the house. I pull my bandana down to be able to breathe better.

"Yeah, we found a necklace, and at first, I didn't recognize what it was until something kept nagging at the back of my head telling me I'd seen it before." Derek takes a deep breath like he doesn't want to say the next part. "Chief, the necklace was Brooklyn Lewis's, the second vic." It takes me a minute to process that information.

"Are you sure it's hers?"

"Positive. After I realized why the necklace was familiar, I pulled up her social media pictures again and you can see her wearing the necklace. It also has the initials BL on it. There's no other logical explanation for why Rachel would have it. They weren't friends, Brooklyn was never in town, so Rachel couldn't have found it somewhere..." He trails off as if he doesn't want to finish his thought.

"Fuck," I say, losing all sense of professionalism. Rachel killed Brooklyn Lewis, and if that's the case, then she also killed Ashley Delmont. "None of this is adding up. I don't understand how any of this fits together," I say both to myself and Derek. I notice Todd, Nathan, and Chad have come outside too, so I put Derek on speakerphone and tell them what he found.

"Chief, I have a theory, but I don't think you're going to like it much," Liam says, also apparently on speakerphone.

"I don't like any of this, so just go ahead and say it," I tell him.

"If you look at the timeline, the murders started right after Quinn got here. I mean she'd only been here a couple of weeks when the first murder happened. What if Rachel has some sort of fixation on her? All of our vics have a certain resemblance to Quinn, so maybe Rachel killed them because she couldn't get who she really wanted. Then tonight, she knew you'd both be working late, and Rachel took her chance at getting Quinn."

God, this kid. If I wasn't about to come apart at the seams, I would be incredibly proud. Todd steps in, knowing I need a minute to gather myself. The idea that Quinn could've been targeted shreds my insides.

"That's a pretty good theory, kid, because we have evidence from the house to believe Rachel might've been the one who broke into Quinn's house."

"Where would she take her?" I ask out loud but mostly to myself. "I don't think she'd take her to the landfill because that murder was more in anger than anything else."

"Is there a place Quinn liked that Rachel would know about?" Liam asks.

I look up at Todd, knowing immediately where we need to go. I just hope it's not too late.

38

COOPER

I speed into the parking lot of the lake and get as close to the tackle shop as possible. Slamming on my brakes, I jam the gear shift into park and jump out. Every second matters right now because if Rachel killed those women, she might've already killed Quinn with a cut that was too deep.

When they first met, Quinn told Rachel her favorite place in Sonoma was the lake, and with the first murder happening here as well, I knew it would be the place Rachel would bring her. I hear Todd's door close and tires screech behind me as I make my way towards where the first body was found. Suddenly, I feel a hand on my arm and whirl around quickly to defend myself but realize it's only Todd.

"I know you need to get there right now, but you need to calm down and be smart. If you come in too hot, she could slice Quinn's throat in a second," Todd says. I know I need to heed his advice but I'm having a hard time not going in there guns blazing.

I take a deep breath and shove everything back into a box to deal with later and try to bring my cop brain back into the forefront. It's not easy, and it doesn't work completely, but

I'm able to focus enough to think about the next steps in order to keep Quinn safe.

"Okay, Todd, you're with me. We'll go in on the left. Nathan and Chad, you guys come in from the right. We don't know what we're going to find when we get there, but we can assume Quinn will be tied down and most likely stripped. We need to proceed with as much caution as possible because we don't know Rachel's mindset right now." I look at Todd, hoping my gratitude for his level head is showing in my eyes. He nods his head in understanding.

We all turn and start towards the forest where the first victim was found. As we get closer, we can hear voices, so I hold my hand up to slow our progress and indicate for the guys to do their best to quiet their steps.

Suddenly, I hear a scream, and everything in me tightens. All four of us bring our guns to attention, and I feel Todd's hand on my shoulder acting as both comfort and restraint. We keep moving forward until they come into view.

With the moon shining through the trees, I can barely make out Rachel hovering over Quinn, and I can't tell if she's alive. The sound of our footsteps causes Rachel to spin around, and I can finally see Quinn. I let my eyes quickly assess her before moving back to Rachel. Her shirt is spread open, and I can see at least one wound down her left side. I force my eyes away because I can't afford to lose focus in case Rachel decides to act quickly and kill Quinn.

"Well, this is a surprise," Rachel says calmly as if it's no big deal we're here. I notice she hasn't moved the knife away from Quinn's body though. She knows what she's doing, and that confirms everything I need to know. I slow my steps and come to a stop several feet away from the two women.

I feel Todd's quiet strength behind me and see Nathan and Chad out of the corner of my eye. Each one of them has my back, so I slowly lower my gun to get Rachel to focus on me.

"Did you think I wouldn't find you, Rachel?" I ask, doing my best to sound nonchalant and not accusatory. If I get her riled, that will only put Quinn in more danger.

"I had my hopes, but I didn't think you'd be able to put it all together this quickly. I'm glad you're here though. Now, you'll finally see me and not her," she says, digging the knife into Quinn's sternum making her cry out.

Silence drops around us as her words sink in.

It was me. It was always about me. Oh god, this is all my fault.

I force myself to focus back on Rachel, again pushing every feeling I have into that box in the back of my head to deal with later.

"You wanted me to see you? I've always seen you, Rachel. You've been my friend for a long time," I say, trying to keep her focused on me. I can see the guys slowly spreading out in my peripherals.

"No, you've never seen me. No matter what I did to get your attention, some other whore was always better. Then, after Riss's car blew up, I thought I finally had my shot." As she's talking, I slowly make my way closer to Rachel.

"How did you know about Riss's car? They were never able to determine if it was an accident or purposeful."

Rachel smiles at me, and it sends a cold chill down my spine. "Oops. Guess the cat's out the bag on that one. She wasn't worthy of you, so I made sure she couldn't come back." Then she giggles like it's the funniest thing.

"Jesus, Rachel," I say before I can think.

"You don't appreciate what I've done for you, do you? God, you're so stupid!" she yells and starts towards Quinn.

Suddenly, Quinn pushes Rachel, taking her by surprise and knocking her off balance and to the ground. Todd and I both move at the same time, him working to keep Rachel down, and me kicking the knife out of her hands. Nathan and Chad come in to help Todd secure Rachel, and I finally get to Quinn.

Falling to my knees, I untie her legs, and since she managed to untie her own hands somehow, she launches herself into my arms. I wrap my arms around her and hold her to me as tightly as I can, one hand on her head, the other wrapped around her waist.

I pull back to look at her face and make sure she's okay. Her eyes are wide with shock, and she hasn't said a word since we got here. I look down to check the rest of her and see blood dripping down her chest and side.

"Fuck, Quinn, we need to get you to the hospital." I lift her into my arms and look at Todd, only now noticing he has Rachel handcuffed and held to the ground as she screams and thrashes in anger. I can hear sirens as the adrenaline from a minute ago recedes, and allows me to focus on more than just getting to Quinn.

"Go, we've got her. There's an ambo waiting, and the guys are coming in now," he says, and I nod, taking off toward the parking lot. Quinn still hasn't said anything, and I look down at her to make sure she's okay. Her eyes are open, but it's almost like there's no life in them at all. If she wasn't fisting my shirt, I'd be worried she bled out.

We make it out to the parking lot, and it's so reminiscent of the first scene that I almost crumble at the thought of how close we came to not finding her in time. The guys look up and immediately jump to action when they see I've got Quinn in my arms. I watch a few guys run into the forest to help Todd, and the paramedics roll the stretcher towards me. I gently lay Quinn down, following closely as the guys push her back to the ambulance.

Everything feels loud and chaotic, but I can't tell if it's in my head or the things around me are actually that way. I start to pull away as the paramedics go to push her into the ambulance when Quinn's hand latches onto mine like a vice. I look in her eyes and, through the fog, I can see my girl in there. For the first time since I saw the video of Rachel knocking her out, I take a deep breath.

She's okay. She's alive and with me, and she's okay. I jump into the back of the ambo, keeping my hold on Quinn as best as I can, sitting down by her head so I'm out of the way of the paramedics. Her eyes are closed now, so I lean in and gently touch my forehead to hers. "You are so brave, and I'm so proud of you," I whisper to her. "I'm so, so sorry." I see a tear slip down the side of Quinn's face, and I gently wipe it with my thumb.

Keeping my head on Quinn's, I watch them tape gauze to the cuts and nicks in her stomach, chest, and legs. They're all over her body, upwards of twenty from what I can tell. God, I can't even imagine what that was like for her. Some are deeper than others, and if we hadn't gotten there when we did, I know they would've progressively gotten deeper until she bled out.

We pull into the ER bay and jump out of the ambo. The doctors take over pushing the stretcher and roll her through the doors and into a hospital room. As hard as it is, I stand back and let the doctors check her over to make sure she's okay. I watch them clean up the cuts and push on her stomach to make sure nothing major was hit.

A few minutes later, the doctor comes out of the room. "I asked Quinn if it was okay to give you an update, and she said yes. From what we can tell, there was no major internal damage, but she will need stitches on a few of the deeper lacerations. She's got a concussion from the head wound, so we'll keep an eye on that for a few hours, but all in all, she's in good shape."

If she was in good shape, she wouldn't need stitches or to be monitored but I don't say that out loud. Instead, I say, "Thanks, Doc," while never taking my eyes off of Quinn.

"They're going to clean her wounds, and then I'll stitch

her up. After that, you should be able to go in and see her. It's going to take about an hour, so if you want to wait in the waiting room, that'd be good," he says as the nurses close the curtains to give her some more privacy.

Everything in me is screaming to stay right there as close to Quinn as possible, but I head to the waiting room. It's empty since it's so late, and I sit down in the first chair I find.

The only thing that keeps going through my head at this point is, this is all my fault.

39

QUINN

For the second time, I wake up groaning. My head is pounding against my skull and my eyes fly open, working quickly to take in my surroundings. Instead of seeing trees and darkness, I'm lying in a bed with machines beeping around me. The events of the night slowly trickle in as I realize I'm in the hospital now instead of tied to a tree.

My heart starts to race as images come to my mind of Rachel's face and her evil knife slicing into my skin.

"Quinn, baby, open your eyes. You're safe now." Cooper's voice sounds far away, and my eyes flit open to figure out if he's actually here or in my imagination. His beautiful face comes into view, eyebrows furrowed, and worry clouding those amber eyes.

"Cooper? What happened? All I remember is being in the woods with Rachel and then nothing. Why can't I remember anything else?" Cooper grabs my hand, moves a chair closer to my bed, and sits down.

"It's probably because of the shock." He squeezes my hand tight. "You're safe, and we got Rachel."

"Will you tell me what happened?"

"Are you sure you're ready to talk about this? I'm not even sure I'm ready to talk about it," he says.

"Yes, I need to know how I got out of there. It'll help to remind me I'm not still in that clearing."

Cooper takes a deep breath. I can see the events of the evening flash in his eyes before he looks back at me. "We found evidence in Rachel's desk indicating she had murdered those girls, and I believed she'd take you to the lake. You'd mentioned to her it was your favorite place in Sonoma, and since it was the location of the first murder, it was significant to both of you.

"When we got there, we weren't sure what we would find, so we came in as quietly as we could. The first thing we could see was Rachel leaning over you, and it took everything in me not to rush at her when I heard you scream.

"I couldn't see if you were okay, just that your feet were spread apart and tied to stakes in the ground. When we pushed through into the clearing, Rachel turned around, and I could finally see you. I saw blood running down your chest and I swear, I would've shot her right then and there if the chances of me hitting you weren't so high."

I squeeze his hand to pull him back to me. As much as I wanted to hear what happened, I didn't think about the effect it would have on Cooper.

I can't take the space between us anymore, so I put my hand on his neck and pull him closer to me, holding his face so he'll lean in and kiss me. He presses his lips against mine so gently and pulls back entirely too quickly, but the little smile on his face tells me it did what I wanted. I nod for him to continue, and this time, he keeps his eyes on me instead of retreating into the memories.

"I distracted her for a little bit, but when she told me she was the one who killed Riss, I couldn't keep up the easygoing charade. I pissed her off, and she turned to take it out on you, but you pulled your hands out from behind you and pushed her. It took us all by surprise, actually."

"The whole time she had me, I'd been working on untying the knot binding my hands. It helped to distract me from the cuts," I say quietly. Cooper looks at me with both pride and sadness.

"You were so brave, sweetheart," he says. "She wasn't prepared for you to attack, so she lost her balance and fell backward. Todd and I subdued her, and then I untied you and carried you out to the ambulance."

As Cooper finishes telling me what happened, little flashes of the night pop into my mind. The moment I saw Cooper come into the clearing, the feeling of the bind around my hands coming loose, being wrapped in Cooper's arms... It comes to me in pictures instead of actual memories. Some of the things she said over the night comes back to me, and my head snaps up, he may not know everything Rachel has done.

"Cooper, it was her. Everything that's happened over the last month, and even before, was all her. She killed those girls, she broke into my house, she was even behind all of the B and Es in Westlake." He puts his hand on my cheek to help me calm back down.

"I know," he says softly. "Well, I didn't know about the B and Es—although it's not a surprise at this point—but I knew about everything else." Shaking his head, he looks down as if keeping eye contact with me is unbearable. "God, Quinn. I'm so sorry. This is all my fault. Everything she did was because of me... Because I didn't notice her obsessions. I should've seen it. None of this would've happened if I did, and I'm so, so sorry." He sounds so broken.

Oh, my poor guy. I should've known this was going to hurt him to his core. His heart is so big he's going to take the full blame for everything that happened, and of course, it's not his fault.

"Oh, my love." I put my hand on his face despite my skin burning as I twist. "There is no way you could've known. Do you know why?" He looks deep into my eyes, searching for hope and forgiveness, too afraid he's not worth it.

"You are so inherently good. You have such a big heart capable of so much love that the idea of something this heinous is unfathomable. Rachel knew this about you and used it to get away with everything she did, which is why the entire blame lays on her shoulders. Not yours."

"But shouldn't I have noticed how evil she was?"

"Of course not, because she didn't let you see that part of her. She was a master manipulator and was able to hide the evil in her to not get caught." I lean back into the bed because both my head and my body are screaming at me.

"I don't know how long it's going to take me to not blame myself. Look at you. You're like a mummy and can barely move. I don't know how you'll ever forgive me."

"There's nothing to forgive. I love you so much, Cooper," I say, my eyes getting heavy as my body relaxes now that I know I'm safe.

"I love you, Quinn. More than I ever knew was possible," I hear him whisper as I drift off.

* * *

"CAN I GET YOU ANYTHING? How are you feeling?" my mom asks for the fifteenth time over the last hour. Cooper called Mom and Dad while I was getting stitched up, and they flew in immediately to help me recover.

They had to stay in a hotel for a couple of nights while Levi got the guest suite finished, and to my complete surprise, they moved in as soon as it was done. I was also moved in within a couple of days. Cooper put his foot down on waiting, and my stuff was moved in pretty quickly after that.

"I'm fine, Mom. I don't need anything," I grit out so I don't yell at her because I know she's just trying to take care of me, but I am not completely helpless. It's been almost two weeks now since Rachel's attack, and while I am still incredibly sore, I'm able to move and do things for myself.

"Are you sure? I could make you a snack or something. Alice sent over a bunch of groceries for us which was so kind of her."

Not only did my parents use the guest suite sooner than I thought, but they also met Cooper's parents this week as well. They got along fantastically, which was a small surprise to me and I guess could be considered a blessing of Rachel's attack.

It's been great having my parents here, but I'm also ready for them to head home. They've been here a couple of days too long for me, and I know my mom is driving Cooper up the wall even though he'd never say anything.

I sigh and slowly get up from the couch, my muscles aching and my skin stretching around my stitches. I walk into the kitchen where my mom is faffing around and gently wrap my arms around her. "You know how much I love you and how appreciative I am that you're here, right?" I ask her.

"I love you too, dear, and we wouldn't be anywhere else after your ordeal."

"Thanks, Mom, but—and remember I love you—you are driving me crazy. I am fine now, albeit a little sore, and you don't need to keep hovering anymore." I look into Mom's blue eyes, the shade very similar to my own. Her long silver-grey hair—which makes her look so dignified—is pulled back into a clip.

She lets out a deep breath and her shoulders droop. "I know you're fine, honey. I promise, I do. But when we got that call from Cooper telling us you'd been attacked, everything in me just froze. I was so scared for you, and even though he told us you were fine, I kept imagining what you had been through, and to see your beautiful body all bandaged up, I just…"

"I can't imagine how hard that phone call was, but you can see me now, I'm a little gimpy but totally fine. I wasn't even in the hospital for very long. On top of all of that, the stitches come out soon, and then everything will be smooth sailing from there."

"Are you sure? I can still help you around the house."

"I'm positive, Mom. I know you've been delaying your travel schedule for me, and while I appreciate it, it's not necessary anymore." She looks me over as if to make sure I really am okay and then nods her head.

"We do need to get back on the road. We were supposed to be helping a clinic in South Africa."

"Well then, let's get you to South Africa," I say with a laugh because that sounds ridiculous coming out of my mouth.

"Quinn, I want you to know that even though we don't completely understand your job in this gallery, we can see how happy you are here, and we're incredibly proud of you. That's all we want, you know. After everything that's happened…we just want you safe and happy."

Despite having missed the launch party, I'm still trying to keep up with the gallery while I heal, and Mom has gotten a small glimpse into what I'm doing now.

"Yeah, I know, Mom, and I am both of those things." I give her one more big hug, and then we work on packing up their stuff and arranging their flights.

Cooper comes in while Mom and I are fixing dinner. He's been helping wrap up Rachel's case. She hasn't said a single word since her arrest, but they've still found evidence tying her to both murders.

I guess she was living with the manager of the impound lot, and that's how she got the key to the car. One of the part-time guys had noticed it missing, otherwise, it wouldn't have ever been reported. So, between my testimony, the evidence they've found, and what she told Cooper at the lake, she's going to be in prison for a very long time.

"How are you feeling?" Cooper asks as he gives me a quick kiss and then hugs my mom.

"I'm doing good today. Moving around a little more to keep from getting too stiff."

"Oh, so he can ask how you are and it's fine, but me, I'm told I'm hovering," my mom says with a huff and a wink at me, telling me she's kidding. That has been one of the greatest things about her being here. We've gotten to know each other so much better as adults than just mother and daughter, and I've learned so much about my mom that I never knew before. Most importantly, her sense of humor.

Cooper looks at me with wide eyes like he stepped into a fight and doesn't know how to fix it, which makes me laugh. I put him out of his misery and tell him she's joking. "Mom and I had a little heart to heart today about them getting back to work because we all know it's time for them to move on, but she was afraid she'd be abandoning me," I inform Cooper. His eyes flash with a huge amount of relief, but he quickly recovers.

"It's been great having you here though, Denise, and knowing that Quinn is being taken care of while I'm at work has been so helpful," he says.

"I appreciate you saying that, but Quinn is right. I have been hovering and it's time to let you guys have some alone time." Cooper just nods his head and smiles at me, and I can already tell he's thinking, thank god.

"Where's Paul at?" he asks about my dad.

"He and your dad were playing golf this afternoon, and we haven't seen them since," I say. My dad and Rob have gotten very close in the almost two weeks my parents have been here. They're like long-lost brothers, and if I'm honest,

Mom and Dad would be more likely to come for a visit to see Rob instead of me.

A few minutes later, we hear them clomping into the house, chattering away like teenage girls. Piper trots in behind them having gone to the golf course with the boys, and Alice sneaks in carrying another bag of groceries. They clamor into the kitchen and hellos are given out to everyone, including Piper.

We all pitch in to set the table for dinner and sit down to share the meal. The whole scene fills my heart with happiness as I watch our two families enjoy each other's company. I've always dreamed of moments like this but never thought I'd get to have it.

I moved to Sonoma in the hopes of finding the same happiness I found every summer all those years ago. I knew being in my grandparents' house was the perfect start, and from there, I could find out who I am and what makes me, me. I had no idea that one decision could lead to me finding the love of my life, the best group of friends, and the home I had always wanted.

I feel Cooper's hand on my thigh under the table and turn to look at him. Every feeling of love and happiness I just had is reflected back at me. It's a look I will never tire of and one I hope I can return for the rest of my life.

EPILOGUE

QUINN

"Babe, are you ready to go?" Cooper asks, walking into our bathroom. I'm standing at the sink in nothing but my underwear, trying to get my hair to do what I want. "I can see the answer is no," he says, walking up behind me and wrapping his arms around my waist.

"We don't have time for any funny business, mister," I say with a smirk, although I could be persuaded into some funny business pretty easily.

"No, we don't, and you still need to get dressed. I will not have my girl parading around in her birthday suit, even if it is her birthday." I laugh and wiggle around, pushing my butt into his crotch. "Stop wiggling and get dressed. We need to get moving," he says, slapping my butt and walking away.

"Tease!" I yell out from the bathroom, making him laugh out loud. Megan and Todd are hosting a birthday party for me tonight, and it'll be the first large gathering I've been to since the attack. Looking at my body, I trace the pink lines on my torso from Rachel's knife.

It's been about two months, and while my physical wounds have healed almost completely, my brain has been a little slower to come around. My therapist says the trauma of experiencing something so violent has made me react to situations as if they'll harm me, even if I know I'm safe. It's been hard, but between Cooper and our friends, I've come a long way. I was even able to start back at the gallery this week which is a huge deal.

For a while, it was hard just walking in the door, so I worked mainly from home, talking with artists and creating my own artwork. Trish has been incredible and so patient while I've been getting back on my feet.

It took a long time to come to terms with what happened for both me and Cooper. It's not exactly been an easy road for either of us, but the best part about the whole thing is that we've gotten a lot closer. It's taken work and a lot of open and honest communication on both our parts, but it's brought us so much closer than I ever thought would be possible.

He's planned this big birthday bash for me tonight, and I am so excited for it. It's the first time I've felt excited about anything in a while, and I know Cooper put this all together for that reason.

After getting my hair pinned up the way I want, I head into our closet searching for my favorite dress, the white one with the maroon flowers on it. It reminds me of who I was before the attack and who I want to find again. She's still there inside of me, begging to come back, and as I slip the dress over my head and look in the mirror, I can see her again for the first time in a long time.

I grab my brown strappy sandals and head downstairs to find Cooper who's sitting at the breakfast bar in the kitchen. He looks so handsome in his khaki pants and blue, striped button-down shirt.

"I'm ready to go. Thank you for being patient." He turns to look at me and freezes. "What? Do I have something on my dress?" I ask, looking down to make sure there isn't a stain. It is white after all. He shakes his head no and walks over to me.

"You look beautiful, that's all," he says, smiling his million-dollar smile at me which, of course, makes me blush. He brushes his thumb across my cheek. "There she is," he says quietly. Instead of being confused by his statement, I know exactly what he means. I'm finally feeling myself again and it's showing.

We walk out of the house, leaving Piper to herself for the evening, and head towards Megan and Todd's. I haven't been there in a few weeks, and it feels so good to be out and about. I know I've got all of the tools I need in case I have a panic attack, so instead of feeling nervous, I'm thrilled. Plus, I have a handsome date on my birthday. How much better can life get?

* * *

Cooper

I CAN'T TAKE my eyes off of her. She's absolutely shining, and no matter how hard I try to pay attention to the people around me, my eyes always go back to her. When she came downstairs and told me she was ready, I saw the sparkle in her eyes that's been missing since the attack, and I'm so happy it's back.

These past few weeks have been hard on both of us, and we've worked tirelessly to move on from what happened. The guilt I carry has slowly diminished, and that wouldn't have happened without Quinn's ability to pull my head out of my ass. Even when she's struggling with her own problems, she still makes sure I'm doing okay. She's proven that I am the luckiest bastard on this planet to have her love me, and I hope to be able to show her how much I love her right back.

A ding from my phone signals a text, and I quickly check it to see if it's who I think it is. I set up a huge surprise for Quinn for her birthday. Everyone we love was able to come in for her party tonight, even her parents, but one person we love just got here. I take another look at Quinn and watch her talking to Megan, Sara, Lucy, and Natalie. We're all standing outside in Megan and Todd's backyard enjoying the beautiful weather and each other's company.

Knowing Quinn is okay for a minute, I head inside to let our new guest in. I open the door and see the blonde little spitfire that helped push Quinn into my arms.

"Hi, Hailey," I say, letting her into Megan and Todd's house and giving her a big hug.

"Hey, Chief Sexy Pants," she says, making me laugh. "How's our girl?" she asks on a more serious note.

"She's really good tonight. She's more herself than she's been since the attack," I tell her.

Hailey has been checking in regularly and knows a lot about what Quinn and I have been going through recently. She wasn't able to take off work after the attack, but she's more than made up for it in daily check-ins for both me and Quinn. She's become a great friend to me and a morale booster for Quinn. I'm so thankful for how much she's helped bring Quinn back.

"I'm glad to hear that. Is this going to be okay? I'm worried about her having a panic attack from being surprised."

"I thought you could call out to her and get her attention from afar. That way you wouldn't be right in her face."

"Oh, that's perfect. I love it."

"Everyone's outside, so let's head back there." I lead Hailey to the backyard and step outside, my eyes automatically finding Quinn. She has her back to the door, so she won't see us coming out. I'm starting to get a little more nervous as the night goes on. I want this to be the best day for her, but there's a lot of surprises happening tonight, so I hope everything goes according to plan.

"God, I could so go for a glass of wine. What are my options tonight, Coop?" Hailey says loudly, making everyone turn. My eyes stay glued to Quinn, cataloging every facial expression to make sure she's okay. Her eyebrows furrow in confusion, and then her eyes widen in surprise. A smile breaks across her face, and she comes running over to Hailey and wraps her in a big hug.

"Yes please, crush my lungs," Hailey says, but you can see she's squeezing Quinn just as hard. They both laugh as they break apart, and I see tears in Quinn's eyes. She turns to look at me. "Did you do this?"

"Happy birthday, babe," I say, and she comes and hugs me.

"Hey wait, I just got here, and you can't have her back yet," Hailey says, making everyone laugh. She grabs Quinn's hand and walks over to the bar area to get a drink. They're both chattering away and catching up like no time has passed since the last time they've seen each other.

"First surprise down. How ya feeling?" Todd asks as I watch my girl laugh and have a good time.

"I'm good. That went better than I thought it would, so I'm ready for the next one," I tell him. I reach into my pocket and find the ring I stashed there earlier. I wasn't sure if tonight would be a good time but seeing the sparkle in Quinn's eyes assures me that tonight is the night.

We all talk and laugh and eat for a couple more hours, but it's starting to get dark, so I know I need to make my move soon. A sudden bout of nerves washes through me as I think about what I'm going to do. I'm not worried she's going to say no exactly. More about what I'm going to say and potentially for her to say not right now.

I find her in the group and she looks up at me, and in that moment, when our eyes meet, I know without a doubt, it's time. Everything I needed to see is in her eyes, and I'm no longer worried about what I'm going to say. I look at Todd and nod my head so he knows it's about to happen.

I walk over to Quinn and lean down to give her a quick kiss for good luck even though she has no idea.

"Can I get everyone's attention?" I say loud enough for everyone to hear. The group turns to look at me and gets quiet. I look around and feel so much love for both me and Quinn.

"First of all, I want to say happy birthday to the girl who's stolen my heart." I turn and grab Quinn's hand while she smiles at me, her cheeks pinking up since I made her the center of attention.

"From the moment I met you, right here in this backyard, I knew you'd be special to me. I remember wanting to follow you around that party like a love-struck puppy. You were magnetic, you drew people to you not because you were the new girl but because you made them feel like they were the only person in the world. You give and don't expect anything in return, and you've made my life so much brighter than I ever thought was possible."

I get down on one knee, and I hear gasps coming from those who didn't know this was happening. Quinn's hand flies to her mouth, and I see tears gather in her eyes. "I love you so much, and I want to spend every day of the rest of my life with you. Would you do me the honor of being my wife?"

"You want me to be your wife?" Quinn asks, making me laugh because she always repeats the question any time I ask her something major.

"Completely. So, what do you say?"

I grin at her, and she flings her arms around my neck, almost making me fall over.

"Yes, absolutely yes!"

I hear everyone cheer, and I think Hailey says, "I told you so." But all I can see is Quinn as I pull back and grab her hand, putting the oval solitaire diamond ring on her finger.

She holds her hand out to look at the ring and then looks back up at me, love shining in her eyes.

"Ready to start our forever?" I ask, and she nods her head, a smile so big stretched across her face.

"Forever," she says, and I kiss her with that promise on our lips.

THE END

ALSO BY SHELBY GUNTER

ACKNOWLEDGMENTS

To you, amazing reader, for making it all the way to the end. I hope you loved these characters as much as I do!

To my husband for his constant love, support, and encouragement. As well as his ability to "MmHmm" at the right moments while I blather on about plot points. I love you very much.

To my family for letting me talk about this book nonstop for months. I am so grateful for your patience and love throughout this whole process.

To Jaime Ryter for being one hell of an editor and encouraging me to push through my doubts and continue writing.

To Luke at Copy Run for taking my very basic thoughts, and creating a cover that matches this story to a T.

To Isa, Tina, Amber, Sue, Dallas, and Trina for helping shape this story into what it is now.

To the RWR group for their constant support and witty humor when I needed it the most.

ABOUT THE AUTHOR

Shelby Gunter is a romance suspense author who loves to write twisted endings you'll never see coming. She lives in Kansas City with her husband and fur baby, and is either writing, reading, or drinking coffee. Sometimes all three at the same time.

You can find Shelby on all social media sites as well as join her Facebook group, Shelby's Gunter's Bookshelf Besties for exclusive content.

Visit authorshelbygunter.com to stay up to date on Shelby's latest releases.

Made in the USA
Columbia, SC
30 August 2024

40751644R00164